REPRISAL
ROAD

REPRISAL ROAD

A
Joe Erickson Mystery

Lynn-Steven Johanson

LEVEL
BEST BOOKS

Praise for Reprisal Road

"Lynn-Steven Johanson creates a compelling cat-and-mouse murder mystery that sends two detectives on the chase of their careers…readers who delight in detective stories that are powerfully rendered will find the characterization, suspense, and puzzle make for compelling whodunit reading."—D. Donovan, Senior Reviewer, Midwest Book Review

"Two young women, both former high school classmates, are found brutally murdered, each with dead long-stem roses by their side. When Chicago police homicide detectives Joe Erickson and Sam Renaldo begin their investigation, they soon learn that two other classmates, one in Indianapolis and one in Milwaukee, have been murdered in a similar fashion. Were the women's deaths the work of a random serial killer, or is there a darker reason in their past that connects them? And who is next? Detectives Erickson and Renaldo race against time to identify the killer before another body drops. *Reprisal Road* is a gripping police procedural that will keep the reader turning pages long into the night."—Gregory Stout, author of the award-winning Jackson Gamble series

"In *Reprisal Road*, Lynn-Steven Johanson serves up an intriguing dish of red herrings, with a side order of meticulous police procedure. Detective Joe Erickson, with the help of his profiler lady friend, methodically follows every lead, determined to stop a murderer from killing again. And their dog is adorable!"—Kassandra Lamb, author of the C.o.P. on the Scene Mysteries

Chapter One

Buzz.

Amber Engstrom, a leggy, twenty-five-year-old ash-blonde, put aside the magazine she was reading, rose from the sofa, walked over to her intercom, and spoke into it.

"Yes?"

"Flower delivery," a male voice replied.

"Flowers?" she asked.

"Yeah. I have flowers for an Amber Engstrom." reiterated the voice.

"Really? Well…okay."

Surprised and curious about the unexpected flowers, she buzzed him in and then preened in front of the mirror for a few seconds. Satisfied she looked attractive enough to impress a delivery man, she moved toward the door in anticipation. *Odd*, she thought. *Who could be sending me flowers?* She wasn't seeing anyone right now. Maybe it could be a thank you for the photo shoot she worked on a few days ago.

Her doorbell rang, and she opened it as far as the chain would allow. Seeing the delivery man, she said, "Yes?"

"You Amber Engstrom?" asked the middle-aged man, his voice muffled slightly by his N90 medical mask.

"I am."

"Got flowers for ya." He held up a white box with a red ribbon, the type used for long-stem roses.

"Just a second," she said as she released the chain and opened the door to accept the box.

The delivery man stepped forward, handing her the box, saying, "Here you go."

As she took hold of the box, his right hand reached forward under the box. Holding the taser close to her midsection, he pulled the trigger. The electrical jolt shook her body and rendered her unconscious immediately, and she fell backward onto the floor along with the box of flowers.

The deliveryman pushed his way into the apartment and locked the door.

* * *

Two days later, Chicago Police Officers from the 19th District arrived at Amber Engstrom's brown brick apartment building on North Clarendon Avenue. They met the building manager, Walter Kowalczyk, a paunchy, balding man in his mid-fifties. Engstrom's mother, who lives downstate in Edwardsville, called the police, asking them to conduct a wellness check. She was worried since she had not heard from her daughter in three days, and her phone calls, emails, and texts had gone unanswered.

Officer Luis Hernandez rang Engstrom's doorbell. Receiving no answer, he knocked on the door.

"Amber Engstrom? Chicago PD. Open up, please."

Still no answer. He knocked harder this time and repeated his call in a louder voice. After a short wait, he looked over at Officer Darius Brown, who nodded and looked at Kowalczyk.

"Open the door, Mr. Kowalczyk."

Using the key he had out and ready, Kowalczyk slid it into the lock and released the door. After gloving up, Brown asked Kowalczyk to step aside. The security chain was not in place, so the two officers pushed open the door and entered the apartment. On a rug near the sofa lay the body of Amber Engstrom, her lifeless eyes staring at the ceiling. Her T-shirt was pulled up, revealing her breasts, and her jeans and panties lay in a pile a few feet away.

"Mother of God," muttered Hernandez after seeing the body. Then he pulled out his phone and took a picture of the victim's face.

Kowalczyk started to enter the apartment, but Brown raised his hand to prevent him from entering.

"You can't come in. This is now a crime scene."

"Is she...is she dead?"

"Yeah," said Hernandez, stepping away from her body. "She's dead, all right."

"Omigod!"

"Can you ID her?" asked Hernandez, pulling up the photo he had just taken of the victim.

Upon seeing the photo, Kowalczyk winced and mumbled, "That's her. That's Amber Engstrom."

Looking at his partner, Brown said, "Better call in the dicks."

Half an hour later, Detective Joe Erickson and his partner, Sam Renaldo, arrived at the apartment in the Uptown neighborhood. Crime scene tape was already in place, and a uniformed officer stood at the entrance door. As Joe got out of his squad car, he saw the Medical Examiner's van pulling up.

The officer who was guarding the front entrance signed them in and said, "Third floor."

The elevator took them to the third floor. When they stepped off, they saw Officer Hernandez speaking to a police sergeant while Officer Brown was interviewing a woman standing one door down and across the hall from the victim's apartment.

As Joe and Sam approached, they pulled their IDs.

"Detectives Erickson and Renaldo," said Joe. "What have you got?"

Hernandez turned from his sergeant and replied, "DB. White female. Probable homicide." Nodding at Kowalczyk. "This is the apartment manager. He identified her as Amber Engstrom, one of his tenants."

"Walt Kowalczyk," said Kowalczyk, extending his hand, which Joe shook. He spelled out his name while Joe and Sam wrote it down.

"Who called it in?" asked Sam.

"Wellness check. Her mother requested it since she hadn't heard from her in three days."

Joe and Sam both looked in the door and saw the body. The one-bedroom apartment appeared to be neat, and from what he could see, it showed no signs of a struggle.

"ME's here," announced Hernandez.

Joe turned and saw the Medical Examiner, Kendra Solitsky, following Officer Kevin Isley out of the elevator. Kendra and Officer Isley were lugging her equipment toward the apartment. She stopped when she saw Joe.

"Well. What kind of excitement do you have for me today, Detective Erickson?" she asked in her usual sardonic tone.

"Young woman. Amber Engstrom. Looks like foul play. Hoping you can tell us more," replied Joe.

"You can put that down," she said to Isley, who was still holding her equipment case. "Time to get to work." Kendra began donning Tyvek coveralls, booties, nitrile gloves, and a mask in preparation for entering the crime scene.

Sam looked at Officer Brown. "You talked with any neighbors yet?"

"Just the one across the hall. She came out to see what the commotion was all about. Didn't know anything."

"You and Hernandez—start knocking on doors on this floor," said Joe. "See if anybody's home. We need to find out if anybody saw anything."

"Got it."

Joe and Sam waited outside the door, anticipating a preliminary report from Kendra. It didn't take long. After a ten-minute examination, Kendra got up and crossed to the door.

She removed her mask and said, "Liver temp indicates she was killed between thirty-six and forty-eight hours ago. There's evidence of sexual assault, and she appears to have been tased. There's what looks to be a taser burn on the front of her torso and a corresponding mark on her T-shirt. Cause of death looks like manual strangulation. I'll know more when I get her on the table." Pulling out her phone, she said, "I'm calling in Evidence Techs."

"How long before we can get in there for a look?" asked Joe.

"Late this afternoon, after the techs have finished. You know how that goes."

"Yeah."

Evidence technicians Art Casey and Jerry Bristow arrived forty-five minutes later and went to work collecting evidence from the crime scene. Joe had worked with them numerous times and knew how thorough and time-consuming their work would be.

Shortly before 1:00 p.m., Kendra completed her work, wheeled Amber Engstrom's body out to the ME's van, and drove back to the Cook County Office of the Medical Examiner. An autopsy would be conducted the next day.

At 4:15 p.m., Casey and Bristow packed up their equipment and secured the evidence collected from the scene. Outside at their van, Art turned to Joe, who had followed them out to the curb.

"You can go into the apartment now," said Art. "We got what we needed."

"It took you long enough," kidded Joe.

"You want speed or accuracy, detective? Your choice."

"Get me something good, Art."

Art snorted a chuckle and replied, "You might want to check out those lovely long-stem roses. I'll send you a picture of the love card that came with them."

Joe and Sam entered the crime scene and began to look around. The apartment was impressively furnished and decorated. Framed Degas and Renoir prints hung from the soft gray walls, and the dark teal modular couch and tables were upscale purchases. The place was neatly kept.

Joe picked up the white box that came from a florist. Opening it, he was surprised to see three dead roses. Petals were falling off, and the leaves were dry and curling up.

"Look at this," he said to Sam.

"Dead flowers?" said Sam, shaking his head. "What's that about?"

"Why only three? Don't they usually come in a dozen or half-dozen?"

Sam shrugged.

Joe's phone beeped, and he checked. It was a message from Art Casey with an attached image of the love note. It read, "Sic semper scortilla!"

What the hell? thought Joe.

Reading the expression on Joe's face, Sam asked, "What is it?"

Joe held up his phone so Sam could see the image. "It's a picture of the card that came with the flowers. 'Sic semper scortilla.'"

"What's that mean?"

"It's Latin. It means, 'Thus always to bitches.'"

"You read Latin?"

"Catholic kid. And I took a semester of Latin in college."

"Wow. Dead flowers and a message, 'Thus always to bitches'? Somebody really had it in for this woman."

"So it seems," said Joe. "You know the phrase, 'Sic semper tyrannus,' don't you?

"Of course. It's what John Wilkes Booth yelled after he shot Lincoln."

"It was."

"I wonder why the person who sent these flowers chose to write a similar message. You think this was an assassination of some kind?"

"It was hate," said Joe. "Booth killed out of hate, and so did our offender."

Joe and Sam searched Engstrom's apartment for clues that could lead them to the person responsible for her death. Sam would need to apply for a search warrant for her laptop and cell phone in order to access her messages. Necessary red tape. Once the search warrant was granted, her laptop and cell phone could be sent to the Regional Computer Forensics Laboratory, where technicians would open the devices and download her messages. Normally, they would have copies of her messages back to detectives in one week's time.

Looking over her kitchen counter, Joe saw several 8X10 glossy photos of Engstrom in various poses, suggesting she was a model. A modeling agency's information was stamped on the back of the photos. Sam looked at them and said, "A model, huh?"

"Apparently. Appears she was working for an agency."

"We need to check with that agency. See if she had any recent modeling assignments."

Joe agreed and took down the agency's information. The search of her apartment failed to turn up any tangible evidence that would point them toward an offender. Hopefully, her computer and phone would provide clues to her killer's identity.

Before heading home, Joe contacted the 19th District Police headquarters and requested the name and contact information for Amber Engstrom's mother. Then he contacted the Police Department in Edwardsville, Illinois, a community of 25,000 located east of St. Louis, and asked them to deliver the sad news of her daughter's death. He provided his phone number so she could call him to learn more about the circumstances.

Chapter Two

J oe was late getting home. He had called Destiny to let her know of his situation while he was still in his office at the Area 3 Detective Division. She understood that crime investigations like this often required extended hours.

When Joe entered the door, Destiny was pouring a glass of his favorite wine, a new Pinot Noir she picked up at the wine sellers.

Autumn, their Lhasa Apso, came running up to Joe, wagging her tail and jumping up on his leg. Joe kneeled down and began petting her. "Hello, Autumn. Are you happy to see me?" She turned a couple of circles and woofed. Joe looked into her face and said, "Oh, I know what you want. A 'treat?'" Autumn barked in response, and Joe stood and picked up one of her treats from a box on the counter. He held it out and said, "Speak!" Autumn responded with a bark, and he held out her treat. She snatched it from him, ran over to her bed, and began chomping on it.

Destiny handed him his wine.

"You're a good girl, too," said Joe.

"Do I get a treat?"

"Of course." And he leaned in and kissed her.

"Busy day, huh?"

"Oh, man. An attractive young lady was sexually assaulted and strangled in her apartment in Uptown," replied Joe before taking a drink.

Joe moved to the kitchen island and sat on one of the stools as Destiny poured a glass of wine for herself. He took a drink, savoring its flavor.

"This is good," he said, holding up his wine glass. "Something new?"

"Uh-huh. It was recommended in *Bon Appétit*."

"That probably means it was expensive."

"No, actually. It wasn't that bad."

While Joe pensively swirled the wine in his glass, Destiny engaged him by asking, "Do you have any suspects yet?"

"Uh, no. No one yet." He went on to tell her about the taser mark, the dead roses, and the card reading, "Sic semper scortilla."

Destiny thought for a moment. "It sounds like the offender was trying to justify killing and sexually assaulting the victim. It's a statement implying she was malicious and deserved what she got."

"You think the offender may hate women?"

"Maybe, but not necessarily. It could be a singular act of reprisal against the victim. And…it may not be a man."

"You think?"

"A sexual assault could be carried out by a woman using an object of some kind."

"That would be a twist. I guess I should keep an open mind until we know more."

"Women can be as vicious as men, but strangulation is not a typical method women use to commit murder."

"It takes a lot of strength to strangle a person."

"If you eliminate guns from the equation, women prefer to kill by stabbing, asphyxiation, and poison. Men go for beating, blunt objects, and strangulation. But there are always those rare cases that don't fit the norm."

"We may know more when Kendra conducts the autopsy tomorrow. She may have recovered evidence already."

"You going to attend?"

"Yeah."

"Any security videos?"

"Uniforms are canvassing the area, and we recovered some security video from the apartment building. It's being analyzed, so we should be able to see it tomorrow. Maybe we'll get a break."

Their conversation grew silent as they both tipped up their glasses. Destiny noticed Joe's sad thoughtfulness and decided to change the subject. "You hungry?" she asked.

The thought of food perked him up. "As a matter of fact, I'm famished."

"I thought maybe we could get something delivered. What are you hungry for?"

"Chinese. What about you?"

"Chinese sounds good. I'll call it in. Your usual? Mongolian beef and fried rice?"

"Uh-huh. And hot and sour soup."

"You got it."

After dinner, Joe and Destiny retired to the living room. Autumn followed them and jumped up on the couch to be near them.

"We're not going to talk shop tonight, are we?" asked Destiny. "You need to leave your work at Area 3."

"I wasn't planning on it."

"Good. I received some news from Jacquie Lambert today."

"Yeah?"

"The assets have been distributed, and Liz's estate's been formally closed. So, you're now free to buy Jared's Camaro from her. If you're still interested."

"I am."

"She made arrangements to have his Chevelle auctioned by Barrett Jackson."

"I'm glad she's taken my advice. It'll bring a premium at auction since it's a flawless, numbers-matching car. And I'll make her a fair offer for the Camaro."

"She trusts you. I'm sure she'll accept what you offer her."

"Was she satisfied with the distribution?"

"She was, and she was grateful Jared's parents didn't contest anything. The fact Jared didn't have a will and Liz did was something they couldn't legally do much about. Aren't you glad I set up that appointment with my attorney so you could have a will drawn up?"

"Yeah. I never thought about it until Liz and Jared died in that plane crash. I'm glad I won't be burdening you with legal stuff if something happens to me. In my line of work, that's always a possibility."

Destiny wanted to move on from the death of her best friend, so she asked, " Do you want to continue watching that series on Netflix?"

"Yeah. That sounds like a plan." After glancing around, he asked, "Where's the remote?"

"I don't know. Maybe you should teach Autumn to fetch it for you."

"Now, there's an idea." He looked down at Autumn and said, "What do you think, Autumn?"

Autumn slowly looked up at Joe. Her mouth opened, and her tongue slipped out.

Joe looked at Destiny and smiled, "I think she just laughed in my face."

Chapter Three

During his morning jog, Joe thought about what Destiny had mentioned the previous evening about "sic semper scortilla" being justification for killing Amber Engstrom. If so, why was she perceived to be a "bitch" by the offender? And why did he feel such a statement was necessary? And why was it worded in this manner? There are many reasons why a woman could be labeled a bitch. Why was she? They would need to interview Engstrom's friends and associates to see if anyone could cast a light on this.

As Joe drove to work, he considered the nature of Amber Engstrom's death. If this was retribution for something, it most likely had a sexual component since she was not only murdered but also sexually assaulted after she was tased. What could she have done that could have infuriated someone enough to kill her? Cheat on a boyfriend? Break it off with a lover? One night stand with the psychopath? Something caused someone to hate her. And he believed it had something to do with sex. His mind was still exploring the possibilities when he turned into the parking lot at Area 3.

Sitting at his desk, Joe began making notes based on the mental brainstorming he had done on his drive to work. Sam dropped by when he arrived.

"I'm going to start working on that search warrant for Amber Engstrom's computer and cell phone. Can you think of anything else?" asked Sam.

"No. I think we need to get those two things to the computer forensics lab as soon as possible."

"I'll write it up and run it down to Judge Warner's office later this morning."

At 10:00 a.m., Joe called Christine Engstrom, Amber Engstrom's mother. He was not looking forward to making the call, but it was necessary to get information to move forward with the investigation. The phone was answered on the second ring.

"Engstrom residence," answered a female voice."

"My name is Joe Erickson, and I'm a detective with the Chicago Police Department. I need to speak with Christine Engstrom."

"Hold, please. I'll get her for you," said the woman on the other end.

After a pause, a woman's soft voice answered, "This is Christine Engstrom."

Joe introduced himself and said, "My condolences for your loss, Mrs. Engstrom. I know you're probably in a state of shock about your daughter, but it would help our investigation if you could answer some questions. Do you feel up to it?"

"The police here didn't give me any details other than she was killed. What happened?"

"I'm sorry to report that we're investigating your daughter's death as a homicide."

Silence.

A few moments later, she softly voiced, "She…she was…murdered? Is that what you're saying?"

"She was. In her apartment."

"Ohhhh, god." Her response drifted off into tears.

"I'm sorry, Mrs. Engstrom. Would you like me to call back later? Or speak with your husband?"

Joe heard another woman's voice in the background asking what was wrong, and Mrs. Engstrom said, "It's all right, Erin."

Engstrom returned on the phone a few moments later, having pulled herself together to some extent. "I'm sorry, detective. My sister…there's no husband. I'm a single mother." She took a deep breath and said, "What would you like to know?"

"Thank you. Well, the first question we always ask is, did your daughter have any enemies or people she may have had run-ins with recently?" asked Joe.

"Not that I know of. She never mentioned anything like that to me?"

"Did you speak often?"

"A couple times a week."

"What about boyfriends? Did she have a boyfriend or romantic interest?"

"Not at the moment. She broke up with her boyfriend a month ago."

"Do you know his name?

"Josh. Joshua Blake."

"Do you have contact information for him?

"Sorry. But I know he works for the Chicago Cubs. I don't know what exactly he does."

"That's okay. We can find out."

"Something to do with management."

"Did she break it off with him, do you know?"

"She did."

"How did he take it?"

"Not very well from what she said."

"Did you ever meet him?"

"No."

"Or know anything else about him?"

"Not really. I didn't get the idea she was all that serious about him."

"I see. We saw some photos in her apartment. It appeared she worked as a model, is that correct?"

"She did. She was trying to establish her modeling career."

Joe looked at his notes and asked, "Do you know if she was working with TGM Talent?"

"Could have been. I don't know for sure. I know she worked for a talent agency."

"Did she have any other jobs?

"No, she received a substantial inheritance from her grandparents, so she had a monthly income from those investments."

"Did her boyfriend know about her personal assets?"

"I have no idea."

"We'd like to contact her friends. Do you have any names of friends here in the city?"

"One that I know of. Olivia Morrison."

"Do you have an address or phone number for her?"

"I have her phone number. Hold on." There was a pause while Mrs. Engstrom looked up Morrison's phone number. "Here it is. It's 312-555-8836."

"That's helpful. Thanks."

"Detective…Could you…Could you tell me how she was killed?"

Joe wished he did not have to reveal the cause of death, but he had no choice. She had the right to know. "She was rendered unconscious by a taser and then strangled. I'm sorry."

There was a gasp. After a pause, Mrs. Engstrom asked in a trembling voice, "Anything else?"

Joe did not want to mention the evidence of sexual assault and upset her further, so he decided not to mention it. Since it was not official yet, he said, "Nothing's been confirmed at this time."

Another pause. Then she asked, "Do you know when I can get my daughter back? I want to have a funeral service down here."

"That'll be up to the Medical Examiner. When she can, she'll contact you so you can make arrangements."

"You said she was tased. Would she have been unconscious when she was…"

"There's a good chance she was. I doubt she suffered if that's what you're asking."

"Thank you. That's…somewhat comforting."

Joe ended his conversation with Christine Engstrom, but only after asking if it would be all right if he contacted her again should further questions arise. She agreed and thanked him for his kindness. Hearing the details of her daughter's death must have been tough, but she got through it. And Joe was able to gain some pertinent information.

Sam walked to Joe's desk. "You know that box the roses came in?" he asked.

"Yeah."

"The florist's name was imprinted on the box. I think it might be a good idea to interview the florist to see if they can provide names of people who purchased long-stem roses in the last month."

"Good idea," agreed Joe.

Lincoln Avenue Florists was located in the Lakeview neighborhood bordering Lake Michigan's shore. Joe and Sam walked under the awning of the brown brick building and entered the shop. The aroma of fresh-cut flowers and plants acted as a natural air freshener. They made their way to the counter, where a middle-aged woman greeted them with a smile.

"Hello. May I help you?"

Joe and Sam presented their IDs. "I'm Detective Joe Erickson, and this is my partner, Sam Renaldo. We have some questions about a purchase of long-stem roses."

"Oh. Okay."

"One of your boxes containing three long-stem roses was found at a crime scene. Do you keep a record of people who make purchases?"

"Credit card records. Yes. Some people make cash purchases, and we also keep receipts for those."

"How often do you sell long-stem roses?" asked Sam.

"Not that often. Maybe three times a week at most."

"Don't people usually buy them in multiples of six?"

"Not necessarily. Sometimes a person will simply come in and buy one."

Joe was interested in how long it would take for roses to wilt and dry up like those found in the box, so he decided to ask. He removed his phone and pulled up a photo of the dried roses found at the crime scene.

"How long would it take for roses to dry up like these?" He showed her the photo.

"Oh, my," she said. "These look like they've been hung up and dried."

"Any idea how long that would take?"

"Well, I've dried roses before. I hung them upside down in my closet, and it took about three weeks for them to dry out."

"Three weeks," repeated Sam. He looked at Joe, who eyed the name tag on the woman's blouse.

"Connie, that's your name?"

"It is."

"Well, Connie, it would help us immensely if you could provide us with the names and contact information of everyone who bought long-stem roses in the past two months."

"Don't you need a search warrant for that or something?" asked Connie.

"Only if you insist on one," said Joe. "But you can save us a lot of hassle if you simply provide us with the names."

"We're looking for an offender who brutally killed a young woman, and we're concerned that he may do it again," explained Sam.

"Chicago PD would appreciate your cooperation," added Joe.

Connie thought momentarily and then said, "We have that information in the computer. I can pull that up for you once we close. Can you come back tomorrow?"

"We can."

Joe and Sam breathed a sigh of relief. They will have their list of possible suspects. After thanking her, they returned to Area 3.

Joe called Engstrom's friend, Olivia Morrison, but his call went to voicemail. He left her a message to call him. By the end of the day, she had not returned his call, so he planned to call her again tomorrow.

Amber Engstrom's autopsy was scheduled for 3:15, so Joe drove to the Office of the Cook County Medical Examiner to attend the procedure. He entered through the back door and checked in with the attending detective. Then, he went to Kendra Solitsky's office to let her know he had arrived. She was already dressed in scrubs.

"My assistant is setting up," she said. "I'll be ready to go in ten minutes."

Joe slipped into an adjoining room and donned scrubs and put on a face shield in case of a rare instance of blood spatter during the procedure. He entered the autopsy room and immediately felt the cool temperature on his exposed skin. Amber Engstrom's sheet-covered body was lying on a stainless-steel table. The autopsy instruments were laid out and ready for use.

Kendra and her assistant, Kenny Miller, entered the room, and the procedure began at 3:15 p.m.

Amber Engstrom was a twenty-five-year-old female, five feet eight inches tall and weighing one hundred fifteen pounds. She had no identifying marks or tattoos. Her four front teeth had veneers applied, and her fingernails were intact. They were scraped, and the scrapings were preserved for forensic examination.

A red fiber was removed from the ligature marks on her neck for later analysis by the crime lab. Her hyoid bone was broken, and her trachea showed signs of trauma from the device used to strangle her.

While examining her lower pelvic region, Kendra found evidence of bruising in the vaginal area. Her pubic hair was combed in an attempt to recover foreign hairs. Swabs were taken for DNA and the presence of semen. She swabbed adjacent areas for samples to send to the lab for DNA analysis. After preparing a slide and peering into her microscope, Kendra looked at Joe as she said, "No sperm cells." Kenny took additional swabs on other areas of her body to discover if there was any DNA transferred from her attacker.

Once the outer body was examined, the Y-incision was made in her chest, continuing down her abdomen. Organs were removed, examined, and weighed, while the stomach was emptied for analysis later. The cranial vault was opened, and the brain was removed, examined, and weighed.

Amber Engstrom was a healthy twenty-five-year-old woman who was strangled to death after being tased and brutally raped by an offender, as yet unidentified.

Blood samples were taken for a tox screen. Once Kendra began preparing tissue samples for microscopic examination, Joe left. He would follow up by calling her tomorrow. He tossed his scrubs into the appropriate receptacle and entered the nearest restroom, where he threw water on his face in an attempt to wash off the death. Back at Area 3, he turned in his squad car. Glancing at his watch, he decided to head home, where a beautiful woman and a loyal dog awaited him.

Chapter Four

The next morning, Joe was sitting at his desk when he received a call from Olivia Morrison. He hoped she would call him back so they could interview her about Engstrom and her relationship with her former boyfriend.

"Thank you for returning my call," said Joe. "I'm calling about your friend, Amber Engstrom."

"Amber? Has something happened?"

Oh, no, thought Joe. *She doesn't know.* He would have to tell her. "I'm sorry to report that your friend was found dead in her apartment two days ago."

Morrison gasped, "Omigod," and began crying. "Wha-What happened?" she blubbered.

"She was killed by an unknown assailant. We're investigating her death. I called you because her mother told me you were one of her close friends."

"I am…was."

"Look, is there a time when I can interview you? Ask you some questions?"

"Oh, god…uh…I'm sorry."

"It's okay. I can call back later. Give you some time to process this."

"This is horrible. I just…"

"I thought maybe you would have heard. It's been in the papers and on the news."

"I was out of town visiting my sister in Minneapolis. I just got back last night."

"What would you like me to do?" asked Joe.

"Can you call me this afternoon?"

"Sure. Around two o'clock?"

"That'd be fine."

"Okay. And I'm sorry for your loss."

"Thank you."

Joe ended the call. He hated delivering bad news about victims to loved ones, and he wasn't expecting that Engstrom's close friend had not heard about her death. Maybe by this afternoon, she would have time to deal with the shock and be able to set up a time for him to interview her.

That afternoon, Joe called Olivia Morrison, and she suggested they meet at 3:30 at The Job Site, a neighborhood bar on North Sheridan Road. She said she would be wearing a dark blue U of I T-shirt.

Joe drove to the Wrigleyville address of The Job Site and walked under the portico of the corner building. Entering the bar, he looked around and spotted a young, dark-haired woman in her twenties sitting at one of the tall tables. She was wearing a blue T-shirt with Illinois emblazoned in orange across the front. She looked up, and as her eyes met his, he gave her a little wave. She responded with a wave back.

Walking up to her table, Joe said, "Olivia?"

"Yes."

"Detective Joe Erickson. Thank you for seeing me so soon." He pulled out a chair and sat down across from her.

"That's okay. I just want to help."

"I appreciate that."

"Can you...tell me how Amber was killed?"

"It appears she opened her door to receive flowers, and the offender tased her and then strangled her." He chose not to mention the rape so it would not upset her further.

Morrison shuddered after hearing the details. "My god!" She picked up her highball glass with a shaking hand and took a drink. She looked at Joe with tears in her eyes and said, "I can't believe this."

"We're just beginning our investigation, so any information you provide could prove helpful. According to her mother, she recently broke up with her boyfriend. Do you know anything about that?"

She nodded. "Yeah. Josh." Rolling her eyes, she said, "Josh Blake."

"I take it you know him?"

"Uh-huh."

By the negative tone of her voice, it appeared she didn't hold him in high regard. "What can you tell me about him?"

"He's a handsome guy. Amber was really into him to begin with. But the more time she spent with him, the more she found out what he was really like."

"And that was?"

"He was abusive. Not physically. I don't think he ever laid a hand on her. But his abuse was psychological. He was controlling, jealous, demeaning…I mean, Amber was a really bright person, and she came to realize that good looks and great in bed only go so far, you know what I mean?"

"Yeah. You said he was jealous?"

"Oh, yeah. If she spoke to another guy at a party, it would set him off. She told me he blew up at her after a party because she talked with a guy who modeled with her on a shoot. He was no threat. The guy was gay. But Josh flew into a rage over it."

"What happened?"

"That was the last straw. She broke it off with him shortly after. Told me she'd had enough."

"How did he take it?"

"Not very well. She threatened him with a restraining order if he didn't leave her alone. And she told him her attorney would contact his place of business and report his abusive behavior."

"Did he stop?"

"She said he did. He apparently loves his job, so he backed off."

A waitress finally noticed Joe's presence and came over to the table. "Can I get you something?" she asked.

"You have coffee?"

"We do."

"Bring me a cup. Black."

"On duty, huh?" asked Morrison.

"Yeah. I have to behave myself."

"She smiled. "That's too bad."

"It is. Let me ask something. How well did you know Josh Blake?"

"Not all that well. I saw him with Amber at parties. And my boyfriend and I went out to dinner with them once."

"And how did that go?"

"Fine. Graham didn't exactly like him. But he played along, and it was a nice evening."

"Do you think Josh's jealousy could develop into the kind of rage where he could do Amber harm?"

Morrison thought for a moment. Shaking her head, she said, "I don't know. I'd like to think not. But who knows what people are capable of, you know? If I can't have her, no one can. Like that, you mean?"

"We have to look at all the angles."

She finished her drink and then held up her glass. The bartender acknowledged and began making her another.

A moment later, the waitress delivered Joe's coffee. "Can I get you anything else?"

"No thanks." He looked across at Morrison and asked, "How long have you known Amber?"

"We met at the University of Illinois. We were sorority sisters."

"Ah. So, you knew her well."

"Yeah. She was going to make it as a model. She had it all. She was starting to get a lot of work around the city, and her agent recently got her a commercial shoot in L.A. Her career was on the rise."

Joe took a sip of his coffee, which caused him to make a face. It was nasty from being in the pot too long. He put the cup down and pushed it away.

"Do you know if Amber had any enemies? People who didn't like her for some reason. Maybe jealous of her success? Anyone she may have offended?"

Shaking her head, Morrison said, "Not that I know of. I mean, she was well aware of her looks, and she had a little attitude that may have rubbed some people the wrong way. But I doubt someone would have killed her for being snotty."

"You'd be surprised what may set people off these days. Can you remember Amber talking about any incidents?"

"Not off the top of my head."

The waitress came with her drink. After placing it in front of her, she picked up her empty glass and looked at Joe. "How's your coffee?"

"Terrible, to be honest. It's been in the pot way too long."

"I'm sorry. I'll get you another cup."

"Don't bother. I'm leaving shortly."

"Well, we won't charge you for it." She picked up his cup and took it away.

Looking amused, Morrison said, "I guess you told her."

"She wanted to know, and I wasn't going to lie." He looked over at her glass. "What are you drinking?"

"Old Fashioneds."

"Well, don't drink too many of those."

"I won't. It's only my second one. I usually quit after two. I guess I've grown up. I can't handle getting hammered anymore." She managed a little smile.

"You and me both," said Joe. He slid his stool back and stood up. "Thanks for your help, Olivia. Your information's been helpful." Placing his card on the table, he said, "If you think of anything else, call me." He laid down enough bills to pay for Morrison's drinks and said, "Take care."

Morrison followed him with her eyes as he walked out of the bar. Then she reached over and picked up his card. After reading it, she placed it in her purse and then picked up her Old Fashioned and took a drink.

Returning to Area 3, Joe wrote up his notes on his meeting with Olivia Morrison. Given what Morrison stated in their interview, Josh Blake appears to be high on their list of suspects. He would explore that tomorrow.

Chapter Five

Joe began investigating Josh Blake the next day. He was born Joshua Allan Blake in Naperville, Illinois, on October 20th. He was twenty-nine years old and graduated from Naperville South High School, where he played football and baseball. Five years later, he earned a Bachelor of Science degree in Sports Management from Illinois State University. Never married, his last known address is an apartment in Lincoln Park. The Chicago Cubs organization has been his employer for the past five years. Before that, he was a scout for the Athletic Program at the University of Illinois at Urbana.

Blake had no record, but police were called to his apartment two years ago when a domestic disturbance was reported. No arrests were made. Shortly afterward, an Order of Protection was filed against him. Interesting.

Joe informed Sam about what he had found.

"We need to bring him in for questioning," said Sam. "You said he works for the Cubs organization?"

"Yeah."

"I'll make some phone calls and find out where he can be reached. And confirm his home address."

"Good. I'll get a warrant to find out who filed the Order of Protection. If he was violent toward one woman, he may have been violent toward another."

Sam was usually the one who wrote out the warrant applications. He liked that kind of work, and Joe didn't mind him doing it because he was good at it. Joe volunteered to write this one himself since Sam had an appointment that took him away from Area 3 for an hour.

Half an hour later, Joe's concentration was broken when he received a phone call from Ronald Wu at the Regional Computer Forensics Laboratory.

"We have successfully opened Amber Engstrom's cellphone and laptop computer. Where would you like me to send the link to her communications?"

Joe gave him his email address and thanked him. He was anxious to read her emails, both incoming and outgoing. Hopefully, they would provide clues as to the person who killed her. When Sam returned, Joe walked over to his desk and let him know about the email message that would be coming from Ronald Wu.

"Let's go through her emails and see what turns up," said Joe.

"If Josh Blake was abusive to her like he was to someone else, we should be able to find something in her emails. You writing up the warrant to find who filed the Order of Protection?"

"Working on it."

"I can take over if you want," said Sam.

"I'm almost finished. But I'd like you to check it out when I'm done."

"Be glad to."

An hour later, Joe finished writing the warrant application and gave it to Sam to look over. When Sam had finished and given the warrant his blessing, he ran it downtown to the office of Judge Frederick Blackman. Usually, he would have taken it to Judge Warner, who was more liberal in signing their search warrants, but Warner was still on leave after undergoing heart bypass surgery. Judge Blackman's administrative assistant, Bret Carlson, received the documents and advised Sam that the judge would read the warrant and have an answer sometime tomorrow.

While Sam was gone, Joe began looking through Amber Engstrom's emails. There was nothing recent that was of any consequence. But he struck gold when he searched through the past dates, starting with Amber's breakup with Josh.

On the day she broke up with him, he sent her a late-night message where he unloaded his wrath. He accused her of being "a bitch," and how dare she dump him after all he had done for her. It was painfully apparent that he had a fragile ego and could not take rejection. Joe wondered if the "bitch" description carried over from his emails to the Latin message accompanying the dead flowers.

The next day, Amber responded to Josh in a polite but firm message, stating why she decided to move on, how his psychological abuse was the main factor, and how being with him was taking a daily toll on her. She gave him examples of his abusive behavior and told him that from now on, she would no longer respond to his email messages.

He shot back with an angry, expletive-laced message accusing her of infidelity and using him to take advantage of his social connections and good nature. Good nature. Now, that was ironic to the nth degree. What shot up a red flag was how he ended the message with a line stating, "I'll make sure you'll regret this."

In an email sent to her mother nine days later, Engstrom said she had to file an Order of Protection against Blake because she spotted him stalking her on two occasions. Her mother became concerned, but Engstrom told her it seemed to work since she had not seen him after the Order went into effect. Her attorney also sent Blake a letter stating he would alert the Cubs organization about his abusive behavior and the Order of Protection, something that would jeopardize his employment. After that, Engstrom emailed her mother and her friend, Olivia, that things with Josh seemed to have settled down. That did not necessarily mean they had, and things could have continued stewing in Blake's mind until his emotions came to a boiling point where he acted out. But given all the bad blood and the Order of Protection, why would Engstrom let him into her apartment? That didn't make any sense.

When Sam returned, Joe handed him a list of emails he found that seemed to implicate Josh Blake. Sam said he would look them over and continue searching for any other suspicious messages. Joe would do the same.

At 2:30 p.m., Joe called Kendra Solitsky. But his call rolled over to voicemail. He left a message for her to call him when she had a chance. At 3:45, his phone rang.

"I got your message," said Kendra.

"Thanks for returning my call."

"I was in the middle of an autopsy when you called. I suppose you want to know if I have anything regarding Amber Engstrom, right?"

"Yeah."

"I'm finishing up the autopsy report as we speak, so I should be sending it over tomorrow morning."

"I appreciate that."

"Well, there's not a lot I can tell you, Joe. At least not until the DNA results come back on the samples we sent out. The red fiber found in her neck is silk, probably came from some sort of apparel. A ribbon or scarf, maybe. The lab may be able to narrow it down once they analyze it. But I wouldn't hold my breath."

"What did you send out for DNA analysis?"

"Swabs from her face, neck, abdomen, thighs, vagina, a loose hair we retrieved from her body–could be hers–but it came out when we combed through her pubic hair. And the scrapings from under her fingernails."

"Is the DNA lab still running way behind?"

"Oh, hell, yes. As always. But I'll let you know as soon as we have their findings."

"Great. Anything else?"

"Yeah. Catch the bastard who did this."

Joe smiled at her response. "We're working on it. Thanks, Kendra."

After ending the call, Joe called the Chicago Cubs Customer Service number and got a recording of a cheerful male voice, giving him numerous wonderful options for directing his call. None of the choices sounded like an appropriate office, so he hung up. He decided it would be most expedient to show up at their headquarters in person.

Joe walked to Sam's desk and asked, "You don't have a phone number for the Cubs office personnel, do you?"

Sam gave him a skeptical look. "Are you kidding? You think I know important people?"

"You don't know until you ask. I can't get through their recorded greeting and their various options. We need to go there if we want to interview Josh

Blake. You have a home address for him?"

"I do, but I don't know if it's current."

"Let's try his residence first. Maybe we can avoid the organization. It's huge."

"You think he could be working from home?"

Joe nodded. "A lot of people do. At least part of the time. He works in their media relations department, so it may not be necessary for him to be in the corporate office every day."

"Okay," said Sam.

"Let's check it out."

They drove to Blake's address, an apartment on West Hubbard Street. They entered the beige-stone building and checked the list of residents. Joe spotted "J. Blake" and pressed the button, hoping for an answer. There was none. When a person came out of the building, Sam grabbed the door before it closed, and they slipped into the lobby.

They took the elevator to the fifth floor, where his apartment was located. Joe rang the buzzer several times and pounded on the door. There was no response. Looking at Sam, Joe said, "Probably at work. You want to call the Cubs organization and see if you can reach him?"

"Why not?"

Joe gave Sam the number for the Cubs Customer Service, and Sam made the call. After listening to the options, he pressed a number, greeted the person who answered the phone and explained who he was and who he wanted to speak with.

Sam looked at Joe and said, "I'm being transferred."

After speaking with someone else, he was transferred again. A woman answered, "Media Relations, this is Christina."

"This is Detective Sam Renaldo, Chicago PD. I'd like to talk with Josh Blake, please."

"He's out of the office today, but he'll be back in tomorrow. Can I ask what this is about?"

"We'd like to talk to him—part of an investigation we're conducting. You wouldn't happen to have a direct phone number where we can reach him, would you? I was transferred all over the place before I got connected to you."

"Certainly."

Sam took Blake's direct office phone number and thanked Christina for her assistance. Then, he began speaking to her in Spanish and conversed with her for a few minutes.

After Sam ended the call, Joe said, "Nicely done, Sam. How did you know she spoke Spanish?"

Sam smiled. "ESP."

"Oh, you're psychic all of a sudden?"

"It was the way she talked. Not that hard to figure out. So, you think we should go pick him up tomorrow?"

"Let's try the phone call first. If he's uncooperative, we can pay him a visit."

"Sounds good."

Chapter Six

Joe made a call to Josh Blake the next morning. His first call went to voicemail. Half an hour later, he called again, and his call was answered.

"Media relations. This is Josh Blake."

"Mr. Blake, this is Detective Joe Erickson, Chicago PD. I'm investigating the death of Amber Engstrom, and we're contacting her known associates. We'd like to ask you some questions."

There was a pause, and after a sigh, Blake said, "I figured somebody would contact me about her."

The tone of his voice suggested he was annoyed. "So, you know about her death?"

"Yeah."

"How did you find out?"

"I got a text. From a friend."

"I see." Deciding he would not get anything from Blake over the phone, Joe decided to move on. "Well...Is there a time when we can interview you?"

"When?"

"The sooner, the better. We can come to your office if you'd like."

Immediately, Blake answered, "No. No, that wouldn't be...convenient. Uh...I could take some time off, and we could meet somewhere."

"How about today?"

"Today? Well...I suppose I could. It's kind of short notice, but I guess I could take some time off this afternoon. I don't have any meetings after two."

"Okay. Say, three o'clock?"

"Uh, yeah. I can make that work."

"Come to the Area 3 headquarters on Belmond," said Joe. "You know where that is?"

"Not exactly."

Joe gave him the street address and said, "When you go into the public access area, have the sergeant there ring for Detective Joe Erickson, and I'll come down and escort you to a room where we can talk. We'll expect you at three."

"Got it. Three o'clock."

Before Joe could thank him, Blake hung up. His tone of voice and guarded responses to questions told Joe that Blake was not thrilled about being interviewed. They would soon see how willing he was to cooperate. Walking to Sam, Joe told him about Blake coming in at three.

"That was fast. Was he agreeable to being interviewed?" asked Sam.

"Somewhat. Said he expected a call from us at some point."

"Then he's going to be prepared. He'll be practicing telling his side of their story."

"We'll see about that. He has a lot of explaining to do based on his email messages and what Olivia Morrison told me."

"By the way, I got the warrant to find who filed the Order of Protection. You know who it was?"

"Amber Engstrom?" replied Joe.

"How'd you know that?"

"She wrote about it in an email to her mother."

"So, we didn't need the warrant after all."

"I didn't see the message until after we sent the warrant to Judge Blackman."

"It turns out it wasn't a total waste. You know what else I found?"

"What?"

"Another woman named Roxanne Wilken also filed an Order of Protection against him almost two years ago."

"Roxanne Wilken," repeated Joe. "We need to find her."

"I'm already on it."

Back at his desk, Joe began his brainstorming process regarding Josh Blake.

Given his temperament and the Order of Protection with at least one other woman, Joe suspected Blake could have retaliated for being spurned. What Olivia Morrison mentioned proved right: "If I can't have her, nobody can."

At five minutes after three, Joe received a call from the sergeant at the public access desk saying someone was asking for him. Joe alerted Sam and then went down to the area to meet Blake. As he entered, he saw a well-dressed young man in his late twenties. He saw Joe entering and stepped toward him.

"You Detective Erickson?" he asked.

"Yes."

"Josh Blake," he said, and extended his hand, which Joe shook. His handshake was overly firm.

"Thank you for coming in. If you'll follow me..." Joe led him up to the interrogation room where Sam was waiting. Blake had movie-star good looks. Chiseled tanned features, dark hair precisely cut, a good physique, and an expensive suit with a shirt open at the neck presented a young businessman representing his organization with professional aplomb.

Joe introduced Sam, and they sat down at the table across from Blake.

"Would you like anything to drink? Soda, coffee, water?" asked Sam.

"Water would be fine," replied Blake.

Sam left the room and came back with a bottle of water. Blake twisted off the top and took a drink. When he was finished, he looked at Joe and Sam, saying, "I don't know what I can tell you. I was in a relationship with Amber up until two months ago when we called it quits."

"Was your split amicable?" asked Joe.

"For the most part."

"What can you tell us about her?" asked Sam.

"She was beautiful and was working on her modeling career. It was just starting to take off. We met at a party where she was paid to be one of those attractive people in the crowd. We talked and then began seeing each other, and over the next couple of months or so, we became a couple."

"Did you move in with her?" asked Joe.

"No. We wanted to keep our own places in case things didn't work out...

Well, you can't always count on relationships lasting, you know? But we spent a lot of time at each other's apartments."

"How long were you two together?"

"About nine months."

"What was her personality like?"

"Sweet, but she could be temperamental at times. Especially if her career wasn't going the way she expected."

"You ever fight?"

"By fight, I assume you mean arguments? Yeah, we had a few disagreements. But as far as fighting goes, it never got physical, if that's what you're asking."

"Did you go out socially much?"

"Occasionally. She had parties she said she needed to attend. And I had events associated with my work."

"She ever get hit on by other guys?"

"Probably. I mean, with her looks, there are bound to be guys who were attracted to her. Wanted to…you know."

"Did you ever witness anyone hitting on her?"

"I don't recall. Maybe."

"And what did you think of that?"

"God…I don't remember. I probably didn't like it," he said, his annoyance growing.

"You ever have words about it?"

Blake was getting frustrated and finally asked, "Why all these questions? I'd think you'd be out looking for her killer."

"We are," said Sam, looking him in the eyes.

Pause. Then Blake concluded, "Am I a suspect here?"

"Maybe," said Joe. He pulled several photocopies from the folder Sam had brought to the room and laid them down in front of him. "You see, we've obtained email records from Amber's laptop and phone. This is not looking good for you, Mr. Blake."

Looking at the highlighted lines, Blake's hostility increased. He clearly took offense at Joe having copies of his correspondence with Engstrom.

"You have no right to our private conversations."

"We have every right. A court order gave us that right," said Sam.

"Those were some nasty emails you sent when she broke up with you, Mr. Blake." Looking at one of the photocopies, Joe went on to say, "I'm not going to read all the nasty shit you wrote in your messages. It's pretty disturbing stuff. But I'm interested to know what you meant when you wrote, 'I'll make sure you'll regret this.'" Looking Blake in the eyes, he said, "Well, Mr. Blake?"

"That was just my anger talking. I would never hurt her."

"Really?" said Sam. "Then why did she file an Order of Protection against you?"

"You'd have to ask her."

"Sounds like she was frightened of you."

"Were you stalking her?" asked Joe.

"No. She saw me in a coffee shop once. Maybe she assumed I was."

"Just once? Then why did she file an Order of Protection if it was only a coincidence?" asked Sam.

"Because she was paranoid? How the hell should I know."

"You have quite a temper, don't you?" pressed Joe. "You can't handle being rejected, can you? In fact, another woman also filed an Order of Protection against you, didn't she?"

"Did you kill her?" asked Sam.

"No!"

"If I can't have her, nobody can?" said Joe. "Is that what you thought?"

Furious, Blake exploded, pounding his fist on the table and saying, "I am not saying another fucking word until I speak with my attorney."

"You're not under arrest, Mr. Blake. But if that's what you want—"

"Can I go?" he asked, his eyes shooting daggers at Joe and Sam.

"Certainly," said Sam. "You're not under arrest. You can go."

"By the way," said Joe, "We'll need an alibi from you for the time of Amber's death."

"You'll hear from my attorney."

"Looking forward to it."

"And don't blow us off," warned Sam.

Blake rose from his chair and left the interrogation room in a huff. Joe looked at Sam and asked, "What do you think?"

Sam rose and said, "Since he left his water bottle, I'll bag it and send it out for DNA analysis. Maybe the crime lab can match it to something."

"We need to find out if he has an alibi. If not, he's looking good for it."

"Yeah, and we have to find the other woman he was dating before Engstrom. Apparently, she broke it off with him, too."

"Roxanne Wilken."

"Yeah."

"I wonder what he did to her."

Chapter Seven

Joe arrived home late that afternoon while Destiny was working away at her laptop. She was consumed with what she was doing and was oblivious to Amber's barking. When Joe didn't see her, he announced, "I'm home."

He kneeled to pet Autumn, who greeted him as soon as he entered.

A moment later, Destiny entered from the bedroom they had turned into an office.

"Hi. I was so lost in thought I didn't hear you come home," she said and gave him a peck on the cheek.

"Autumn heard me."

"I heard her bark. Lhasas instinctively alert their masters to intruders."

"So, I'm an intruder, now?"

"So to speak."

Joe reached for a glass and poured himself a glass of water from a pitcher in the refrigerator.

Afterward, Joe sat on a stool at the kitchen island. Destiny joined him.

"How was your day?" she asked.

"Progress. I think we have a suspect in the Amber Engstrom murder. Her former boyfriend. She broke it off with him, and he didn't take it very well. Vile emails and threats. She ended up filing an Order of Protection against him."

"Rejection issues?"

"Apparently. But I'm still bothered by the dead flowers she received and the fact she was tasered. It doesn't seem like something a spurned lover

36

would do."

"Did she open the door for her assailant?

"It looks like she opened the door to receive a flower delivery. We think that's how the offender gained access to her apartment."

Destiny thought momentarily and asked, "Why would she open her door for someone she filed an Order of Protection against? That doesn't make sense. Did she have a chain on her door?"

"She did. You'd think if she recognized him, she wouldn't have opened her door to accept anything from him."

"Do you suppose he could have used an apology and the flowers to get her to open the door? Then he could have talked his way in."

"Or barged in and tased her if the door wasn't chained. The chain wasn't broken. Once inside, he could have raped and strangled her while she laid there helpless."

They continued discussing the crime for the next ten minutes. As Joe took his last drink, Destiny said, "This whole scenario would have taken a lot of planning on the offender's part. Obtaining a taser, learning how to use it, and securing three dead flowers."

"And what's the significance of just three dead flowers and the Latin message on the card?"

I don't know. It doesn't seem to be the act of a rejected lover. Chances are, a rejected lover would act more spontaneously."

Joe thought about this briefly and then asked, "But what about a jealous, insecure man seeking revenge? Does it make sense that he planned it down to the last detail and then acted on it?"

"Anything's possible, but the one thing he couldn't plan for would be her reaction to seeing him at her door. If she filed an Order of Protection, she clearly feared him. You would think her reaction would be closing the door and calling the police."

"You'd think. But if the door wasn't chained and he forced his way in…"

"Does your suspect have an alibi?"

"We don't know yet. We asked him to provide one during the interview, and he told us we'd hear from his lawyer."

"Lawyered up, huh?"

"Yeah. We went at him pretty hard, and he decided he needed to speak with his lawyer. At that point, our interview ended."

"Well, I wouldn't rule him out," said Destiny. "As a profiler, I see some things that don't fit. But there are always exceptions to the norm."

"I know," said Joe. He rose and placed his glass in the dishwasher. "What shall we make for dinner?"

"I thought we could prepare that Parmesan-crusted tilapia we fixed last month. We could make roasted brussels sprouts, and I have all the ingredients for a green salad with apples, cranberries, and pepitas to go with it."

Joe was pleased with Destiny's suggestion. They made the same dinner for themselves last month, which was wonderful. Although Destiny is a vegetarian, she occasionally ate seafood. Technically speaking, that made her a "pescatarian." In any case, this was a terrific recipe. He volunteered to prepare the tilapia while Destiny agreed to make the salad and the vinaigrette.

Their dinner was a culinary delight, and after cleaning up, they adjourned to the living room, where they tuned in to the next episode of a Swedish crime drama they had been watching on Netflix. By 10:00 p.m., Joe was tired and losing focus by the time the episode ended. He went to bed, and Destiny followed, not wanting to doze off and wake up on the couch at midnight like she had done the night before. It made going back to sleep difficult.

The next morning, while Joe was jogging, he thought about Josh Blake's efforts to access Engstrom's apartment. The more he thought about it, the more he dismissed Blake as a viable suspect. Too much about the scenario didn't fit, but to rule him out, they would need to get a search warrant for his residence to see if he had remnants of dried roses, a taser, and anything made of red silk that could have been used to strangle the victim. If there was something, they could have it tested to see if it matched the fibers Kendra found on Engstrom's body. They could also have it tested for Engstrom's DNA. That would be conclusive, and speculation about how he got into her apartment would not matter.

Before they sought to secure a search warrant, they would need to speak with his former girlfriend, Roxanne Wilken. Sam had said he would work on locating her. Maybe he would have a lead on her whereabouts sometime this morning.

Chapter Eight

As Joe drove to the office, he was still thinking about what Destiny said yesterday. He trusted her opinions since she had worked on many criminal cases as a profiler. And when she said things didn't fit, he began thinking more and more that someone other than Blake may be a better suspect. But Blake was all they had at the moment, and they needed to focus their efforts on gathering more evidence. Joe hated men who abused women, and he was trying not to let his feelings cloud his judgment about Blake.

Joe and Sam met first thing to discuss what their next steps would be in their investigation. Sam said he would concentrate on tracking down Roxanne Wilken, while Joe would look into who Blake's friends were.

By noon, Sam had located a Roxanne Wilken who fit the age range. Looking her up on the Illinois Driver's License database, he found her photo and address. Her photo revealed she was an attractive young woman with ash blonde hair whose weight was listed as one hundred twenty pounds. The twenty-eight-year-old lived in the Uptown neighborhood. She was the same physical type as Amber Engstrom, and he thought maybe these were women who Blake would seek out. By searching other databases, he acquired her cell phone number and her employer, a law firm where she worked as a paralegal.

At lunch, Joe and Sam talked, and they agreed their next move should be setting up an interview with Wilken. At 1:15, Joe called the number Sam had given him. His call went to voicemail. Thinking she did not answer unknown callers, his next move was to contact the law firm where she worked.

Friesen & Hartley, Attorneys at Law, had an office on West Jackson Boulevard. When he called their office number, a woman's voice answered.

"Friesen and Hartley Law Offices, may I help you?"

"This is Detective Joe Erickson with the Chicago Police Department. I'm calling to see if Roxanne Wilken works in your office."

"She does. Can I ask what this is about?"

"She hasn't done anything wrong, but her name came up during one of our investigations, and we'd like to speak with her. Is she in?"

"She is. Let me transfer you."

Joe was put on hold and endured golden oldie music for about a minute. Then, a female voice answered.

"This is Roxanne Wilken. How may I help you?"

After introducing himself, Joe said, "Your name came up during one of our investigations."

"Oh?" she replied. "In what context?"

"Are you the Roxanne Wilken who once dated Josh Blake?"

Joe heard an exhale of breath. Then she answered, "Oh my. That was some time ago."

"We'd like to interview you regarding our investigation. Particularly about you filing an Order of Protection against him."

"Wow. Uh, okay."

"Is there a time my partner and I could meet with you?"

"Let me check my schedule...let's see...Uh, I could see you this afternoon at 2:30 or tomorrow morning at 10:15."

"Let's do it today at 2:30. Where would you like to meet?"

"Why don't you come to our office? We have a conference room where we can talk. Do you know the address?"

Joe repeated the address Sam had given him for the Friesen and Hartley law firm, and she confirmed it was correct. Joe ended the call and told Sam about the scheduled meeting. Joe glanced at his watch and figured he had enough time to research Roxanne Wilken.

Wilken was born in Chicago twenty-eight years ago to Frank Joseph

41

Wilken and Judy Marie Mattox Wilken. She was the oldest of three siblings. She graduated from Holy Trinity High School and the College of DuPage with an Associate of Applied Science degree in Paralegal Studies. She has been employed by Friesen and Hartley, Attorneys at Law, for the past six years, having been previously employed by the Illinois Office of the State's Attorney. She lives on North Sheridan Road in the Uptown neighborhood. She is a registered Democrat and volunteers as an election judge. Not married and no arrests, not even a traffic citation. *Looks like a solid citizen*, Joe thought.

Joe and Sam got to the office of Friesen and Hartley a few minutes before 2:30. The receptionist picked up the phone and announced their arrival. Moments later, an attractive young woman dressed in a mauve business suit greeted them.

"I'm Roxanne Wilken," she said, her manner assertive and business-like.

Joe and Sam showed their IDs and introduced themselves. After shaking hands, she said, "If you'll follow me, please. The conference room is down the hall."

The receptionist appeared interested in what was happening, and when Joe looked her way, her eyes darted back to her desk. Her timid reaction amused him.

They followed Wilken into a wood-paneled room with a long table. She indicated chairs for them to sit and she sat opposite them.

Before Joe could say anything, Wilkin spoke up. "On the phone, you said my name came up regarding an Order of Protection I filed several years ago. Care to elaborate?"

Joe took the lead by asking, "Sure. Why did you file the Order of Protection against Joshua Blake?"

"Can I be frank?"

"Please.

"He's a fucking asshole."

Sam smiled and repeated Wilken's words, "Care to elaborate?"

"We began a relationship after meeting at the wedding of one of my friends. It turns out he was a friend of the groom. He was a really good-looking guy and came across as charming and witty. I was bowled over, to be honest, and we started seeing each other and began a relationship a couple of months later. During the next few months, I found out what he was really like."

"And that was?" asked Sam.

"He was a control freak. And he got jealous if I even looked at another guy. Over the time we were together, he began minimizing me. Suggesting I was stupid, implying he was more intelligent than me because he had a four-year degree, accusing me of cheating when I went out with my girlfriends. He wanted to know everything I did and at what time. According to him, I could never do anything right. I got fed up and told him I never wanted to see him again. That's when it got physical."

"He got physical with you?"

"He grabbed me by the arm, threw me down on the couch, and started screaming all sorts of obscenities in my face. I had bruises from where he grabbed my arm so hard. I fought back and slapped him across the face and told him to get out. He hit me back and bloodied my lip. Finally, he got up and left. As he was going out the door, he turned and said he wasn't through with me. That scared me, so the next day, I filed an Order of Protection against him. An attorney in our office tried to get me to go to the police, but I figured since I slapped him, it might be seen as me initiating the violence. But John—that's the attorney from our office who I talked to—he said if he violated the Order of Protection, he would go after him."

"Did he violate the Order?" asked Joe.

"He sent me abusive emails where he said some horrible things. I showed them to John, and he sent Josh a letter threatening to take legal action if he didn't cease and desist. After that, I never saw him or heard from him again."

"Nice guy," said Sam.

"Yeah. Real nice."

"We're investigating him because a woman who recently broke up with him was found murdered in her apartment," explained Joe.

She gasped. "Omigod."

"He sent her abusive emails, and she believed he was stalking her, so she filed an Order of Protection against him, too."

"And she was killed?" asked a horrified Wilken. "And you think Josh may have done it?"

"He's a person of interest at the moment, but we have no evidence that proves he's the offender."

"My god...I can't believe it."

"Our victim was tased, raped, and strangled in her apartment. In your opinion, do you think he's capable of doing such a thing?" asked Joe.

Wilken was silent for a few moments, processing the information. Then she looked up and said, "Josh may be an asshole, but...it's hard for me to believe he would do something like that. He reacts on the spur of the moment. This murder sounds calculated."

"But he was physically abusive to you in the end," said Sam.

"He was, but he only hit me after I hit him first. That's what brought it on. I can see him abusing other women psychologically like he did me. But killing someone...that's a leap, I think." Shaking her head, she added, "I...I don't know if he would go that far."

"Did you ever think he was stalking you?" asked Sam.

"No, I never saw him any place where I was. I think the letter John sent him must have scared him off. He valued his precious job with the Cubs too much."

"We'd like to interview Josh's acquaintances," said Joe. "Would you happen to know the names of any of his friends?"

"Oh, jeez. Uh...there's Rob Cragar and a guy named Dino. Don't remember his last name. Sorry. They're the only ones I can think of."

"You know how we can get ahold of Rob Cragar?"

"He's some kind of cybersecurity expert. Last I knew, he worked for a place called...uh... Ingram...Interventions. No, wait_Ingram Innovations. That's it."

"Ingram Innovations," repeated Sam.

"That's it. I think he works in the Loop somewhere."

After a few more questions, Joe and Sam felt they had all the information they needed, so they thanked her for her assistance and concluded the interview. On their drive back to Area 3, Sam asked, "What do you think?"

"I agree with Wilken that Blake is a 'fucking asshole,' as she put it, but there are some problems I see with the way he could have gotten into Engstrom's apartment, given she would have recognized him at the door. Why would she allow him in?"

"Good question," said Sam. "But he could have if he still had a key. I think we need to search his apartment."

"Agreed. Let's apply for a search warrant."

Joe looked into Ingram Innovations to locate Blake's friend, Rob Cragar. It turned out that Ingram Innovations was a technology firm located in the Loop on South Wacker Drive. His call to their number was answered by a recording giving him options. *Wonderful.* He pressed number nine to get him to a "customer representative."

"Ingram Innovations, Kara speaking."

"Hello, Kara. This is Detective Joe Erickson with the Chicago Police Department. During one of our investigations, the name of Rob Cragar came up. We were told he was employed by Ingram Innovations, is that correct?"

"Let me transfer you to Personnel. Hold, please."

After a minute on hold, a female voice answered. "Leticia Evans. May I help you?"

Evans listened as Joe explained who he was and asked if the company employed Rob Cragar.

"He is presently employed with our company."

"Does he have an extension so I can speak with him?"

"Can I ask what this is about?"

"An investigation we're conducting. He's an acquaintance of a person of interest, and we would like to speak with him. He's not in any kind of trouble. We're just looking for information."

"All right," said Evans. "If you hold, I'll contact him and see if he's available to take your call."

Again, Joe was put on hold. After listening to their music for a couple of minutes, Evans returned to the line and told him she was transferring his call to Cragar's extension. As his call was being transferred, the line went dead. "Dammit!" said Joe as he slammed down his phone in frustration and got up from his chair. His outburst caused other detectives sitting around him to look at him.

"You all right, Joe?" asked Marv Hopkins, who worked property crimes.

"Yeah. I'm all right," replied Joe. He walked to get coffee and popped a pod in the Keurig since he saw there was only sludge in the coffee pot. That added to his annoyance.

"You know how to run that thing?"

Joe turned and saw Detective Michelle Cardona smiling ever so slightly.

"I need coffee, and this is the only way I can get a cup, given what's in the pot."

"I see what you mean," she said as she emptied its sludge into the sink and began making another pot. "You look pissed off. Something happen?"

"You ever get shuffled from one person to another, to another, and to another during a phone call, and when you're finally being transferred to the one person you need to speak with, your call gets cut off?"

Cardona snorted a laugh. "Sounds like you need more than coffee."

"I'm hoping coffee will suffice."

After the Keurig filled his mug, he looked at Cardona, who was scooping coffee into the filter. "It's this case that's getting to me."

"What case is that?"

"A young woman was tased, raped, and strangled in her apartment. And a box with dead flowers was found next to her. No evidence pointing to an offender so far. Only a former boyfriend as a person of interest. Maybe DNA will give us something. You know how that goes."

"Hurry up and wait."

Joe responded with a mirthless chuckle.

"Good luck," she said.

"Yeah," said Joe, and he returned to his desk.

He was not in the mood to try contacting Rob Cragar's office again, so he chose to wait until tomorrow when he was in a better state of mind. If his call was cut off again, he would go to his workplace and speak with him face to face. *You'd think a company named "Innovations" would have a more innovative phone system,* he thought.

Chapter Nine

The next day, Joe received an email message from Kendra saying, "I have something. Call me." Joe dialed Kendra's number, and she picked up right away.

"I received your email. You have some information?" he asked.

"I do. You know that loose hair I retrieved from Amber Engstrom's body?"

"Yeah?"

"Well, it was not a match to her. Thought you'd want to know. It's been sent out for DNA analysis, but as you know, that'll take some time. I'll let you know when we get the DNA information back. Hopefully, it will lead you to a suspect."

"Could you tell if it was from a male or female?"

"No, we couldn't determine that. But it looked different under a microscope."

"Our offender, maybe."

"It's possible, but not necessarily. It could also be from someone she had intercourse with before she was attacked."

"Got it. We collected a water bottle our person of interest drank from. Maybe the DNA from it will be a match to the hair."

"One more thing. The lab came through on the red fibers. They're from a silk scarf. Unfortunately, these scarves are not unique, and a lot of different budget stores around the city sell them."

"Wonderful."

"Sorry about that. But the lab may get more specific evidence for you when the DNA results come back."

You'll let me know?"

"ASAP," replied Kendra.

As soon as the call ended, Joe told Sam about Kendra's call. "Maybe we'll get a match from the water bottle Blake drank from."

"We were lucky he didn't take it with him when he left," said Sam.

"Are you going to write up a request for a search warrant on Blake's apartment?"

"Working on it as we speak."

Later, Sam ran the application for the search warrant down to Judge Blackman. The judge was in court, and his administrative assistant, Bret Carlson, told Sam that Blackman would look it over later today. After reading over the request, he felt Blackman would probably sign it. Hopefully, he was right.

* * *

In a better state of mind than he was yesterday, Joe made another call to Ingram Innovations, and this time, he got through to Rob Cragar's extension. Cragar agreed to be interviewed for their ongoing investigation, but Joe avoided informing him it would involve Josh Blake. It was better to keep it vague so he would not react unfavorably or contact Blake about it, since they were friends.

Rob Cragar came to Area 3 Headquarters for the interview a day later. Joe was talking to Lieutenant Bellamy at the time, so Sam brought Cragar to the interrogation room. He asked for coffee, and Sam left him there while he fetched a cup. Spotting Joe leaving the lieutenant's office, Sam signaled to him.

"Cragar got here early. He's in the interrogation room."

Joe followed Sam into the room and saw Cragar standing with both hands in the pockets of his khaki pants. He was in his late twenties, and he was checking out his hair in the mirror when the two detectives entered. Joe introduced himself as Sam placed the coffee on the table where he wanted Cragar to sit. After the introductions and handshakes, they all sat down.

To establish a friendly rapport, Joe asked a personal question to begin the interview.

"Out of curiosity, what do you do at Ingram Innovations?"

"I set up computer systems for our clients, some well-known corporate entities. They explain what they want, and I'm one of the guys who makes it happen."

"So, you set up your clients' websites?"

"We have people who do that, but I design systems used specifically by employees within a company. It's a lot more sophisticated than the design of a personal website."

"I understand."

Cragar looked from Sam to Joe and asked, "You said you wanted to interview me because of some sort of investigation?"

"That's right. We're investigating the death of Amber Engstrom."

"Oh."

"Did you happen to know her?" asked Joe.

"I basically knew who she was. My wife and I went out with her and one of my buddies a couple times."

"Josh Blake?"

"Yeah. I only knew her because she was dating Josh. I wouldn't have known her otherwise."

"What can you tell me about their relationship?"

"It didn't last."

"Can you be a little more specific?"

"For some reason, Josh's relationships don't stick. He hooks up with beautiful women, and after a few months, they break it off with him."

"So, they break up with him?"

"Yeah."

"Do you have any idea why his relationships fail?"

"Not really. He's never shared that kind of stuff with me."

"How many relationships has he had since you've known him?"

"Well...three that I know of."

"We know about Amber Engstrom and Roxanne Wilken," said Sam. "Who was the third one?"

"Uh, that was…sorry, I'm bad with names. "It was uh…Chastity…no. No, it was Charity. Yeah, Charity Allyn."

"You wouldn't happen to know her whereabouts, would you?"

"Josh told me she was moving back to Oregon because her father was ill."

"Did you believe him?"

"I dunno," Cragar shrugged. "That's what he told me. Maybe he was saying that to save face. Who knows?"

As Joe was writing this information down, Cragar asked, "What's all this have to do with your investigation, anyway?"

Looking up from his notepad, Joe replied, "Josh Blake is a person of interest in the death of Amber Engstrom."

"Holy shit," mumbled Cragar, squirming in his seat. He pulled a handkerchief from his tweed blazer and began mopping his brow.

"So, anything you can tell us about him could eliminate him from consideration."

"From what we know so far," said Sam, "both Engstrom and Wilken broke up with him because he was psychologically abusive. They feared him enough that both took out Orders of Protection against him."

Silence. After taking a sip of his coffee, Cragar spoke. "That's news to me. He never let on about it when we talked. Wow."

"Did you ever witness anything like a temper flare-up or spite toward anyone?"

"No, not at all. He seems like a pretty cool-headed guy when I'm around him."

"Did you ever see another side of him when he was with a girlfriend?"

"Not really. I mean, he would get annoyed once in a while. Like poor service at a bar or lousy drivers, but I never saw him really pissed off, if that's what you're asking."

"Do you think him capable of raping and strangling Amber Engstrom?"

Cragar's face registered shock, and he sputtered, "Is—is that what happened to her?"

Joe nodded.

"That's not the Josh Blake that I know at all...no. He couldn't have done that."

"Did he ever talk about payback or getting even with anyone?" asked Sam.

"Never."

Joe and Sam continued questioning Cragar for another fifteen minutes, but the picture he painted of Blake was that of a good friend. He didn't recall Blake showing any hints he was capable of violence, much less first-degree murder.

Joe ended the interview by saying, "We'd appreciate you keeping this interview to yourself and not mentioning anything about it to Mr. Blake. It could hinder our investigation."

Cragar agreed, and Sam escorted him out to the parking lot. When Sam returned, Joe said, "We need to speak with Charity Allyn."

"You think she's in Oregon like Cragar said?" asked Sam.

"Maybe. Maybe not. It could have been a lie, Blake made up to explain their breakup."

"She never filed an Order of Protection against him. That much we know. Maybe she wasn't afraid of him."

"Or she moved halfway across the country because she was, and she wanted to get away from him."

"Or...he made her disappear," suggested Sam."

Sam's suggestion stopped Joe in his tracks. "I hope to hell that's not the case."

"We'd better do some checking."

Chapter Ten

Joe began researching Charity Allyn. He found a record of her in the Illinois Driver's License database. Her photo revealed an attractive twenty-three-year-old blonde. Her appearance suggested she was the same type as Blake's other girlfriends. But there was a problem. The license was expired. It should have been renewed two years ago.

Further research revealed that she was living in Salem, Oregon, the state's capital. As he was trying to locate her current address and phone number, he received a phone call from Michelle Cardona.

"Remember when you told me about your case? The one with a young woman who was tased and killed in her apartment. Box of flowers present?"

"Yeah," replied Joe with suspicion in his voice.

"Well, my partner and I were called in on a homicide case. It looks like the same M.O. for your murder case. Thought you'd want to know."

Her call took Joe aback. After a moment, he asked, "Are you at the scene?"

"We are."

"Where is it?"

She gave him the address—an apartment on North Broadway Street.

"We'll be there shortly. Thanks for the heads up."

After notifying Sam, they drove to the North Broadway address given to them by Detective Cardona. They arrived at the modern, upscale apartment building and saw the Medical Examiner's van parked out front. They badged their way past the officer at the front door and entered the building. A uniformed officer stood there talking with the woman in the lobby. After showing their IDs, he logged them in and directed them to the third floor.

They got off the elevator and walked down the corridor to where two uniformed officers, Detective Cardona and her partner, Detective Rick Murphy, stood outside Unit 319.

As they approached Cardona and Murphy, Joe asked, "What have you got?"

Cardona responded, "Regina Fischer, twenty-six. Her friend, Ashley Grimaldi, found her. She had a key to her apartment so she could water her plants when she was out of town. She lives down the hall in Unit 306. She's there now."

They peered inside the door and saw the room. It had light gray walls with modern art hanging here and there. A white couch, two gray chairs, and glass tables made up the living room. On the oak floor next to the living room area rug was a young woman's body. Naked from the waist down, her blouse was open, and her breasts were exposed, much like Amber Engstrom's body. A box from a florist lay a short distance from the door.

The ME, Frank Barstow, was dressed in Tyvek coveralls, boots, gloves, and a mask. He was working over the body and looked up to see Joe and Sam standing outside the door, looking in. Acknowledging them with a nod, he went about his business for another ten minutes before packing up his equipment and walking to the door.

Pulling off his mask and hood, Barstow stood before the detectives. He was fifty-something with many years of experience with the medical examiner's office. Well-known to the detectives, he had been called in on numerous cases they had investigated.

Looking at Cardona, Barstow said, "She was killed approximately eighteen hours ago. There's a taser burn on her abdomen, and she was sexually assaulted. Cause of death was strangulation with some kind of ligature."

"Ligature," repeated Sam. "With a red silk scarf, maybe?"

Barstow raised an eyebrow and replied, "Well…it's possible. I'll know more during the autopsy when I can look for microscopic particles in her neck. Why do you ask?"

"Everything about this death appears to be a copy of a murder we investigated a week ago. Kendra Solitsky was the attending ME on that one," replied Joe. "Did you examine the contents of the flower box by any chance?"

"No. I've called in Evidence Techs. I'm sure they'll be checking that out."

"Since this appears to be connected to your investigation, you want to take over the lead on this one?" asked Rick Murphy. "That way, we won't get in each other's way."

"You made any progress on the other case?" asked Cardona.

"Some. We have a person of interest, but not enough evidence to arrest him. We'll have to see if he has a connection with this victim. You know what she did for a living?"

"Her friend told us she was a model."

"A model?" reacted Joe. He looked at Sam and saw the surprise on his face. "Yeah. Why?"

"Our first victim worked as a model, too," said Sam.

Cardona considered what Sam had said and then looked from Sam to Joe. "This is no coincidence. You suppose they knew each other?"

"I don't know, but we'll find out," said Joe.

Looking through the apartment door, Sam remarked, "Pretty spiffy digs."

"Models can make good money," replied Barstow as he removed his Tyvek coveralls. "My daughter worked as a model before she got married. Told me if you work for a famous designer or get featured in the media with a product, you can make a bundle."

"Let me know when the autopsy is scheduled. I'll want to attend," said Joe. "You bet."

Joe hoped the Evidence Techs would be Art Casey and Jerry Bristow, who worked the first case. But it was Big John Gustafson and Connie O'Connell who arrived to go over the apartment with a fine-toothed comb. He was called Big John because he stood about six feet six and weighed around two-forty-five, just like the song.

Joe greeted Gustafson and said, "There's a box from a florist in there. I'd be interested to know what's inside it."

"We'll check it," he replied.

Five hours later, Gustafson and O'Connell had completed their work and were packing out the equipment and samples they had taken.

Joe approached Gustafson and asked, "What about the flower box?"

"It contained four dried-out roses with this note," said Gustafson, handing Joe a plastic sleeve containing a card. It stated, "Sic semper scortilla."

"Thus always to bitches," said Joe. "Just like the card found at Amber Engstrom's apartment." He handed it to Sam, who looked it over.

"It's the same M.O. down to a tee," said Sam, returning the sleeve to Gustafson.

"Not quite," said Joe, looking at Gustafson. "You said there were four dead roses, not three?"

"Yeah. Four."

Overhearing Joe and Sam's conversation, Gustafson said, "You said you've seen this same evidence before?"

"Another homicide a week ago. Casey and Bristow worked the scene."

"Then I'll coordinate with them."

"Was there a computer and cell phone in there?" asked Sam.

"Yeah. Both.

"We'll get a search warrant for those and send them out to the Regional Computer Forensics Lab," said Joe. "Her messages may lead us somewhere."

As Gustafson and O'Connell were securing their equipment, Joe looked at O'Connell and asked, "Is it all right if we go into the apartment?"

"Yeah. We're done," said O'Connell.

"Let me know if you find something."

"Of course," she replied. Then she and Gustafson began walking down the hall with their evidence samples and equipment.

Joe and Sam gloved up and entered the victim's apartment. The living room area, with its carefully chosen furniture pieces, wall hangings, and accessories, suggested a professional decorator's touch. The victim's laptop computer sat on an antique secretary's desk with a laser printer positioned on a short, square vintage stool next to it. Framed photos of what looked like friends and family members lined the top of the secretary's desk. There were plants ranging from philodendrons to Chinese evergreens and palms strategically placed in various places throughout the apartment.

"This lady really liked plants," said Joe.

"No wonder she needed someone to water them for her. She has a small fortune tied up in greenery," replied Sam.

Her cell phone was on a glass table beside the couch, along with a copy of Richard Helms' novel, *A Kind and Savage Place.* When Joe saw it, he thought, *How ironic is that?*

Joe moved on to the bedroom while Sam began checking the kitchen. Everything in the bedroom was neat and in its place. The bed had multiple pillows coordinated with the comforter and curtains. There were no articles of clothing lying about. This woman kept her apartment as neat as a pin.

After inspecting the drawers in her bathroom, Joe found nothing unusual and nothing suggesting a male partner who may have been staying here regularly. After he had looked over both rooms, he walked to the kitchen where Sam was completing his search."

"Find anything of interest?" asked Joe.

Closing the door to the refrigerator, Sam replied, "Looks like she enjoyed cooking. Lots of spices, cooking utensils, and cookbooks. Leftover linguini in white clam sauce in the fridge. Making me hungry for some good Italian food!"

"Carolyn doesn't cook for you?"

"Sure, she does. But she cooks all that healthy stuff."

"That's because she cares about you."

"I know, but once in a while, I wish she'd care a little less."

Joe chuckled and said, "There's nothing I can see in the bedroom or bathroom that might be relevant. What about you?"

"Nothing," replied Sam. "Let's hope forensics can turn up something."

"And her phone and computer."

"I'll send through a search warrant for those when we get back to the office."

They left the apartment and attached the crime scene tape across the door. Upon leaving, they told the attending uniformed officers they could remove the crime scene tape from outside the building's entrance doors.

Joe and Sam began canvassing the occupants of apartments on the same floor as the crime scene. No one saw anyone delivering flowers to Regina

Fischer. Then they rang Unit 306, the apartment of Ashley Grimaldi, who discovered Fischer's body. She opened her door a crack and peered out at them.

"Ashley Grimaldi?"

"Yes."

"Chicago PD. Could we speak with you?" Joe held up his ID so she could see it."

Undoing the security chain, she opened the door. Still holding up their IDs, Joe and Sam introduced themselves.

"Come in," said Grimaldi. She appeared to be about the same age as the victim. Her eyes were red and puffy from crying. They followed her into her apartment, which was decorated in a bohemian style that reminded Joe of Liz and Jared's home. Black and white framed posters hung from the teal walls, and brightly colored throws and pillows were abundant on the light beige couch and rattan chair. She shared Regina Fischer's love of plants, as large dieffenbachia, rubber plants, pothos, and other assorted potted plants were placed throughout the room.

"Have a seat," she said, indicating the couch. She sat in the rattan chair opposite them.

"How did you know Regina Fischer?" asked Joe.

"We bumped into each other in the hall a few times and eventually began talking. She found out I was a plant person, and having that in common is how we got to know each other."

"You had a key to her apartment, right?"

"Uh-huh. I agreed to water her plants. She was gone a lot because of her modeling jobs and didn't want them to go without water."

"What can you tell us about her?"

She was really smart and well-traveled. She liked to talk, and I liked to listen, so we were good conversation partners. She was a good cook, too. Seems she was always trying out new recipes and testing them on me. I...really liked her."

"She was very attractive. Did she have a boyfriend?" asked Sam.

"She was gay. Something else we had in common."

"Oh."

"Does that surprise you?"

Sam shook his head and answered, "No. You're cool."

"Nothing surprises us anymore," added Joe. "Thanks for being forthcoming."

She pulled a handkerchief from her jeans and blew her nose. "Sorry...to answer your question: no. She wasn't in a relationship or seeing anybody. She would have said something to me if she was."

"So, you and Regina were close enough that she would confide that in you?"

"Yeah. But if you want to know if we were lovers, no. We weren't."

"Did she ever talk about enemies or people she had problems with?"

"Not really. She could be critical of people, especially some of the people she worked with, but she never mentioned anybody she was afraid of or worried about."

"Do you know who her next of kin would be?"

"She has a sister. She lives in Bolingbrook. Works as a physical therapist at a hospital."

"You know her name?"

"Megan. Megan Fischer. She isn't married, or at least she wasn't last I heard."

"What about her parents?"

"I don't know their names. She told me they moved from Chicago to Ft. Lauderdale. That's all I know.

Joe was writing all this information down when she asked, "Can I go in and check on her plants? To see if they need water."

"Right now, it's a crime scene," said Sam. "But it'll probably be released in a few days. Don't go in while the tape is on the door."

"If Regina didn't water them when she got back, they may need it. That's why I went down there. Can you let me in so I can check on them? They can't go for another week without getting stressed."

"You know where she was when she went out of town?"

"No. She told me she'd be gone for a week. I didn't know she'd come back."

Joe and Sam agreed and took Grimaldi to Fischer's apartment, where they observed her checking the soil and watering several of the plants. When she finished, they reattached the crime scene tape and escorted her back to her apartment.

After a few more questions, they ended the interview with Grimaldi. As Joe and Sam began leaving the building, they met a man entering the vestibule from the street. Sam stopped him, showed his ID, and asked, "Excuse me. You live here?"

"Yeah. Up on the third floor. Why?"

"Did you happen to see anyone delivering flowers yesterday?"

"Yesterday? Uh…yeah, I did, actually. It was late in the afternoon."

"Can you describe him?" asked Joe.

"I didn't pay much attention, but he was about average height. And he was wearing a cap and sunglasses—and one of those Covid masks."

"Was he young, old?"

"I don't know. Middle-aged, I guess."

"Anything else you can remember?"

"Like I said, I didn't pay much attention. Sorry."

"Well, thanks. You've been helpful," said Sam.

"Why all the questions?" he asked with a curious look.

Sam glanced at Joe, who was still writing in his notebook. He decided to tell him. "A person was found murdered here earlier today."

He gasped, "Are you kidding me?"

"Afraid not."

"Who was it?"

"One of the residents on your floor. Regina Fischer. Did you know her?"

"No. I might have seen her at some point, but I didn't know her. You know how it is. People don't get to know other residents."

"Thanks for your help," said Joe. "What's your name?"

"Jim Wells."

"Thanks again, Jim," said Sam. Wells left the vestibule, presumably on his way to his apartment.

As Joe drove back to Area 3, Sam said, "We need to search Josh Blake's place as soon as possible."

"Agreed," replied Joe. "Check to see if Judge Blackman signed it, and we'll serve the warrant."

Sam pulled out his phone and checked his email. There was a message from Judge Blackman's office. "He signed it."

"Good."

Chapter Eleven

Back at his desk, Joe called the Bolingbrook Police Department, asking them to make a death notification. He gave them the information about Regina Fischer's sister, Megan, telling them she was a physical therapist at a hospital. He had located an address for her on the Illinois Department of Professional Regulation website, where one can search for anyone holding a state license. He gave them the address he had found, along with his phone number, so she could call him to get details about her sister's death.

After obtaining a copy of the search warrant, they drove to Blake's residence on West Warren Boulevard in the Near West Side neighborhood. A black iron fence surrounded the red brick condominium building, a feature present on several other buildings on the block. The Near West Side is a neighborhood popular with young professionals and is replete with many restaurants, bars, and condominiums, so it wasn't surprising that Blake chose to live there.

Joe and Sam entered a small vestibule and pressed the button for Blake's 2E condo.

"Yes?"

"Chicago PD," replied Joe. We need to speak with you."

"What about?"

"You need to buzz us in, Mr. Blake. We have to speak with you in person."

"All right." The tone of his voice reflected his annoyance. Joe thought to himself, *He'll be even more annoyed when he sees the search warrant.*

The door unlocked, and Joe and Sam took the stairs to the second floor and Blake's 2E condominium. Joe rang and the door opened, revealing Josh Blake in a tee-shirt and jeans. Apparently, he was working from home today.

"What is it?" asked a surly Blake.

Sam shoved the search warrant in his face and said, "We have a warrant to search your condo, Mr. Blake."

Before Blake could protest, they barged past him and began gloving up. Blake hit the ceiling, sputtering obscenities and threatening them with a lawsuit. After hearing enough of his belligerence, Sam responded.

"Shut up, you peckerhead, or I'll arrest you for obstruction!"

"I'm calling my attorney," said Blake as he pulled out his cell phone.

"Go right ahead. By the way, you'll need to wait in the hall."

Blake moved into the hall, his phone up to his ear and a frown on his face. After Sam closed the door, they began searching Blake's apartment for any red fabric and evidence of dead flowers, floral boxes, a taser, and DNA evidence. While Sam began searching his refrigerator and kitchen cabinets, Joe went to his bathroom, collected hair from his hairbrush, and bagged his toothbrush. After searching the bathroom, Joe moved to the bedroom, where he searched all the drawers in his dresser looking for a taser or any scarves with red fibers.

When Joe moved on to his closet, he noticed a small, dark circle above the closet doors. He reached up and touched it. It had a smooth surface, like glass. He opened the closet door, and inside he saw a small wire running along where the wall meets the ceiling. It ran to a small video recorder hidden under a sweater. Since the camera was pointed at the bed, Joe suspected Blake may have been recording his sexual encounters.

Leaving it in place, he moved to the living room and searched the drawers in a cabinet under the television. One particular drawer was filled with DVDs. Looking them over, Joe saw they were all porn videos. "Found a stash of porn here," he called out.

"Oh, yeah?" replied Sam, and he walked over to take a look. He picked up a couple of DVDs and looked them over. "Quite a collection."

"Nothing illegal since the cover images don't suggest children."

"Just a nice over-sexed heterosexual," quipped Sam.

"Yeah...hold on...look at these," said Joe, holding up a blank DVD case marked "Amber." It contained a DVD also labeled "Amber." There were other such cases and DVDs marked "Karla," "Charity," "Roxanne," and "Tess."

"What the hell...?" muttered Sam.

"He has what appears to be a hidden camera pointed at his bed. I'd be willing to bet he's been recording himself having sex."

"Sick bastard. You suppose Amber Engstrom found out he was recording their romps in the sack and threatened to go to the police?"

"It could be another reason why she dumped him. When she spoke to her friend, she referred to him as a 'creep.'"

"What do you want to do? The search warrant doesn't specify DVDs."

"Let it go. I'll let Roxanne Wilken know what we found. I'm sure she'll go after him for recording her having sex with him."

Sam returned to searching the kitchen while Joe checked under the furniture and behind the books in a bookcase. When he finished, he stepped to where Sam was working and began helping him check the kitchen cabinets.

After an hour of searching, they concluded there was no additional evidence specified by the search warrant.

As they were concluding their search, a middle-aged man opened the door to the condo and entered, scratching his bald pate. His demeanor suggested a terrier looking for a rat.

"What the hell is going on here?" he asked in a loud voice.

"Who are you?" asked Joe.

"Howard J. Stein. I'm Joshua Blake's attorney."

Joe stopped what he was doing and approached Stein. "Well, Howard J. Stein, I assume you read the search warrant?"

"I have."

"Then you know we're conducting a legal search of your client's residence."

"This is outrageous. It's a violation of my client's rights," Stein replied.

"I don't care what you think," replied Joe calmly. "We have the right to search this apartment. I suggest you leave while we complete our work here. Interfering with our search will be considered 'obstruction.'"

After glaring at Joe briefly, Stein turned and walked into the hall and began conferring with Josh Blake. Fifteen minutes later, Joe and Sam completed their search, failing to find anything to implicate Blake in the murders of Amber Engstrom and Regina Fischer. Joe hoped the DNA evidence he collected might match the foreign hair found on Amber Engstrom's body.

Joe and Sam entered the hall where Stein was conversing with his client and explained they had completed the search of Blake's condo.

"Hey! That's my toothbrush!" cried Blake after he saw it in an evidence bag.

"No shit, Sherlock," said Sam. "It's evidence."

"For what?"

"DNA."

Blake began complaining to Stein, but Joe intervened before it got out of hand. "Before we go, we have a few questions for your client, Mr. Stein."

"May we go inside rather than answer your questions in a hallway?" asked Stein.

"Of course."

As they entered the condo, they gathered in an area close to the door.

Blake objected to answering any questions, but Stein instructed him to cooperate. "If you don't answer their questions here, they can take you in, and you'll be answering questions in their interrogation room."

"Been there, done that," said Blake. He looked at Stein momentarily, then said, "All right. What do you want to know?"

"Where were you yesterday between five and seven o'clock?"

Blake looked at Stein, who nodded he should answer. "After work, I went downtown to pick up a couple of tickets for a play I want to see. Then I went to a sports bar to meet a woman for drinks."

"Can you verify that?" asked Sam.

"If I have to, I suppose I can. Why?"

"A young woman was found murdered in her apartment. The same M.O. as the murder of Amber Engstrom."

"And you think I was responsible for her death now?"

Stein spoke up, saying, "Don't say another word." Then he turned to Joe and Sam. "If you don't have evidence implicating my client, I suggest you leave. This is bordering on harassment, and we won't tolerate your witch hunt. From now on, if you have questions for Mr. Blake, you contact me."

"Fine," said Joe. "But we'll expect documentation of your client's alibi." Then, looking at Blake, he said, "Soon." He nodded to Sam, and they left the condo, drove back to Area 3, and logged in their DNA evidence.

Chapter Twelve

Joe met with Sam the following day to determine the next steps in their investigation. Over the last few days, he was becoming less convinced that Josh Blake was Amber Engstrom's killer. And if he came through with a solid alibi for the Regina Fischer murder, he could be off the hook for the Engstrom's death, unless the DNA was a match.

An email message came in from the Office of the Cook County Medical Examiner. It was from Frank Barstow. It said the autopsy on Regina Fischer was scheduled for 3:00 p.m.

At 11:00, he called and left a message on Roxanne Wilken's answering machine, asking her to call him. Half an hour later, she returned his call.

"I got your message," Wilken said.

"We obtained a search warrant for Josh Blake's apartment, and we found a hidden camera in his bedroom and some DVDs with women's names on them. One was marked 'Roxanne,' and I thought you should know about it."

She gasped. "That son-of-a-bitch!"

"You didn't hear it from me. Our warrant didn't specify videos, so we couldn't take them. But you might want to expose him. There were other DVDs with women's names on them."

"You didn't watch them, did you?"

"No, we didn't."

"Thank god for that."

"That particular Roxanne could be someone else."

"I doubt it. Thanks for letting me know. What should I do?"

"Contact our Vice Unit and see if they can help you. Say that I referred you."

Joe gave her the contact information for the Vice Unit and told her to ask for John Chamberlain, a vice officer he knew.

Shortly after 1:00 p.m., Joe received a message that Howard J. Stein had arrived at Area 3 and was asking to see him. Joe met Stein and brought him up to the interrogation room. Sitting across from Joe and Sam, Stein opened his briefcase and pulled out two documents. He had not spoken to them until this point, other than to say he had "something" they would be interested in seeing.

Pushing one document to Joe and another to Sam, Stein explained, "The first is a copy of a sworn deposition from Callie Hessler stating she met Josh Blake for drinks and dinner at the Irish Bar & Grill and was with him in the late afternoon and early evening, on the day and time of Regina Fischer's death. The second document is a copy of Josh Blake's credit card charge for theatre tickets at Steppenwolf Theatre. The time on the receipt corroborates my client's statement that he purchased theatre tickets after work."

Joe and Sam swapped the documents and read them over. After a moment, Joe glanced at Sam, who handed the document back to him.

"Do you find this satisfactory?" asked Stein.

"It looks acceptable," replied Joe.

"Then, you'll stop harassing my client?"

Rather than address Stein's assertion of harassment, Joe stood up and said, "I think we're done here."

"Thanks for coming in," added Sam, even though he didn't mean it.

Closing his briefcase, Stein rose and stepped to the door. "I can find my own way out. Good day, gentlemen."

As they watched him leave the room, Sam said, "I guess this pretty much exonerates Josh Blake in Regina Fischer's murder."

Joe picked up the documents and sighed. His disappointment was palpable, though he had misgivings about Blake as a suspect.

"This will let him off the hook for Engstrom's murder, too."

"Yeah," said Joe. "He's not our guy. No need to contact Charity Allyn."

"Think Roxanne Wilken will try to have him prosecuted for his sex videos?"

"Oh, yeah. She was really pissed off about it. I told her to contact John Chamberlain in Vice."

After leaving the interrogation room, Joe made photocopies of the documents Stein provided and filed copies in both the Amber Engstrom murder file and the one he had started on Regina Fischer.

What was nagging at Joe was the connection between the victims. Did someone have it in for models in general or just these two? Why were there three roses at Engstrom's apartment and four at Fischer's? Were there two more models killed, and Engstrom and Fischer made it three and four? And did they know each other? He wondered if the same modeling agency represented both Fischer and Engstrom.

He checked the notes he took on the Amber Engstrom case and saw the name of the modeling agency that had been stamped on the back of her photos: TGM Talent. Looking it up, he found their office was located in the Loop on Dearborn Street. He wanted to go there, but he had to attend Fischer's autopsy. It would have to wait until tomorrow.

Joe had attended numerous autopsies on homicide victims. Frank Barstow was conducting this one, and he knew his work to be thorough.

After donning scrubs and a face mask, Joe walked to the autopsy room where Lane Sherwood, Barstow's assistant, ensured all the instruments were laid out and ready.

At 3:00 p.m., the autopsy began. Barstow confirmed that Fischer's cause of death was strangulation with a ligature. He found microscopic evidence of red fibers in the wound around her neck. He also confirmed that she had been sexually assaulted, but there was no sign of semen, and found no foreign hairs on the body.

Like Amber Engstrom, Fischer had dental veneers to make her teeth look perfect. She also had hair extensions to add length and volume. He scraped her fingernails for possible forensic evidence.

After swabbing various areas on her skin, he began the Y-incision and proceeded to open up of her chest cavity. The autopsy went along without any surprises. Barstow concluded she was a healthy, twenty-six-year-old female who had never given birth. Cause of death was manual strangulation.

When tissue dissection began, Joe left and went into the bathroom to throw water on his face and wash his hands. After changing out of his scrubs, he left and drove back to Area 3. He informed Sam that Barstow found microscopic red fibers in the ligature marks on her neck.

"I think we can assume the same offender was responsible for both attacks."

"If they get a match on the red fibers from each victim, it'll be conclusive," remarked Sam.

Sam and Joe agreed that their next step should be contacting the florist whose box contained the dead roses found in Fischer's apartment. Flowers & More. was located on the ground level of a red brick building on West Division Street. Upon entering, Joe and Sam were greeted by the smell of fresh flowers. On their way to the counter, they walked past shelf displays of ceramic planters and vases. Joe spied a planter that matched the one Destiny had placed in their living room.

No one was present behind the counter. Sam looked around and was about hit the bell on top of the counter when the cooler opened, and a middle-aged man wearing a green apron appeared carrying a handful of carnations. He looked a little surprised when he saw Joe and Sam.

"Oh...you must have just come in."

"We did," said Joe.

Putting the flowers on a nearby table, he asked, "What can I help you with?"

Joe showed his ID and said, "I'm Detective Joe Erickson, Chicago PD. This is my partner, Detective Renaldo." Seeing a name embroidered on his apron, Joe asked, "Are you Alex?"

"Yeah. Alex Pappas. I'm one of the owners.

"Do you keep records of purchases by customers?"

"We do. We would have that information if a purchase was made by a credit or debit card. Why are you interested?"

"A box with your imprint was found at the scene of a homicide we're investigating."

"Oh, dear."

"It contained four long-stem roses. They were most likely purchased within the last sixty days by a man. Can you check your records and provide us with a list of male customers who bought long-stem roses?"

"The last sixty days?"

"Yes."

"I can pull that information up in our system, but I'm busy right now. Can I get back to you?"

"Certainly," replied Joe. "You don't happen to remember a man buying long-stem roses, do you?"

Alex laughed and said, "Which one? Almost all of our customers buying long-stem roses are men."

"I suppose that makes sense. We think the man who made the purchase may be the offender, so your assistance would be appreciated."

"How soon do you need it?"

"As soon as you can get it to us."

"I can have that ready tomorrow morning."

Sam asked, "Do you have security video in your store?"

"No, we don't. We probably should, given the possibility of robbery and vandalism. But it's an expense we can't justify at the moment."

At this time, a woman entered from a door at the back of the store. She walked up to the counter and addressed Alex.

"Everything's unloaded."

"Thanks," said Alex. "My wife, Sophia." Looking at his wife, he explained, "These are police detectives. They need a list of men who bought long-stem roses during the past sixty days."

"It's part of an investigation we're conducting," said Joe.

"I told them we could pull up that information on our system."

Nodding, Sophia replied, "We can do that. But some people pay in cash, and we wouldn't have a name. Only a record of the purchase."

"Do you remember any men who might have paid in cash, or remember any man who may have stood out for some reason? He might have been wearing a ballcap and a medical mask."

Alex and Sophia thought momentarily, and then Sophia said, "I remember someone like that. That was some time ago. But I can't recall anything specific about him. Sorry."

"I don't remember waiting on somebody like that," said Alex. "Unless it involves something odd, or they're repeat buyers, I generally don't remember customers."

"What about someone who bought just three or four rather than a dozen?" asked Sam.

Alex shook his head and looked at his wife. "Nobody like that," she replied.

Joe handed Sophia his card and said, "If he happens to come in again, please call me. He could be a killer, and we need to get him off the street."

"Oh, my," responded Sophia. "That's disconcerting."

"One last question," said Sam, pulling his phone from his pocket. Showing her a photo of the dead roses. "How long would it take for fresh roses to get to this state?"

"Can I see that?" she asked. Taking Sam's phone, she looked closer at the dead roses. After a moment, she returned his phone, saying, "It depends. Without watering them, it could take a month or so. But you could hurry that along by drying them in an oven on low heat or in a food dehydrator. That could just take a day."

"Good to know. Thanks."

As Joe and Sam walked to their car, Sam asked, "You think our offender would buy again from the same store?"

"Not if he's smart, and I think this guy is smart."

Chapter Thirteen

Following his two days off, which he spent at home with Destiny and Autumn, Joe returned to Area 3, raring to go. After dropping off his lunch and getting coffee, he looked up TGM Talent and wrote down their phone number. A few days ago, he found they had an office located on Dearborn in the heart of the Loop. Their website stated they opened for business at 10:00 a.m.

Shortly after ten, Joe called TGM's number. A woman's perky voice answered.

"TGM Talent. Gayle speaking."

"Good morning," said Joe. "I'm Joe Erickson, a homicide detective with the Chicago Police Department. I need to speak with the person in charge."

"That would be Elizabeth Traynor. She's the 'T' in TGM Talent. Can I tell her what your business is?"

"Murder."

"Oh," she said as her voice trailed off. "Uh…Let me transfer you."

"Classical music played for a minute or so, and then he heard a woman's voice. "This is Elizabeth Traynor. May I help you?"

Joe introduced himself and said, "It's come to my attention that you employed Amber Engstrom. Is it correct to assume Regina Fischer also worked for your agency?"

"Yes."

"Were you aware that both of these women have been killed?"

Silence. Then Traynor responded, "Regina, too?"

"I'm afraid so. I take it you were aware of Amber Engstrom's death?"

"Yes, it was in all the papers."

"We believe they were killed by the same offender."

"Omigod," she said, her voice going soft. Joe heard a sniff and an intake of air. It was clear she was shocked and upset by the news. "This…this is…terrible."

"I'm sorry to deliver such bad news, but my partner and I are investigating both deaths, and given that your agency employed each of them, we'd like to ask you some questions. Do you have time for an interview today?"

"Let me see." Joe could hear papers rustling. "I can cancel my appointment for two o'clock if that works for you."

"That works." Joe confirmed TGM's Dearborn address. "We'll see you then."

Joe ended the call and informed Sam of their upcoming afternoon interview.

"You thinking it could have something to do with their work for the agency?" asked Sam.

"It's a place to start."

Joe and Sam reached the Dearborn tower a few minutes before two o'clock. They got off on the fourth floor and found Suite 405, the address of TGM Talent. Upon opening the door, a receptionist rose from her seat and greeted them. She looked like a model, with perfect makeup and mid-length feathered honey-blonde hair.

"Good afternoon, gentlemen," said the same perky voice he heard on the phone that morning. "I'm Gayle. Would you happen to be Ms. Traynor's two o'clock appointment?"

"We are," said Joe.

"Wonderful. If you'll follow me. She's expecting you."

They followed Gayle down a short hallway to a double door with the name plate, "Elizabeth Traynor." Opening the door a crack, she said, "Your two o'clock is here."

"Show them in, Gayle," came a voice from inside.

The receptionist opened the door and said, "You can go in, gentlemen." As Joe and Sam entered, the door was closed behind them.

Rounding a large walnut desk was a woman in her forties who greeted them in a business-like manner. Joe's first impression of Elizabeth Traynor was she looked as tough as boiled owl. A young man in his twenties remained standing behind her desk. "Come in," she said. "I'm Elizabeth Traynor, the owner of TGM Talent." Referring to the young man, she said, "This is my assistant, Ethan Andrews. Their clothing was tailored and professional, and Sam noticed she was not wearing a wedding ring, something he always picked up on.

In addition to her desk, the large office had a burgundy leather couch and two matching chairs with a short table in the center. The ivory walls were filled with framed photos of young men and women in print advertising for major magazines and television commercials.

Joe and Sam showed their IDs and introduced themselves. Traynor said, "Why don't we have a seat over here," indicating the leather sofa and chairs. She sat on the sofa with Andrews sitting next to her while Joe and Sam seated themselves on the chairs.

Once everyone was comfortable, Joe began. "As I mentioned on the phone, we're investigating the deaths of Amber Engstrom and Regina Fischer."

"It's just awful. You said you believe they were killed by the same person?"

"Evidence indicates the same offender."

Traynor sighed, "It's hard for me to process this. It's not only a tragedy for their families and those of us who knew them, but it also shines a bad light on our company."

"Can you tell us about their last modeling assignments?" asked Joe.

"I looked that up before you came. They were two of five models featured in a photo shoot for a new line of clothing by Pierre Aubert."

"And where did this take place?"

"The studio of Damien Bose, the photographer. He's quite well-known as a fashion photographer. I have some photos of the shoot if you would like to see them."

"We would," replied Joe.

She looked at Andrews and said, "Ethan, would you get the file on my desk?" Looking back at Joe and Sam, she said, "Just a moment." Andrews walked to her desk and picked up a manila folder. Before sitting, he handed the file to Traynor, who laid the color 8X10 photos on the table so Joe and Sam could see them. There were individual photos of the two victims and group photos with all five models. They were wearing sportswear of various kinds against the background of a tropical island.

"Did they work a lot for you?" asked Joe.

"Amber was one of my top models. She was going places. Pierre Aubert showed an interest in bringing her to Paris, but that still needed to firm up. We employed Regina fairly often. I guess you could say she was a regular. Regina had training as an actress, and because of that, she's obtained work in television commercials and music videos."

"Did they know each other?"

"They did, but I don't know if they were friends outside of work."

Joe considered that and thought they might be able to find out when the contents of their cell phones and computers came back. Maybe it wasn't important, or…maybe it was.

"Did they work often enough to support themselves without having outside jobs?" asked Sam.

"Regina occasionally appeared in some of the television shows that are shot here. I can't tell you if Amber supplemented her modeling income with other jobs. But they always made themselves available when I needed them."

Joe considered Engstrom's problem with Josh Blake and asked, "Do you know of any romantic problems, stalkers, or confrontations they may have had?"

"No, not really. Amber mentioned she broke up with her boyfriend some time ago, but they don't share much personal information with me. We tend to keep things professional. The only reason I know about Amber's former boyfriend is because she told me that going to Paris for an extended period wouldn't be a problem since she'd broken up with him."

Sam was examining the photos Joe placed on the table, and held up the photo of all five models in the picture. "Who are the other three girls?"

Traynor said, "Models with our agency. Why do you need to know?"

"Because two of the women in this photo are dead, and it may be possible our offender could be targeting all five."

"Oh, no. Surely not."

"We have to look at all the possibilities," said Joe. "So, we'd like to interview each of them. I'm sure after hearing about Amber and Regina, they're wondering if they could be next."

"Sometimes clues can be found where you least expect them," added Sam.

Traynor proved amenable to providing the contact information for the other three models and asked Andrews to generate a list. He sat down at her computer and began typing.

"Why would anyone want to harm my girls?" asked Traynor.

"That's what we want to find out," replied Joe. "Did either of them mention anything about an argument or disagreement they had with anyone?"

Traynor thought for a moment. "Well, this may not mean anything, but Amber said the photographer was rude during her last photo shoot. She felt he was picking on her, and she was upset about it."

"Have your clients worked with this photographer previously?"

"They have." She sighed and said, "Look. He's an artist, and he can be temperamental and difficult sometimes. We've had complaints about him before, but his photos get our clients into magazines, so we put up with his…eccentricities."

"Has he ever gotten physical with any of your models?" asked Sam.

"No. It's all been verbal. So far as I know, he's never laid a hand on any of our girls. If he did, we'd never work with him again."

Looking up from his computer screen, Andrews piped up, "But he's been known to sleep with certain models working on his shoots."

Turning to Andrews, Joe said, "Oh? And you know this how?"

"Gossip. I hear things."

"From your clients?"

"Among others," he said, looking back at his computer screen, and beginning to type again.

"That's helpful," said Joe in a mildly sarcastic tone. He looked back at Traynor, who gave him a shrug.

Joe heard the laser printer, and he hoped Andrews was printing out the list of the other models who worked on the shoot. After a moment, Andrews rose from the chair and pulled two pages from the printer. He walked to Joe and Sam and handed each of them a page.

"Here you go," he said.

As he sat next to Traynor, she said, "Thank you, Ethan."

Looking at the paper, Joe saw the contact information for Hanna Zimmer, Lisa Alessandro, and Desiree McMillan. "Ms. Traynor, I think it best if we spoke to these women together. It would save us a lot of time. Would it be possible for you to arrange a time when we can meet with all three of them? Here in your office, maybe?"

"Of course," replied Traynor. "I can bring them in. I don't want anything to happen to them."

"Call me with a time, and we'll be here," said Joe.

Looking at Sam, Joe gave him the "are we finished?" look. Sam nodded.

Picking up the photos, Sam asked, "Is it all right if we keep these?"

"Certainly," replied Traynor.

"Gonna use 'em to get off?" asked Andrews in an attempt to be witty. It didn't work.

"What did you say your name is?" asked Sam, offended by his lack of respect.

Taken somewhat aback, he said, "Ethan Andrews."

"And where were you on June 4th and June 26th, Mr. Amusing?"

Flustered, he said, "Uh...I dunno. I'd have to check."

"You'd better have an alibi for both dates because that's when these women were killed. And I'm not ruling you out as a suspect."

Traynor was not pleased with her assistant's attempt at humor. Joe saw her shoot Andrews daggers after he made his quip. Sam noticed, too.

"We'll expect your alibis by noon tomorrow," said Sam, who handed him his card. "You can email or text me. But you'd better not blow me off!"

Andrews looked pale and shrank into the couch. Traynor looked at Sam and said, "You'll have to excuse my assistant's attempt to be amusing. He clearly needs to mature."

Sam slid the photos back into the folder and rose from his chair.

"I think we have what we came for," said Joe.

"Thank you for your time," added Sam.

"You have my phone number, so if you need anything or have questions, feel free to call," said Traynor. "I hope you catch who did this."

They left TMG Talent, and on the way to the car, Joe said, "You came down pretty hard on Traynor's assistant."

"That little piss ant needed a comeuppance."

Joe chuckled and said, "Yeah. Traynor wasn't too pleased with what he said. The look she gave him was enough to kill."

"She's probably ripping him a new one as we speak."

"I don't know," said Joe. "He looked like a boy toy to me. He might get a finger wag. You going to hold him to reporting his alibi?"

"Damn straight."

Chapter Fourteen

Back at his desk, Joe entered the contact information for the three models into his computer and then placed the hard copy in a file folder. It was only half an hour before Miller time, but Joe was curious about the supposedly temperamental photographer, Damien Bose.

He began a search for a criminal record on Bose. He found that he was arrested five years ago on a battery charge after a scuffle with another photographer at a fashion show. After pleading no contest, he received probation and a $2500.00 fine. In addition to his criminal record, he has had two traffic citations for speeding. While the traffic citations were of little consequence in their investigation, the battery charge sent up a red flag as it proved he was capable of violent behavior.

Looking at his watch, Joe could see it was time for him to leave for the day. As he drove home, he thought about what could have motivated a photographer to kill two of his models. It didn't make sense, but many murders didn't initially make sense. Did something happen to cause him to hate these two women? Payback for something they had done to him or not done with him. Interviewing the remaining three models may provide a clue.

When he reached home, he parked under the carport and entered through the garage. He walked past Destiny's Mercedes and the partially assembled Camaro he was storing for Jacquie Lambert, the sister of Destiny's late friend, Liz. It belonged to Liz's husband, who had perished with Liz in a plane crash. Jacquie agreed to Joe's offer to buy it from her while Liz's will was going through probate, and at this point, he had to wait to make the financial transaction and receive the vehicle registration so it would be officially his. He turned to look at it, something he did nearly every time he came home. He was itching to begin working on it, but until he had it registered in his name, all he could do was look and dream a little.

With her superb hearing, Autumn started barking when Joe pulled into the carport. She learned to recognize the sound of his car and always alerted Destiny when he returned home. Autumn was the first to greet him when he came through the door.

Joe kneeled and petted her as he talked to her. Then he gave her a treat, something that had become a daily ritual upon his return home.

He walked to the office and found Destiny on the phone. She waved to him and signaled with one finger that her conversation would end in another minute or so. Turning back to the kitchen, he opened a new bottle of Pinot Noir and poured himself a glass. Destiny entered as he began to sit at the island.

"Hi," she said and kissed him. "You make any progress today?"

"Some."

"Some?" she asked.

"Yeah, we may have a person of interest, but I'm not so sure right now. We'll be meeting with the three other models who were hired for the photo shoot. I'm hoping they can provide us with something helpful."

"Are they hot?" she asked, teasing him a bit.

"They're beautiful. But they don't hold a candle to you."

"Aww…" That was worth another kiss. "You know how to charm a woman."

Joe looked at his wine and asked, "You want me to pour you a glass, too?"

"No, thanks. I took some ibuprofen fifteen minutes ago. Working at the computer all day gave me a headache."

"How was your day? Other than the headache."

She sat down on a stool next to him. "I was on the phone with Miami PD when you came in. They have a serial rapist down there, and the head of their task force wanted to know if I'd be interested in creating a profile."

"Mm. You going to do it?"

"I said I'd let them know. I wanted to run it past you first."

"Go for it," said Joe. He didn't have to think twice since he always supported her work as a profiler. "When would you have to leave?"

"The day after tomorrow. Is that all right?"

"Sure."

"Fine. I'll call him back tomorrow morning and tell him it's a go."

"Well, then. We should do something special tonight since you'll be leaving."

"What do you have in mind?"

"One of your favorite restaurants, maybe?"

"Perfect," she smiled. "I'll call for a reservation at The Art of Dining." Destiny reached for her cell phone and made a call. Joe liked that restaurant and had been there several times with Destiny. It was only ten minutes from their home. After ending the call, she looked at Joe and said, "Seven o'clock."

"Great."

"That gives me an hour. I'd better call my mom and let her know I'll be heading to Florida."

"And I'll take Autumn for a walk, unless you've done that already," said Joe.

"I haven't."

Following a vigorous walk around the block, Joe and Autumn returned to the house. After removing her leash, he tossed a ball into the living room, which Autumn chased and started throwing around. Their walk invigorated her. While Joe sat at the island and began finishing his wine, Autumn got the "zoomies" and ran at full speed into the kitchen, around the island, into the living room, around the coffee table, and back again. Joe had to laugh at her zoomy run, and after about three laps, she stopped, jumped up on his leg, and gave a woof.

"You want another treat?" he asked. "Is that what you're telling me?"

In reply, Autumn gave a short bark, so Joe dug into the treat bag and tossed one to her. She sniffed it, picked it up from the floor, trotted to her bed, lay down, and began crunching on it.

When Joe and Destiny returned from the restaurant, it was nearly 8:30 p.m., and they found themselves in the living room with Autumn lying at Destiny's feet.

"So, tell me about your 'dead models' investigation. I'm intrigued."

"Our next step is interviewing the three other models from the photo shoot. The owner of the agency is setting that up for us."

"And then there were three. I hope it isn't a case of Ten Little Indians."

"Let's hope. I'm interested in the photographer in charge of the photo shoot. He's been described as difficult. Temperamental. And he had been previously charged with battery."

"Sounds like a pleasant guy. But why would he kill two models from his session?"

"I know," replied Joe. "It doesn't make sense at the moment. But we'll see. If we get stuck, I may have you create a profile on the killer."

Destiny smiled. "It'll cost you."

Smiling back, Joe said, "How much?"

"We'll work something out. You want to play a game?"

"As long as it isn't Twister."

"Aw, I was envisioning an invigorating game of Strip Twister."

"I'll bet you were."

Destiny laughed. "Not after the dinner we just had. Besides, we don't have the mat. How about Trivial Pursuit? We haven't played that in a long time."

"You're on." He rose and went to find the game. Returning, he set things up on the coffee table. "I swear, I'm going to beat you this time."

"Good luck. You'll need it."

They played for the next hour and a half, and after the score was tallied, Destiny won again. Joe could not seem to beat her at this game. While putting the cards away, he asked, "Tell me. How is it you know that yak's milk is pink?"

"Common knowledge," she said, suppressing a grin.

"You got that question one other time, didn't you?"

Sticking by her guns, she repeated, "Common knowledge. How did you know there are five stars on the Chinese flag?"

"Observation. I've seen it."

"No wonder you're such a good cop."

"I'm only as good as the latest case I investigate."

Joe returned the game to the hutch and poured himself a glass of filtered water from a pitcher in the refrigerator. Destiny turned off the light in the living room and joined him in the kitchen.

"You going to turn in?" she asked.

"Yeah. It's been a long day."

"I could make it longer."

Joe looked at her and said, "Tell me what you have in mind."

Chapter Fifteen

The following day, Joe and Sam were called out to a suspected homicide in Gill Park on West Sheridan Road.

They met a uniformed officer standing at the entrance to the children's play area. After he logged them in, they made their way under the crime scene tape. They approached another officer, who was standing a short distance from the body. Joe noticed the name "Madden" on the name badge attached to his uniform.

"What have you got?" asked Joe.

"DB. We were called in early this morning when an employee arrived at the park. His name is Otis Tripp."

Joe thought, *Otis Tripp. Otis Tripp. Where have I heard that name?*

"According to his driver's license," continued Madden, "he was fifty-nine years old. We thought it may have been a heart attack at first until we took a closer look."

"And…" asked Sam.

"He was hit in the back of his head. You have to look close to see it. He must have fallen forward and died in that position because there's no blood near the body."

"Who found him?"

Consulting his notes, he replied, "Carol Peterson. She came to work, looked out the window, and saw the body. She went out to check on him, thinking he might be in trouble. After she saw he was deceased, she called it in."

"Got it," replied Joe. Looking over his shoulder, he saw the ME, Kendra

Solitsky, walking into the playground area. She acknowledged him with a nod and stopped when she got to him.

"Good morning, so to speak. What do you know?" she asked.

Joe looked at Officer Madden and said, "Go ahead."

Madden reeled off the same information he had given to Joe and Sam. Kendra looked at the thick gravel on the playground and said, "How many people have been around the body?"

"Just the woman who found him and me," said Madden.

"Okay." She set down her equipment and began suiting up in her Tyvek coveralls and booties. After pulling on her mask, she slipped on gloves and moved to examine the body. Fifteen minutes later, she walked to where Joe and Sam were standing.

"Death occurred between eleven and twelve o'clock last night. COD appears to be blunt force trauma to the back of the head. I'll know more when I get him on the table." She handed Joe an evidence bag containing a wallet. "I'm going to need some help pushing the gurney through this gravel."

"No problem," said Sam. He got Madden's attention, saying, "Officer. We'll need your help."

Kendra returned to the ME's van, followed by Sam and Madden. She unloaded the gurney, and the three of them pushed it next to the body. After closing the body bag, Sam and Madden lifted it onto the gurney and helped her push it through the gravel to the van.

While the others were moving the body, Joe gloved up, looked through Otis Tripp's wallet, and noticed Tripp lived at the same address as Regina Fischer. Then it dawned on him. Pulling his notebook, he began checking his notes. Suddenly, he saw the entry. Otis Tripp was the super for Regina Fischer's apartment building.

Joe recalled Tripp was not interviewed since he had nothing to do with the crime scene or the discovery of Fischer's body. He was simply present in the hall during their investigation. Joe looked over toward the ME's van and saw Sam standing there. Waving him over, he asked, "You remember the super of Regina Fischer's apartment building?"

"Uh...vaguely," said Sam.

"He's our victim."

"What?"

"This is the Otis Tripp who was standing in the hall while we investigated Fischer's murder."

"Why's he turned up dead?"

"Maybe he saw something, or the killer thought he did. And out of caution, he took him out," said Joe.

"That or maybe he recognized him," replied Sam.

"If he did, why didn't he say something when he had the chance?"

Sam shrugged his shoulders in frustration and shook his head, saying, "Yuh got me."

"What could he have been doing here around midnight, anyway?"

"Good question," said Sam. "Meeting somebody, maybe?"

"It's only a mile from his address on North Broadway. He may have been lured here by the killer."

"If his death has any connection to Fischer's murder. On the other hand, it could be a coincidence he's turned up dead."

"A coincidence?" asked Joe skeptically.

"I know, I know. There's no such thing as a coincidence in our business. But we shouldn't rule it out."

Nodding, Joe said, "I think we have to see what kind of guy he was and go from there. We'll need to search his apartment and talk to some of the building's residents."

They walked back to Kendra and asked if they could release the scene.

"Go ahead. I'm done here. I see no reason to bring Evidence Techs in on this."

"You'll let me know when you'll conduct the autopsy?" asked Joe.

"Sure. It'll be sometime tomorrow. I have a full schedule today."

Joe and Sam drove to Otis Tripp's apartment on North Broadway. They entered the vestibule and looked on the intercom for a listing for "Tripp." Seeing it, Joe pushed the button, and a female voice answered, "Yes?"

Detectives Erickson and Renaldo, Chicago PD," said Joe. "We need to speak with you."

A moment later, they heard a buzzer, and the door to the lobby opened. Tripp's apartment was Unit 101 at the end of the hall. A brass-colored plate on the door read, "Superintendent." Joe rang the doorbell, and the door opened as far as the chain allowed. A woman in her sixties peered out, and Joe held up his ID so she could read it. "Okay," she acknowledged, removing the chain and opening the door.

"Are you Mrs. Tripp?" asked Joe.

"No, I'm Helen Sackett," she replied in a soft, raspy voice.

"Does Otis Tripp live here?"

"Yes. He's my brother."

"We need to come in," said Joe.

She opened the door, and they stepped past her. The apartment was neatly kept, with crocheted doilies on older furniture and framed landscape pictures on the walls. It smelled of recently baked bread.

"Is something wrong?" she asked.

"I'm afraid there is. I regret to inform you that your brother was found deceased this morning."

She gasped and became weak in the knees. Joe and Sam took her arms and helped her to an overstuffed chair in the living room, where she began to cry, saying, "I can't believe it."

"I'm sorry," said Sam.

"Are you sure it's him?"

"We're sure."

"Can I get you anything?" asked Joe. "A glass of water or—"

"No, thank you," she said through tears, pulling a handkerchief from her apron and dabbing her eyes. "What...what happened?"

"He was found this morning in Gill Park," replied Sam. "Maybe you know it? It's about a mile from here. I'm sorry to say we're investigating his death as a homicide."

"Someone killed him?"

"I'm afraid so. Around midnight last night."

"Omigod." She blew her nose into her handkerchief.

"I know this is a bad time, but it would be helpful if you could answer some questions. To help our investigation."

Looking up, she nodded and said, "Of course."

"Would you know what he was doing in Gill Park last night?" asked Joe.

"No."

"Did he get any phone calls last evening?"

"Not that I'm aware of."

"Did you think it odd that he didn't come home last night?"

Struggling to keep her composure, she said, "I…I go to bed early…around nine…so he must have left after I'd gone to sleep."

"And were you concerned he wasn't here this morning when you woke up?"

"No. You see, he usually gets up about five, and a lot of times, he's gone by the time I wake up. But he's always back here for lunch unless a resident calls with a problem."

"Could I ask where he goes?" asked Sam.

"Besides this building, he manages the Greystone Apartments a couple blocks from here."

"I have to ask this, so I apologize in advance," said Sam. "But did your brother use drugs?"

Taken aback by his question, Sackett responded indignantly, "Absolutely not."

"Okay."

"Do you know if he had any enemies?" asked Joe.

"No, he wasn't that kind of person. He was easygoing with a sense of humor. People liked him."

"Did he have confrontations with anyone? People who lived in his apartment buildings?"

Wiping her eyes again, she said, "Just that poor girl who was killed on the third floor. The model. He was quite upset about that."

"Did he say anything about it? Like seeing anyone suspicious or someone he saw that didn't belong here?"

"Not that he told me. He just talked about what people would think about living here. This building has a reputation as a safe place to live. There haven't been any crimes here."

"What about his habits? For instance, did he drink, gamble, owe money to anybody?"

"Nothing like that."

"One more thing," said Sam. "Did your brother own a car?"

"Uh-huh. But he took it in to be repaired a couple of days ago. He was supposed to get it back today."

"Was he in the habit of walking? You know, for exercise?"

"No. He was lazy. Didn't like exercise. He'd walk to and from the other apartment building, but that's about it."

After several more questions, Joe and Sam felt they had all they needed and decided to end the interview.

"I think we're done here," said Joe. "Is there anyone you would like us to call? Friend, clergy…?"

"No, thank you. With Otis gone, I'll have no place to go," she said, beginning to cry again.

Joe handed her his card. "If you need help, please call me. I don't want to see you out on the street."

Taking his card, she thanked him and walked them to the door.

"You sure I can't call anyone for you?" asked Joe.

"I have a sister who lives in Rogers Park. I need to call and let her know what happened to Otis. But I appreciate your offer."

Helen Sackett was a sweet woman, and Joe felt sorry for her since she would probably lose their apartment to the next person hired to be the building's superintendent. He wondered if the frail woman was financially able to find another place to live.

On their way back to Area 3, Sam thought about their interview with Sackett. "Nice lady," he said, thinking out loud. "Too bad we didn't get any useful information from her."

"Yeah."

Upon returning to their Area 3 office, Joe found an email message from Elizabeth Traynor stating she had scheduled a meeting at 10:00 a.m. tomorrow morning with the three remaining models from the photo shoot.

He copied Sam on her email, and a few minutes later, he strode to Sam's desk.

"That was fast," said Sam. "I expected it would be weeks before she could get them together for an interview."

"I think she's concerned about the safety of her other models."

"And it casts a shadow over her agency, too. She probably wants this solved ASAP."

"So do I," said Joe. "So do I."

Chapter Sixteen

Joe skipped his daily jog the next morning since Destiny was leaving for her profiling job in Miami. He made a breakfast of Eggs Benedict using vegan Canadian bacon. He cheated and used a packet to make the Hollandaise sauce rather than taking the time to make it from scratch, like he usually did.

Destiny came out of the bedroom looking ready to travel. Joe poured her a cup of coffee and then began to poach the eggs.

"What are you making?" she asked, sitting at the island.

"Eggs Benedict."

"Nice. Thank you for a great sendoff breakfast."

Popping English muffins into the toaster, he said, "Nothing's too good for you."

"You're sweet."

Whenever Destiny was leaving for a consultation, Joe wanted to make her a special breakfast before he left for work. It was a throwback to his Swedish grandmother, who believed cooking for people was a way of showing her love for them.

They enjoyed their breakfast together, and after they were through, it was nearly time for Joe to drive to work.

Destiny was catching an Uber ride to the airport at nine o'clock. He said he wanted to stick around so he could see her off. But while she appreciated his gesture, she felt it was important that he get to work on time.

"You need to go to work," she said. "Your meeting with the models is crucial, and you and Sam need to be prepared for it."

"I know. Let me know when you arrive, okay?"

"Of course." She embraced him, kissed him, and said, "I love you."

Kissing her back, he said, "Love you more."

She grinned. "Doubt it." Releasing their embrace, "You'd better get moving, or you'll be late."

On his drive to work, Joe tried to relax and concentrate on the unusually heavy traffic. Pulling into the Area 3 parking lot, he saw Sam walking toward the door. Recognizing the sound of Joe's car, Sam turned and waited for him to park. They walked into the building together. While filling their mugs with coffee, Sam volunteered to check out a squad car for their trip to the Loop and their interview at TGM Talent.

Joe sat at his desk, logged into his computer, and began transferring his notes from the Otis Tripp case into the database. After what seemed like a short period of time, he felt Sam's hand on his shoulder.

"Ready to go," asked Sam.

"Uh, yeah," Joe replied, rising from his chair. Hours had slipped by.

They drove from Area 3 to the Dearborn Street address in the Loop, where TGM Talent was located. Walking into Suite 405, they approached the receptionist's desk and saw Gayle, the young woman, who greeted them on their previous visit. Upon seeing them, she rose from her chair.

"Good morning, detectives. You're expected in the conference room. Follow me, please."

Joe and Sam followed her down a hall, where she opened the first door and announced, "The detectives are here."

"Show them in," said Traynor.

Three women were seated at the table along with Elizabeth Traynor. Looking at the three models, Joe was struck by how different they looked from their appearance in the photos from the photo shoot. Two were wearing minimal makeup, while the third was not wearing any and had her hair pulled back in a ponytail. Not much glamour today. Traynor rose from her chair.

"Good morning," said Joe. "Thank you for meeting with us. I'm Detective Joe Erickson, and this is my partner, Detective Sam Renaldo."

Sam nodded and said, "Hello."

"Good morning," replied Traynor. "I'd like to introduce Hannah Zimmer, Lisa Alessandro, and Desiree McMillan." The three women acknowledged each other with nods and smiles as they were introduced. "Please be seated."

Joe and Sam took chairs on the opposite side of the table and pulled notebooks and pens from their pockets.

"As you may already know," began Joe, "we're investigating the homicides of Amber Engstrom and Regina Fischer."

Before he could continue, Zimmer pushed back her blonde hair and asked, "Are their deaths related?"

"They are. Each was tased, sexually assaulted, and then strangled. There's overwhelming evidence these crimes were committed by the same offender."

The three women looked at each other with apprehension, and then McMillan flashed her brown eyes at Joe and asked, "Am I in danger?"

"You mean, are *we* in danger," corrected Zimmer. McMillan responded with an eye roll. "I think that goes without saying."

"We can't say for sure at this point," said Sam. "But I would advise you to be proactive regarding your safety."

"We know the offender posed as a man delivering flowers from a florist for each victim," explained Joe. "That's how he gained entrance into their apartments. From a witness, we know he was wearing a blue baseball cap and a medical mask. So, you should take great care when accepting a flower delivery. Especially if it was not expected."

Sam added, "In both cases, the flowers were long-stem roses. We found the boxes at the crime scenes."

"That's horrible," remarked Alessandro, flicking her dark hair back. "Why do you think they were targeted?"

"We're working on that. And that's the reason we wanted to talk to you."

"Did you know the victims?" asked Joe.

"Not really," replied McMillan, reaching back and adjusting her ponytail. "This is the first time I'd worked with either of them."

"I knew them both from other shoots, but I didn't know them personally," remarked Alessandro, making eyes at Joe. Her big brown eyes could have reduced a lesser man to putty.

"I knew Regina," said Zimmer. "She was a nice person. And I'd worked with Amber once before. I didn't care for her that much."

"Why's that?" asked Sam.

"Well...She had a little attitude. But it's not like we had words or anything. I just didn't care to get close to her, that's all."

"I noticed that about her, too," added Alessandro.

"Can you tell us anything else about Amber?"

"I liked her," replied McMillan. "She was going places, and I felt happy for her. She had a little attitude, sure, but I think it was because she was a perfectionist. She was always friendly to me. I have to tell you I cried when I heard what happened to her."

"What can you tell us about the photo shoot you were on?" asked Joe.

"Typical," said McMillan.

"Except for the photographer," interjected Alessandro.

"Care to explain?"

"One of those egomaniacs. He didn't treat us very well," explained Zimmer.

"That's putting it mildly," added Alessandro.

"He can be temperamental," added Zimmer. "I worked with him before. He's always condescending to his models."

"But..." Traynor cut in, "Damian Bose is a world-class photographer, and his photos get you into top magazines. That's why he gets work. Our clients have gotten a lot of print exposure because of him. It's a case of taking the good with the bad."

"I don't care how big an asshat he is," said McMillan. "If he gets me into *Cosmo* or *Vogue*, it's worth it."

"Not all photographers are like him," said Zimmer. "But not all of them are as talented as he is, either."

"I'd work for him again. I can ignore his crap," admitted McMillan.

Joe felt Alessandro's eyes on him while he was writing notes. When he looked up quickly, her eyes darted away. He smiled to himself. When he finished writing, he asked, "Did you notice anything odd or unusual during the shoot? Regarding Amber or Regina?"

After a moment, Zimmer spoke up. "I saw Damian speaking with Amber during one of the breaks. I was too far away to hear what they were talking about, but it looked a little intense."

"Did she say anything afterward?"

"No. She seemed to have shrugged it off because it didn't appear to bother her."

"Do you know if they'd worked together before?"

"Many times," answered Traynor.

"It was rumored they had something going at one point, but I can't say for sure it was true," said Alessandro.

"Was there any tension between them afterward?" asked Sam.

"As far as I know," replied Zimmer, "once the shoot was over, she left while he and his assistant were packing up their equipment."

"I didn't notice anything," said Alessandro.

"Neither did I," replied McMillan.

"She's such a pro. She wouldn't have shown any emotion while she was working," added Zimmer. "Whatever it was about, she didn't let it bother her."

"Did he pay any special attention to Regina?"

The three looked at each other, and then McMillan stated, "No, not really." Alessandro and Zimmer shook their heads in agreement.

"What about Bose's assistant? Anything unusual about him?" asked Joe.

"He hardly spoke," said Alessandro. "What was his name...?"

"Daniel," replied Zimmer. "I don't know his last name."

"He just stood around and did what he was told," added McMillan.

Joe and Sam continued to write notes when Traynor asked, "Do you think some madman is after my girls?"

"That's what we're trying to find out," said Joe. "Until we know, I would advise being diligent about your safety." Looking specifically at Traynor, he said, "And that goes for you, too."

"Me?"

"Since you're a part of this agency, the offender could be targeting anyone associated with TGM Talent."

"Maybe I should buy a gun," mumbled McMillan.

"I would not advise doing that," said Sam. "Anyone who buys a gun should be trained in how to use it. A lot of untrained gun owners wind up accidentally shooting themselves or somebody else."

"That's good advice," said Joe. "Out of curiosity, do any of you know a man named Otis Tripp?"

Deer-in-the-headlights looks appeared on everyone's faces. "No?"

They shook their heads, and Traynor asked, "Is he a suspect?"

"No, he's a person somewhat related to the case. Just wondering. "

"He's definitely not a suspect," assured Sam.

"Is he what you'd call a person of interest?" asked McMillan.

"No," replied Sam. "Actually, he's dead."

"Oh!"

There was a lull in the conversation. Looking at Sam, Joe asked, "You have any other questions for these ladies?"

"No, I think we got what we came for."

Joe and Sam rose from their chairs. "Thank you for your time," said Joe. "This has been helpful." He left several of his cards on the table, as did Sam. "You can reach us at the numbers listed on our cards."

Traynor and her models rose, came around the table, and shook hands with Joe and Sam, expressing their thanks. As Joe turned to go, he felt a tug on his sleeve. Turning, he saw Alessandro.

"Can I ask you a question?"

"Of course," replied Joe.

"Do you think I should hire protection?"

"That's up to you, but if you're careful and don't open your door to anyone you don't know, you'll probably be fine."

Holding up his card, she asked provocatively, "So, I can call you if it's…an emergency?"

Joe knew what she was up to and wanted to let her know he wasn't interested in any funny business. He looked her in the eyes and said, "Only and <u>only</u> if it's an emergency. Understood?" he stated in no uncertain terms.

Alessandro looked deflated by his answer. "Understood."

As Joe and Sam rode down the elevator, Sam joked, "Looks like Miss Alessandro has the hots for you."

"Yeah. Those are the perils when you're knockdown handsome."

Sam laughed out loud. "Yeah, you're the best-looking thing since sliced baloney."

As Sam drove them back to their office on Belmond, they discussed the next step in their investigation.

"Damian Bose seem like a person of interest to you?" asked Sam.

"Oh, yeah. We need to take a real good look at him," said Joe.

Joe's phone beeped. He checked and saw a text from Kendra about Tripp's autopsy.

"Otis Tripp's autopsy is scheduled for 2:30. So, I'll be gone for most of the afternoon."

"Should I be focusing on Tripp's murder or the girls?" asked Sam. "We have a lot on our plate right now."

Joe thought for a moment and said, "You might check to see if Gill Park has any security footage from the night Tripp was killed. I'll start researching Damian Bose when we get back."

"Sounds good. We need to split up some of this stuff if we're going to make progress on these cases."

Chapter Seventeen

Sam dropped Joe off at Area 3 and proceeded to Gill Park to inquire about security footage. Joe got coffee, grabbed his lunch, and sat down at his desk. After logging into his computer, he began to research Damian Bose.

The internet search brought up Bose's website. It featured many of his published photographs, a biography, contact information, and awards he had received. It was an impressive website, professionally executed by a company called "WebArtSites." He made a mental note, thinking it might be a company useful to Destiny for redesigning her own website.

Bose's website's biography page stated he was born in Stuttgart, Germany, 46 years ago. He emigrated to Chicago with his parents when he was two years old. His father was an executive with Mercedes-Benz America. Bose studied photography at the Art Institute of Chicago and became an assistant to noted French photographer Francois Labiche in Paris for three years. He left Labiche to work as a freelance photographer back in America and gained a reputation after his fashion photos began appearing in Vogue and Elle magazines. Since then, his career has blossomed, and his photos have appeared in every major fashion magazine in both America and Europe.

Impressive career. When Joe dug deeper into Bose's personal life, he found he was never married. However, he has been sued twice, once by a woman for sexual harassment and by another for non-payment of child support. His driver's license information stated he was born on January 16th, is five feet ten, and weighs 165 pounds. Like many driver's license photos, his was unflattering unless one finds the disheveled perpetrator look appealing. His

Greektown address matched the one that was listed on his website.

Further searches revealed Bose has several unpaid parking citations and one careless driving charge after being involved in a car accident five years ago. He was arrested for assault nine years ago and pleaded no contest. He got probation and has had no further arrest incidents. Vehicle registration showed he owns a two-year-old Porsche 911 and a Ford van.

Joe took particular notice of the harassment and assault charges. Wondering if Bose would be capable of carrying out a fatal attack against a woman, he decided to call him to arrange an interview. His call went to voicemail, and he left a message emphasizing the urgency of a response to his call.

The alarm Joe set on his watch buzzed, and he realized it was time for him to drive to the Office of the Cook County Medical Examiner for Otis Tripp's autopsy. He met with Kendra beforehand, and she told him she had already taken several DNA samples.

"He had what looked like tissue under his fingernails. I've already sent that out for analysis. He may have fought with his assailant," she said.

Joe sat through the autopsy, listening and making notes about what Kendra found during the procedure. It turned out Otis Tripp was a type 2 diabetic and showed evidence of emphysema and atherosclerosis. These findings indicated some serious health issues. Tripp may or may not have been aware of these health problems, but they were not responsible for his death. Upon examining the posterior region of the skull, Kendra found significant fractures caused by a blunt object. When his brain was examined, she found small pieces of skull embedded on the back of the brain. She determined a brain bleed caused his death.

When Kendra began the tissue dissection, Joe left. The autopsy confirmed what Kendra said upon her initial examination: death due to blunt force trauma to the back of the skull. He would get a copy of the ME's autopsy shortly. It would be about two weeks for the results of the toxicology report to come back.

Joe hoped Sam could discover security video of Tripp's confrontation with a suspect unknown. With a little luck, video footage of the incident might help to identify the offender.

When Joe returned from the autopsy, he saw Sam sitting at his desk. He walked over and said, "Any video footage from the crime scene?"

"I got their tapes," replied Sam. "It looked like one of their cameras captured the assault on Tripp. It's being examined as we speak. The quality isn't very good, but the lab thinks they can enhance it so we can get a better look at the offender."

"Did they indicate how soon we can have the video?"

"A week."

"Okay. Let's focus on the model murder cases until we get that back," said Joe. "Given what I learned about Damian Bose, I think a little chat's in order. I left him a voicemail earlier. We'll have to see how fast he responds."

Joe filled Sam in on what he had discovered about Damian Bose, and Sam agreed his past suggested he could be a person of interest. They definitely needed to interview him.

When Joe arrived home, he took Autumn for a walk around the block. Once they were back inside, Joe began preparing dinner. Since Destiny was gone, he decided to cook the steak he picked up on the way home. An inch-and-a-quarter thick ribeye was his protein, and together with a Caesar salad, he'd be dining "high on the hog," as his father used to say. As he was putting his steak on the grill, his cell phone rang.

He didn't recognize the number but decided to answer it anyway. It was some man with an Asian accent wanting to know if he received his new Medicare card. Joe wasn't old enough for a Medicare card and said so in unkind terms. Looking down, he saw Autumn was eyeing him.

"You don't get junk calls, do you?" She perked up her ears. "You're lucky you're a dog, Autumn."

She put her head down on her paws and looked sad.

"Treat!" said Joe. Autumn jumped up and ran over to the door. His steak was now cooked to medium rare, so Joe put it on a platter and entered the house. Putting down the platter, he gave Autumn one of her small treats. She practically inhaled it and then looked up at Joe. "You only get one," he said. "Sorry. But if you're good, I'll give you a taste of my ribeye."

Forty-five minutes later, he had finished his dinner. The grilled ribeye steak with Bearnaise sauce was perfect, and the Caesar salad was an excellent complement. And Autumn gobbled up her ribeye morsel like she had been starving for a week. After cleaning up, he walked into the living room and sat down. Autumn jumped up beside him. He was about to turn on the TV when his phone rang. It was Destiny.

"I made it, and I'm settled in," she said. "I rented a car and drove from the airport to the hotel. Have you ever driven in Miami traffic?"

"Never been there."

"It's crazy. I thought Chicago was bad."

"Do you have to drive to the police department?"

"No, someone's picking me up at ten o'clock. I'll be meeting with the head of the homicide unit to get all the information. How's Autumn?"

"She's fine. She was kind of moping around because you're not here, so I gave her a morsel from my ribeye. Now, she's my best friend."

"You know how to win over a girl's heart. Did you have your meeting with the three models?"

"We did."

"How did it go?"

"Well, besides one of them coming onto me, I think we may have discovered a person of interest."

"One of the models came on to you?" asked Destiny, sounding a little amused.

"Afterward. But I shut her down."

"Was she pretty?" she asked, trying to put Joe on the spot.

"She wasn't bad. I mean, she was bad but not bad-ass. In other words, you don't have anything to worry about."

"I trust you."

"I know you do."

"So, who's your new person of interest?"

"The photographer who was shooting the ad. We'll be looking into him more closely tomorrow."

Joe went on to explain why they were going to investigate Damian Bose, who he was, and what his record revealed about him. They talked for another fifteen minutes, then said good night to each other and ended their call.

Joe was wondering why Otis Tripp would be at Gill Park around midnight. So, in order to find out if something funky was going on there during these late hours, Joe decided to drive to Gill Park at eleven o'clock and observe the area where Tripp was killed.

He arrived and parked a block from the park. Wearing black clothes to be as inconspicuous as possible, he moved to the park and took up a position behind a large maple tree where he could see the playground area. Joe waited and saw no one for almost forty-five minutes. A little before midnight, he saw a man walking down the street who turned and entered the playground. The light was poor, so Joe could not see details other than he was male. The subject seemed to be waiting for someone.

Five minutes later, another person entered from a different direction. He entered the playground area and said something to the man waiting. At that point, they made a quick exchange and parted ways. A few minutes later, another person entered the playground, and another exchange was made. Joe was more interested in the seller, and when he left the area, he trailed him to a car. When he got in, Joe ran up to the car and pointed his Glock at the driver's window.

"Police! Hands on the steering wheel," ordered Joe.

The shocked man complied. Joe opened the door.

"Get out of the car and put your hands on the roof."

The man did as he was told, and Joe frisked him. When going through his pockets, Joe pulled two plastic bags of what he suspected was marijuana. From another pocket, he removed several wads of cash.

Pulling his hand behind his back, Joe began cuffing him, saying, "You're under arrest for selling a controlled substance."

"Oh, come on, man," whined the suspect. "What's a little weed? Shit's legal now, ya know."

"It's legal if people get it from a licensed dispensary, not from you," said Joe.

"I'm just trying to make a buck, man. I'm not hurtin' anybody."

Joe could see he was just a kid. College-age. And he didn't look like a grubby street dealer. "How many times a week do you come here at night?" he asked.

He didn't answer. "Come on," pressed Joe.

"Three or so."

"So, you have regular customers?" The kid didn't answer. "You're going to help yourself if you answer my questions."

After a few moments, the kid said, "Yeah."

Were you here last night?"

"Yeah."

"Did you see a man get attacked on the playground?"

"Shi-i-i-t."

"Well, did you?"

"Yeah."

"The man who was attacked—was he a customer of yours?"

The kid was conflicted about answering, but he finally acknowledged with a nod. "He was gettin' it for his sister. Said she has cancer and needs it for the pain."

Did you get a look at the offender?"

"Sorta."

"You've seen him before?"

"I think…I dunno…maybe."

"You know who he is?"

"No."

"Could you identify him if you saw him again?"

"Maybe. I dunno. He was wearin' a hoodie, and it was kinda dark."

"What did he use to attack your customer?"

"It looked like a little baseball bat," he said.

Joe knew what he was talking about. His father once had a miniature Louisville Slugger about eighteen inches long. It would have been a formidable weapon.

"Why do you think he did that? Any ideas?"

Shrugging his shoulders, the kid said, "Maybe he came here to rob me. I make close to a grand some nights."

"Did he search the victim after hitting him?

"Yeah. But he didn't take anything I could see."

Joe looked through the kid's wallet and took a photo of his driver's license. His name was Jamal Taylor.

"If we arrest the offender, can you testify you saw him hit Otis Tripp in the head with a baseball bat?"

"Shit, man. Muthafucka'd kill me if I do."

"Not if he's in prison. We need your help, Jamal."

Joe released him from his handcuffs.

"What's this? You lettin' me go?"

"Yeah."

"How come?"

"You're more valuable to us as a witness than a pot seller. But if you renege, I'll come looking for you and the deal's off."

"Okay."

"So, you've seen this guy before?"

"I didn't get a real good look at him. Like I said, he was wearing a black hoodie. But he looked kinda like a guy I saw here at the fitness center."

"Yeah? Can you describe him?"

"White dude, thirty, maybe. Shaves his head. Has this tattoo of a snake on one arm."

"Thanks, Jamal. Now, be on your way."

"I can go?" Jamal asked.

"Get out of here," said Joe.

The kid left quickly, and Joe walked back to his car. Driving home, he was pleased with himself for making the effort this evening. They now had a lead, and it appeared Tripp's murder may not be connected to Regina Fischer's after all.

Chapter Eighteen

When Sam came into work, Joe needed to tell him about what he saw at Gill Park the previous night.

You went to Gill Park?" asked Sam.

"Yeah, last night at eleven. I got a wild hair and decided to check it out. I waited, thinking I might see something that could cast some light on our victim."

"You see something?"

"Yeah. I watched a kid selling pot to a couple of people, and afterward, I apprehended him at his car. He thought I was going to bust him for selling, but I told him I was only interested in what happened to Tripp the night before. Kid's name is Jamal Taylor, and he admitted he was there and saw the person kill Tripp."

"So, what was Tripp doing there?"

"Taylor said Tripp bought pot for his sister, who needed it because she was suffering from cancer."

"And he actually saw the attack?"

"Yeah. Said a guy in a hoodie hit Tripp with a baseball bat and then searched through his pockets. He thinks the guy had come there to rob him and mistakenly attacked Tripp instead."

"So, this Jamal Taylor…he's a drug dealer?" asked Sam.

"Yeah. Sells pot. May sell other stuff, too. But he just had pot on him last night."

"You think he was telling you the truth?"

"For the most part. He knew about Tripp getting hit in the head. How would he have known that if he hadn't seen it?"

"Or did the deed himself."

Sam brought up a good point. Taylor could have known about it if he was the offender. But it didn't make sense for him to kill one of his regular sources of income.

"I don't think so," replied Joe. "My gut tells me he was telling the truth."

"What did you do with him? He had illegal pot on him, right?"

"I let him go. He was more important as a witness, and I thought some goodwill might convince him to help us in the future."

"So, Tripp was scoring pot for his sister. I got the impression she wasn't well when we saw her."

"Yeah," agreed Joe. "I had the same feeling." Helen Sackett's skin color, her thin body, and the cheap gray wig suggested chemotherapy. Marijuana may have been a way for her to relieve the side effects she was experiencing from chemotherapy treatments.

Sam had an idea. "You think the guy who killed Tripp might try again, knowing he screwed up his first attempt?"

"Possibly."

"You think Taylor would work with us to take down this guy?"

"Set up a surveillance of the playground, you mean? Use him as bait?"

"Yeah. And intervene when the offender tries to rob him."

Joe didn't know anything about Jamal Taylor and didn't know if he would be willing to set himself up as bait. But eliminating a potential killer and overlooking his pot selling could be an incentive Joe could use to bring him on board.

"I can ask him. Doesn't hurt to ask."

Joe decided to return to Gill Park that night to see if Taylor would be there. But today, he wanted to focus on Damian Bose.

"I think we should see if Bose bought any roses," said Joe.

Sam agreed, and they decided to split up to cover more establishments. Sam printed off a list of the florists, and they each took half the list.

Joe spent all morning approaching florist shops and asking if they had a record of a sale to Damian Bose. Beginning their search at ten o'clock, when most businesses opened their doors, Joe had covered five florists by noon. No luck.

He called Sam, only to learn he had no luck, either. All the walking and the frustration of finding parking places had whetted his appetite, so he stopped at a bistro for lunch. Forty minutes later, he was on a mission to check out the next florist shops on his list. He struck out three more times.

It was mid-afternoon when he entered Windy City Floral on East Superior Street. As he pushed through the door, a bell attached to the top of the door announced his entry into the shop. He was getting used to all the florist shops smelling the same way, but this one had the scent of potpourri in the air. It was pleasant and refreshing.

A middle-aged woman was behind the counter, cutting off flower stems to create an arrangement in a glass vase. She smiled at him as he approached the counter.

"Hi, there," she said, holding a flower in one hand and scissors in the other.

"Good afternoon," said Joe as he produced his ID. "I'm Detective Joe Erickson with Chicago PD."

After seeing his ID, she put down the scissors and the flower on the counter. "What brings you into the shop?"

"I'm investigating a person of interest in a criminal case, and I'd like to know if he purchased roses here. Do you keep records of people making purchases?"

"We do," she replied.

"That's good news. Could you check if a man by the name of Damian Bose made a purchase? The last name is spelled B-O-S-E."

"What kind of crime is it?" she asked with growing concern.

"I'm not at liberty to say. He's only a person of interest at this point and may not have committed any crime. Do you remember the name Damian Bose?"

"No. The name isn't familiar."

"Could you check and see if he purchased roses? Uh, sorry…what's your name?"

"Della."

"Thank you, Della."

Della stepped to her computer and began punching keys. "You said the last name is spelled 'B-O-S-E?'"

"Yes. Damian."

While waiting for the computer to pull up the information, she looked at Joe and said, "Sorry, the computer's a little slow today.

"That's all right," he assured her.

"Ah! Here we go. Damian Bose. It looks like he made two purchases of roses on different dates."

"Can you tell if they were long-stem red roses?"

"Sorry, I can't, but given the price, I'd say that's what he got. And it doesn't state the color. But he purchased a dozen each time."

"Could you print that for me?"

"Sure." A moment later, a laser printer pushed out a copy. She handed it to Joe, and he saw the dates were within weeks of the model murders. Time enough to dry them out so they looked dead.

He thanked her and asked, "Could you tell me what the wonderful fragrance is? I smelled it when I came in, and I like it."

She walked over to a display of packages of dried leaves in transparent packages, and tied with a colorful ribbon at the top. Picking up a package, she brought it back to Joe and handed it to him.

"Take a whiff," she said.

He held it up to his nose and took in its fragrance. "That's it. Very nice." He returned it to her, saying, "I'll take it."

"Have you ever used potpourri before?"

Joe admitted he had not. She explained how to use it and where to store it so it would not lose its scent. He thanked her and left with the potpourri and the printout of Damian Bose's purchases. When he reached the car, he called Sam.

"I found where Bose bought roses," said Joe. "Windy City Floral. He made two purchases that were dated within weeks of the two murders. It's possible they're the ones we found at the crime scene."

"Good work," said Sam. "I've come up empty at every place I tried."

"See you back at the office."

Joe returned to Area 3. Sam had beaten him back to the floor, and Joe found him sitting at his desk. He made a photocopy of the florist's sales to Bose. Then, he walked to Sam's desk and placed the photocopy on his desk. Sam picked it up and then turned to him and remarked, "What's that smell?"

"What smell?" asked Joe.

"You. You smell like a fancy gift shop."

Joe chuckled and said," Oh, I bought some potpourri at the florist's. It must have rubbed off on my clothes."

"Well, you've smelled worse."

"And so have you."

"Hopefully, it made the squad car smell better. Where do we go from here?"

"I'm going to call Damian Bose again and set up a meeting with him."

"Okay."

"And I think I'm going to check out Gill Park tonight. See if Jamal Taylor shows up."

"You want me to join you?"

"Sure, if you want to. Meet me there at eleven o'clock."

Joe called Damian Bose and left another message for him to call. Once again, he emphasized the urgency of his inquiry and explained the call concerned the photo shoot he'd done involving Amber Engstrom and Regina Fischer. In addition, he also sent him an email stating the same thing. Hopefully, Bose would respond to one of the two messages.

Joe returned home after work and placed some of the potpourri in a crystal dish on the dining room table. He held out the package to let Autumn sniff it. She backed away and sneezed. She gave him a look, walked to her dog bed, and turned her back to him. "Okay, Autumn, I get the point."

He cooked salmon and used the remainder of the Bearnaise sauce on it. Afterward, he set a reminder on his phone for 10:30 p.m. in case he fell asleep on the couch while watching television. He did not want to miss his Gill Park surveillance.

When the alarm went off, Joe drove to Gill Park and left his Camaro a block away. As he was getting out, he received a call from Sam.

"I saw you drive by. I'm parked half a block away on Sheridan. I've got a clear view of the playground."

"I'm going to watch from behind a large maple tree like I did before," replied Joe.

They kept watch until one o'clock. Nothing. Joe called Sam, and they agreed to cut their losses and try tomorrow night.

Chapter Nineteen

When Joe and Sam met the next morning, Sam asked, "Have you gotten a response from Damian Bose?"

"Not yet," replied Joe. "It hasn't been twenty-four hours yet, so I'm hoping he'll contact me sometime today. In the meantime, let's concentrate on the Tripp case."

Having heard nothing from Bose by two o'clock, Joe called him once again, and once again, his call went to voicemail. He left another voicemail message emphasizing the urgency of the situation and sent him another email to that effect. He got the impression Bose was purposely ignoring him.

Joe and Sam drove to Jamal Taylor's address on West Grace Street. It was an apartment building six blocks from Gill Park. Standing at the entrance door, Joe looked at the intercom and pressed the button for Unit 4, which was listed on Taylor's driver's license address. A female voice answered.

"Yes?"

"I'm Detective Joe Erickson with the Chicago Police Department. We need to speak with Jamal Taylor," said Joe.

"He's not here?"

"And you are?"

"His mother."

"Do you know where he is?"

"He's at work."

"Where does he work?"

"The Coffee Cafe on Broadway."

Joe thanked her, and they drove to The Coffee Cafe, a short distance from

Gill Park. They entered the establishment and walked up to the counter. Joe recognized Taylor, who was working as a barista. When he saw Joe, his eyes suddenly grew wide.

"Uh…hi…" he stammered. Then he quickly pulled himself together and said, "Can I get something for you?"

"Yeah," said Joe. "I'd like a large whole milk Cappuccino and a few words."

"Make that two," said Sam.

"Okay. Coming up."

After paying for their Cappuccinos, Joe asked, "You have a couple of minutes to talk?"

Taylor said, "Let me get Tommy to take my place." He stepped to the back of the bar and spoke to a girl, who was apparently 'Tommy.' She stopped filling a hopper with coffee beans, and after speaking with her, he returned and said, "We can talk in a booth over there," indicating a row of booths against the wall.

Joe got straight to the point after they sat down. "Are you going to be in Gill Park tonight?"

"Well, I uh…," he hesitated, then cracked a mirthless smile.

"Look, we don't care about the little business you have going on," said Joe. "We're not vice cops interested in busting you for that."

"Oh, yeah?"

"Yeah. My first question is, 'Are you planning to be there again tonight?'"

After a few moments of consideration, he answered, "Uh-huh."

"Good. Because we think the offender who mistook Otis Tripp for you might make an attempt to rob you tonight."

"And we want to be there to apprehend him when he tries," added Sam.

"Whoa," reacted Taylor. "You think this guy is going to try again?"

"Yeah, we do. And we want to protect you."

"And, in doing so," said Joe, "we plan to apprehend this offender. You saw what he did to Otis Tripp."

Joe could see Taylor running this through his mind. Then he spoke. "And you won't bust me or any of my customers?"

"No," replied Joe. "Like I said, we're not interested in your nocturnal activities. At least for now."

"Let me get this straight. You're gonna use me as bait?"

"We prefer to say you'll be a participant in the arrest of a dangerous felon."

"As opposed to busting you for selling a controlled substance," reminded Sam.

"Damn and shit," Taylor muttered to himself.

"Nobody will know you were part of this setup. You can say you were being surveilled for selling pot, and a guy attempted to rob you."

After a few moments of consideration, Taylor looked at Joe and Sam. "Okay," he said. "I guess I'll do it. I don't want that guy whacking me with that bat."

"If the offender asks for your money, give it to him," said Joe. "Don't resist. We'll take him down and we'll give your money back."

"Shouldn't there be a signal or something? So, I can tell you I'm in danger?"

"All right," said Sam. "If it makes you feel better."

"What would you like to do?" asked Joe.

Taylor thought for a moment, "How about I put both my hands up like this?" He demonstrated by raising his hands as if an Old West sheriff yelled, "Hands up!"

Smiling, Sam said, "That works for us."

Shortly before eleven o'clock, Joe and Sam staked out the Gill Park playground. They waited, and at 11:05 p.m., Taylor walked into the playground with his backpack and waited behind a slide. Ten minutes later, a man showed up, and he made a buy from Taylor. A short time later, another man entered the playground and exchanged money for a bag of pot. Time passed, and then an older woman appeared and purchased several bags.

It was now midnight, and it appeared Taylor was getting ready to leave. But as he began walking out of the playground, a man in a black hoodie appeared behind him and said something that got his attention. Surprised by the man's sudden presence, Taylor turned to face him. When he did, the man brought up a small bat he had been pressing against his leg. Frightened, Taylor raised both his hands, signaling Joe and Sam.

"Give me your money," the man said as he began threatening Taylor with the bat. When Joe and Sam saw the man in the hoodie, they began moving in with weapons drawn.

As he got close, Joe yelled, "Police! Drop the bat!"

Taylor quickly backed away. Not seeing Sam, the man began to run toward his position.

Stepping out to block his way, Sam pointed his service weapon and yelled, "Police. Freeze!" The man stopped.

"Drop the bat," yelled Joe. "Hands on top of your head!"

Realizing he could not escape the man dropped the bat and slowly placed his hands behind his head. Joe moved in close, his Glock aimed at the man. "Down on your knees, keep your hands behind your head." The man hesitated. "Do it!" demanded Joe.

The man complied. Sam held his gun on him as Joe cuffed him. Then Joe pulled back the man's hoodie to reveal his identity. He was a middle-aged white guy with a shaved head. Joe pulled up his sleeves, which revealed a tattoo of a snake on his right forearm.

Reaching into his back pocket, Joe removed the man's wallet and checked his driver's license.

"His name is Glen Schuler, and his address is on North Fairfield Avenue," said Joe. "You have a wife, or you live alone, Mr. Schuler?

"Live alone."

"Sam, you want to bag the bat?"

"Sure." Sam slipped on gloves, walked to where Schuler dropped the bat, and pulled a large evidence bag from his pocket. The bag was too small for the bat, so Sam let the handle part of the bat stick out of the bag in an attempt to preserve possible blood evidence on the blunt end.

"You're under arrest for attempted robbery, Mr. Schuler. At least to start with." Joe read him his rights.

"Robbing a drug dealer? Really?" chuckled Schuler.

"How about the murder of Otis Tripp? You find that funny, too?"

"I want to speak with a lawyer."

"I'll bet you do. You're going to need one."

Sam joined him with the bat in an evidence bag. Joe pulled Schuler to his feet, and they led him to Joe's car. They placed Schuler in the back seat of Joe's Camaro. It was a tight squeeze into the Camaro's back seat, but Sam managed to slide in next to him. They drove to Police District #19, where Schuler was booked and incarcerated. The bat was placed in evidence, and it would be sent to the lab for DNA testing. If the bat was used to kill Otis Tripp, there was a good chance his DNA would still be on it.

Joe checked his voicemail as well as his email account, and there was still no response from Damian Bose. He was not pleased and would deal with him tomorrow.

After driving Sam back to his car, Joe returned home and arrived at 1:30 a.m. He went straight to bed. It was going to be a short night.

Chapter Twenty

When the alarm rang at five o'clock the next morning, it came way too early. With less than four hours of sleep, Joe reluctantly rolled out of bed and put on his jogging clothes. He ran just two miles, a mile less than he usually did. He exercised Autumn, and following their round-the-block walk, Joe made the bed, showered, dressed, and ate breakfast. The exercise and two cups of coffee perked him up, and he felt alert while driving to work. The lack of sleep would hit him tonight.

At ten o'clock, Joe walked to Sam's desk. "I think it's time we pay Damian Bose a visit."

"He hasn't responded yet, huh?" asked Sam.

"No. We've given him plenty of time. He's either ignoring us, or he's in a coma."

They drove to Bose's studio on South Halsted Street in Greektown. Greektown got its name from Greek immigrants who settled in Chicago's Near North Side neighborhood beginning in the 1840s. Today, Greektown is a popular area teeming with restaurants and businesses.

Joe and Sam entered the double doors leading to the lobby of the Art Nouveau-style building. They took the elevator to the second floor and entered Bose's studio. They were met by a young man in his twenties. He had light brown hair and looked annoyed they had entered the studio without a prior appointment.

"You can't come in. There's a photo session going on," he said in a hushed but intense tone.

Joe and Sam held up their IDs.

"Detectives Erickson and Renaldo, Chicago PD," said Joe. "We're here to see Damian Bose."

The young man looked frantic and replied, "Mr. Bose is working right now. He's not available."

"Then make him available," stated Sam.

"Tell him he needs to take a break," added Joe. "By the way, who are you?"

"Dan McCarthy," said the young man. "Mr. Bose's assistant."

"Go get him."

In a confidential manner, the man replied, "He's going to be pissed off."

"So?"

"All right. You're asking for it." Then McCarthy turned and went through a door, carefully closing it behind him.

Joe looked at Sam, who said, "He's going to be pissed off."

"I heard something to that effect."

"Just how pissed do you think he'll be?"

"On a scale of one to ten, I'd guess an eight."

"Only an eight?" asked Sam.

"Maybe a nine."

A few moments later, the door flew open, and Damian Bose appeared, followed by McCarthy.

"How dare you interrupt me when I'm working," snarled Bose. "I'm paying those two models five hundred bucks an hour. Each!"

"We need to speak with you on a police matter," said Joe. "And I've tried to contact you several times by phone and by email. It's obvious you've been ignoring me."

"I'm a busy man. Time is money, and I don't have time for your so-called investigations."

His response riled Joe. "Well, now you need to make time. You're coming with us."

"Like hell, I am. I'm in the middle of a photo shoot."

"Not anymore," replied Sam. "Your photo shoot is shut down." He grabbed Bose's arm and said, "Let's go."

Bose resisted, saying, "Wait, wait, wait." Then he turned to McCarthy.

"Send the girls home. It looks like we're done for the day."

"Let's go," urged Sam, gripping Bose's arm firmly.

Bose reacted to Sam's grip, saying, "Hey! Easy on the arm, dude."

"Would you rather go out in cuffs, 'dude'."

"All right, all right. Ease up, will ya."

Bose was driven to Area 3, where he was placed in the interrogation room. Joe and Sam let him sit alone and observed him through the two-way glass. He was antsy, pacing, sitting down, getting up, checking his teeth in the mirror, anything but sitting still. He made a call on his cell phone and spoke to someone for a short time. Joe figured it was an attorney. After ten minutes, Joe and Sam entered the room.

"It took you long enough," complained Bose.

"Sorry about that," said Joe. "Something came up."

"I'll bet it did."

"You know why you're here?" asked Sam.

"No. Evidently, it's 'urgent,'" said Bose with contempt.

"So, you did get my messages," said Joe.

Bose didn't answer. He just glared at him. Sam glanced at Joe and continued. "You're here, Mr. Bose, because you haven't been cooperative, and that makes you look suspicious."

"Suspicious?" reacted Bose.

"We're investigating the deaths of two models who were working on one of your recent photo shoots," said Joe. "Amber Engstrom and Regina Fischer. They were murdered."

"Did you hear about it?" asked Sam.

"Of course."

"And you were seen arguing with Ms. Engstrom on the set. Witnesses reported it was heated."

Bose just sat there, refusing to comment and bathing in his contempt.

"What do you have to say about that?" asked Joe.

"Nothing."

"Were you engaged in an argument with Amber Engstrom or not?"

Bose was silent.

"You're not helping yourself here, Mr. Bose. You look like you're hiding something."

"Like hell I am."

"You look guilty," added Sam.

Silence.

"During one of the interviews, an individual who knew Amber Engstrom told us the two of you had a relationship in the past. Is that true?"

"What of it?"

"Did she break it off with you?"

Bose still refused to speak.

"Did that make you angry?" asked Sam. "Is that why you killed her?"

Bose looked up and growled through his teeth, "I didn't kill anybody!"

Joe decided to move on to questioning him about Regina Fischer. "Did you sleep with Regina Fischer, too? Or did she tell you to get lost?"

"I had nothing to do with Regina."

"No? That's not what we heard." It was not something anyone told Joe and Sam, but Joe wanted to squeeze Bose about her.

"You heard wrong."

"I'll tell you what we think," said Sam. "We think you killed Amber Engstrom and Regina Fischer because they both dumped you, and your ego couldn't handle it. And you hated them for it."

"Is that why you killed them?" pressed Joe. "To get revenge? Soothe your ego?"

"That's a crock," replied Bose.

"We don't think so. We think you killed both of them."

"You bought roses shortly before each woman was killed. We found a box with dead roses next to their bodies. Did those roses come from you?"

"No, I bought roses for my girlfriend."

Sam pushed further. "Did you tase, rape, and strangle both of these women?"

Joe didn't give him time to answer before he asked, "Where were you on June 4th and June 26th?"

"Killing these women?" asked Sam, leaning on him harder.

Bose exploded, "Fuck you, you assholes! I'm not saying another word until I speak with my lawyer."

"You're not under arrest, Mr. Bose," said Joe in a calm voice.

Bose glared at him and folded his arms, refusing to speak any further. Joe and Sam rose and left the room, leaving Bose to stew in the interrogation room.

"We need to interview that girlfriend of his," said Sam.

"Yeah," replied Joe. "If he has one."

Fifteen minutes later, a woman showed up, stating she was Bose's attorney. She was forty-something, and she did not look happy.

"I'm Alana Barton, Mr. Bose's attorney. I'd like to see him, please."

"Certainly," said Joe. "If you'll follow me." He opened the door to the interrogation room and let her in. Joe went to get a cup of coffee and met Sam there.

"What do you think?" asked Sam.

"I don't know," replied Joe. "Bose is a jerk, but we don't have enough to charge him."

"Let's see if he can produce an alibi for the times of the murders."

Ten minutes later, Barton emerged from the interrogation room and approached Joe and Sam, who were waiting outside the door.

"Are you going to charge my client or not?"

"Not at the present time," replied Joe.

"So, is he free to go?"

"He is."

"Once he can check his calendar, he will provide his whereabouts on the days in question. He also told me he bought roses for a particular young lady, and he's sure she'll verify receiving them."

Joe acknowledged her, saying, "That would be most helpful. If your client would have cooperated with our investigation in the first place, he would have saved himself a lot of trouble."

"Look, detectives. I've known Damian Bose for a long time. He may be a temperamental, arrogant ass, but he's no murderer."

"We'll see about that, won't we?" replied Sam.

"So, he's free to go?"

"For now," said Joe.

Barton walked back into the interrogation room. A couple of minutes later, she and Bose walked out. As he passed Joe and Sam, he turned and said, "You cost my client several thousand dollars today. You'll pay."

"Good luck with that," replied Sam.

"Come on," urged Barton. "Let's get out of here." They continued walking toward the exit as Joe and Sam watched.

"You think his latest squeeze can verify receiving roses?" asked Sam.

"My question would be: 'Would she lie for him?' I'm sure he'll be calling her when he gets a chance. I'd be more inclined to verify where he was when Engstrom and Fischer were killed."

Chapter Twenty-One

With the next two days off, Joe decided to go to the Art Institute of Chicago to see the new Picasso exhibition. He found the Art Institute relaxing, always stimulating his appreciation for great art. Not only that, it cleared his mind of thoughts he carried with him from work. When he returned to the office, his mind would be fresh, and he could view things in a new light.

Before attending the exhibition, he ate lunch at one of his favorite places, a Russian restaurant on Adams Street, a short distance from the Art Institute. Following a lunch of Classic Beef Stroganoff, he strolled to the Institute and straight to the Picasso exhibition. After an hour, he toured the Impressionist rooms, which displayed some of his favorite artworks. By the time it was four o'clock, he decided to leave for home so he could exercise Autumn.

As they walked around the block, his mind wandered, and before long, he was thinking about the double homicide case. If Damian Bose provides alibis for the times of death, and if his girlfriend verifies that he gave her roses on two occasions, then their investigation would be back to the starting point. Who killed these two women? The murders could not have been random. What common link do these two women have with their killer? He needed to find a new avenue to pursue if they had to eliminate Bose as a suspect.

Joe prepared a dinner of white fish piccata with asparagus spears, served with a glass of Sauvignon Blanc. Afterward, he tossed a ball with Autumn for a while before entering the living room. She accompanied him, jumping onto the couch as soon as he sat down.

After surfing through the channels and finding nothing worth watching, he went onto Netflix. He pulled up *Darkness*, the sequel to an Icelandic mystery series he enjoyed several months ago.

"Are you up for a brooding Scandinavian crime series, Autumn?" he asked.

Autumn looked at him with her sweet brown eyes. Then she turned and lay down facing away from him.

"My, we're moody tonight, aren't we?"

The first episode of *Darkness* hooked Joe on the series. The story was good, and the dubbing was excellent.

As he began the second episode, Destiny called.

"Hi," she said. "What are you up to?"

"I found a new crime series on Netflix. From Iceland. The first episode was great."

"Nice. How's Autumn?"

"Moody. She's not appreciating the plot."

Destiny laughed. "Maybe she would've preferred watching 'My Dog Skip.'"

Joe laughed, looked at Autumn, and asked, "Want to talk to your mom, Autumn?" She acknowledged him with a look and then laid her head down. "I guess not. Told you she was moody."

"That's okay. She probably misses me."

"That could be it."

"How's your latest case going?"

Joe explained about Damian Bose and why they consider him a possible suspect. They talked for another ten minutes about her work in Miami.

"I'll be presenting my profile at nine tomorrow morning, and I'll be flying back right afterward. My flight leaves at 11:15 your time."

"Good. I'm sure Autumn will be glad to see you," said Joe, tongue fully in cheek.

"What about you?" asked Destiny.

"Oh, yeah. I probably will be, too."

"You're so bad!"

Chuckling, Joe said, "I know. I'll be a lot happier to see you than Autumn. Don't expect me to turn in circles and bark, but I'll give you kisses."

"But not the kind Autumn gives, right?"

"Definitely not."

They joked around and laughed for a few more minutes before saying goodnight. Joe watched two more episodes of *Darkness* and then decided it was time to hit the hay. He took Autumn outside so she could potty one last time. At ten o'clock, the July air was still warm and humid. After returning to the house, Joe gave Autumn a treat and went to bed. Sleep came soon after.

* * *

Even though it was his second day off, Joe got up at the usual time and went for his three-mile jog. As he was halfway through his first mile, he began thinking about the case. Why would Damian Bose kill two of the top models in Chicago? He made money photographing them, and the session would have to be re-shot with two new models. The client would not want to promote their line of clothing with photographs of dead women. The more he thought about Bose, the more he began questioning him as a suspect. Even though he found him repugnant, it didn't make him the killer.

After taking Autumn for her morning walk, Joe showered and ate breakfast. He poured himself a second cup of coffee and began researching Amber Engstrom and Regina Fischer more deeply. They were both models, but what else could they have in common?

Joe pulled up Amber Engstrom's Facebook page and reviewed her photos, posts, and personal information. He was looking for anything that could be a clue to a connection with Regina Fischer. After studying her social media for over an hour, he moved on to Fischer's Facebook page. And bingo! There it was. Both Engstrom and Fischer graduated from Clinton College Prep High School on North Wells Street. According to rankings, it was one of the top high schools in the city, with a total enrollment of over 1100 students. He wondered if they knew each other or had mutual acquaintances while attending the school.

He continued exploring Regina Fischer's Facebook page and other social media platforms. By the time he finished, the only apparent connection he could find led back to high school. It wasn't much, but it was something to explore when he returned to the office.

To pass the time until Destiny arrived home and to take his mind off the case, Joe entered the garage and began looking over the 1969 Camaro he had been storing until he could buy it from Jacquie Lambert. The project was started by her sister's husband, Jared Harlow. But when the Harlows were killed in a plane crash, he offered to buy the dismantled car from Liz's sister, who inherited their property. She agreed, and since the estate had been recently settled, he was ready to cut her a check. The only problem was logistics. She lived in Hawaii and would have to travel to Chicago, so details like payment, the car's registration, and the accompanying documentation could be finalized.

Joe grabbed his clipboard and began noting what he needed to do to continue building the car. The body was bolted to the new aftermarket chassis, and the engine and transmission had been set in place, but that was about it. Jared was in the early stages of putting it together. Joe had already gone through and labeled the multitude of boxes containing parts. Jared once told him he had everything he needed to complete the build, and he was right. Nothing seemed to be missing, but assembling all the parts would take time and a lot of thought before the car could go to a body shop for paint and then to an upholstery shop.

By the time noon rolled around, Joe was getting hungry and decided he had finished making notes about the Camaro project. He had not thought about anything for lunch, so he decided to eat out. He drove to the Wilderness Bar and Restaurant on North Broadway, an upscale Irish pub that served good food and opened at noon daily.

After a lunch of corned beef, potatoes, and cabbage, he drove home to await Destiny's call. At 2:45, his phone rang.

"We just arrived. I'm just getting off the plane right now."

"I can drive out there and pick you up if you want," said Joe.

"Thanks, but I can get a taxi right away and be home by the time you'd get here," she replied. "I'll see you soon."

Forty-five minutes later, Joe saw a taxi pull in front of the house, and he went outside to help by bringing in her suitcase.

"How was Miami?" asked Joe after kissing her.

"Hot and muggy. It's good to be back home."

They entered the house and were greeted by an excited Autumn, who seemed happy Destiny had returned home. She danced and barked, jumping up on Destiny's leg, demanding attention.

Kneeling to pet her, Destiny said, "Are you happy I'm back home?"

"I think she missed you," said Joe.

"Well, of course you did. Didn't you?" said Destiny. Autumn nuzzled her and licked her hand. "Aw, you have kisses for me, too?"

Joe took the suitcase into the bedroom and returned to see Destiny giving Autumn a treat. Then Destiny turned to Joe and said, "I'd better call my mom and let her know I made it home."

"You want something to drink?"

"Is there any white wine in the refrigerator?"

"Yeah, there's a bottle of Sauvignon Blanc I opened yesterday."

"That would be nice," she said as she dialed her phone. Joe poured her a glass of the dry white wine. Destiny spoke with her mother for ten minutes, a short period compared with their usual phone calls, which often went on for an hour or more. That's one of the differences Joe noticed between men and women. Men's phone calls seldom lasted more than two or three minutes, or at least that was his experience. *What do women talk about for hours at a time, anyway?*

After the phone call, Joe asked, "Have you spoken to Jacquie now that Liz's estate has been settled?"

"No, not recently."

"I was wondering because I figured she'd like me to pay her for Jared's Camaro. I'd like to get the registration in my name so I can begin working on it."

"I can call her and mention it. I should give her a call anyway to see how she's doing."

"Thanks."

After Destiny finished her wine, they decided to take Autumn for a walk.

As they strolled down the block, Joe asked, "How was your experience with Miami PD?"

"Good. I think they were satisfied with my profile. I hope they apprehend the assailant soon before he can victimize more women."

"They'll let you know when they make an arrest?"

"Yeah. Captain Reyes said he would keep me apprised." They turned the corner, and she asked, "How's your double murder investigation going?"

"We've got a person of interest, but I'm growing skeptical. He was the photographer for the photo shoot I told you about. Temperamental artist-type. He supposedly had a relationship with one of them in the past. But I don't see a motive for killing two of the models he was working with. We brought him in, and he lawyered up. So, we'll see if he has an alibi for the times of their deaths."

"So, where does that leave you if he does have an alibi?"

"Back to square one. But I just found out the two victims graduated from the same high school. Same year. It may be nothing, but I'm going to pursue that tomorrow."

"Sounds like you may have another lead."

"We'll see."

Amber stopped to sniff some unidentifiable, raunchy smear near the curb. Whatever it was, it intrigued her. "Don't sniff that. Yuck!" said Joe as he tugged gently on her lead. "Come on. Let's go." Autumn chose to obey and continued trotting down the street, with Joe and Destiny strolling alongside.

"Dogs," chuckled Destiny. "It looks disgusting to us, but she's simply trying to understand what it is and where it came from."

Joe looked at her and said, "Curiosity killed the cat, right? Just erring on the side of caution."

Chapter Twenty-Two

J oe was sitting at his computer the next day when he received a call from the detective in the public access area. Bose's attorney, Alana Barton, was asking to see him.

Joe alerted Sam to her arrival and then escorted Barton to the interrogation room. After pleasantries were exchanged, Barton removed documents from her attaché case.

Handing them to Joe, Barton said, "These are affidavits from Mr. Bose's friend, Megan Walker, and from Michael Brice, a representative of designer Vera Wang. As you can see, Miss Walker stipulates she received roses from him on two occasions and was with Mr. Bose on a flight to New York on June 4th. And Mr. Brice states he was in meetings with Mr. Bose in Los Angeles on June 26th. We can produce a record of his airline tickets if you insist."

Joe and Sam looked over the documents, suppressing their feelings of dismay. When he had finished, Joe looked across the table at Barton, whose cavalier expression rubbed him the wrong way.

"It looks as though your client has an alibi for the dates in question, Ms. Barton," said Joe.

"So, should I assume Mr. Bose is no longer a suspect?"

"If these check out, we won't be considering him a suspect any longer," replied Sam.

"If they check out?" protested Barton, apparently offended by his answer. "You've heard of due diligence, haven't you?"

Barton rose from her chair, picked up her attaché case, and said, "I believe we're done here."

Following her lead, Joe and Sam stood and moved toward the door. Joe opened it for Barton, and she passed through on her way to the exit.

"Thank you for coming in," said Sam. She did not acknowledge him. With a smirk, he looked at Joe. "Good riddance."

"Yeah."

"Back to the starting gate, huh?"

"Yup," replied Joe, holding on to the affidavits.

Joe made a copy of the two affidavits and placed them in the file for each victim.

With no suspect, Joe began exploring Engstrom's and Fischer's high school years. He searched online for a high school yearbook for their senior year. Upon finding it, he looked through it page by page but found nothing other than formal senior photos of both Engstrom and Fischer. Neither were athletes, and neither one appeared in any photos of extracurricular activities. Maybe the principal would remember them, given both of their alumni were models who had appeared in print advertising—such accomplishments a school would be proud of.

He called the school, introduced himself, and asked to speak with the principal. She put him on hold, and he soon heard a big, baritone voice come on the line.

"This is Bob Hymes. How can I help you?"

"I'm Detective Joe Erickson, Chicago PD," Joe began. "We're investigating the deaths of two of your former students and–"

"Oh, no..."

"I'm afraid so. And I'd like to speak with someone who might remember them."

"Okay."

"Is there a time convenient for me to speak with you?"

"Let me check my calendar. Make sure I don't have meetings scheduled."

Joe heard him typing on his keyboard. "I have an hour open this afternoon from one-thirty to two-thirty. Does that work for you?"

"It does," replied Joe. "I'll be there at one-thirty."

"We have a security system, so you'll need to identify yourself before the door can be opened. Just give your name and say you have an appointment with me. Joe Erickson, you said. Right?"

"Yes."

"I'll put you on my schedule. They'll confirm and unlock the door for you. One of those necessary security measures we need to have these days."

Joe thanked him and let Sam know about his appointment. Sam suggested he stay at Area 3 since he was expecting a phone call from a friend of Regina Fischer.

Joe secured a squad car for his trip to the school, which he estimated to be a twenty-minute drive. Leaving shortly after one o'clock, he arrived at the imposing brick building a few minutes early. He parked in the visitors' lot and waited a few minutes until it was nearly one-thirty. He pressed the button on the intercom, and a female voice answered. Joe identified himself, and she gave him directions to Hyme's office. The door buzzed and unlocked so he could enter.

The directions he was given were easy to follow, and a few minutes later, he was standing in front of the principal's office. Since it was July, there were no students in the halls.

When he entered, a woman rose from behind her desk to greet him. She gave him a friendly smile and said, "Welcome to Clinton Prep, Detective Erickson."

"Thank you." Joe glanced around and joked, "This is the first time I've been to the principal's office since I punched Bruce Heller in high school!"

She laughed and said, "Well, I assume you're not here for punching another student."

"Afraid not."

"I'm Sandra Donovan, Dr. Hymes's secretary. I'll let him know you're here." Her lithe and graceful movement across the room made Joe wonder if she was once a dancer or gymnast. She knocked on a door and opened it a crack, saying, "Detective Erickson is here."

"Thank you. Send him in," came an intimidating voice from within.

Donovan opened the door for Joe and told him to go in. As he entered, Dr.

Hymes was already up and walking toward him. Hymes was as intimidating physically as he was vocally. He was a towering African American man who stood six feet four inches and weighed well over two hundred pounds.

"Bob Hymes," he said as he shook Joe's hand.

"Joe Erickson," replied Joe. "Thanks for seeing me."

"Come in. Have a seat," said Hymes, indicating the chair in front of his desk. Joe seated himself as Hymes walked back behind his desk and sat down. "You said on the phone two of our former students have been killed?"

"They have. They were both twenty-six years old and graduated eight years ago. Amber Engstrom and Regina Fischer."

"Killed as in…"

"Murdered," said Joe, finishing his sentence.

"Dear god. That's terrible. You know who was responsible?"

"That's what we're trying to find out. They both worked as models in the fashion industry, but we don't know if that had anything to do with their deaths. I was thinking maybe you had some recollection about them as students."

"I hate to disappoint you, but I've only been here five years. Before that, I was finishing my doctorate."

"I see," said Joe, clearly disappointed.

Reading Joe's disappointment, Hymes said, "I think I know someone who may be able to help you, though. One of our guidance counselors, Gary Richardson. He's been here a long time. Let me call and see if he's in his office."

Hymes picked up his phone and punched in some numbers. After a moment, he said, "Mr. Richardson, there's a detective from the police department in my office asking about a couple of former students…yes…they were students here before my time…You have a few minutes? Good. Come to my office." He hung up and said, "He'll be here shortly."

"I appreciate your help."

"No problem. You said both girls were models?"

"They were. You may have seen them in magazine ads. They were both quite attractive and had bright futures in the business."

CHAPTER TWENTY-TWO

"That's a shame."

Joe and Hymes conversed briefly before the door opened, and Donovan announced, "Mr. Richardson's here."

"Send him in," said Hymes.

Upon first glance, Richardson reminded Joe of one of his high school teachers. He was in his forties, balding, with a physique suggesting a former athlete gone to seed. Joe noticed a small port-wine stain birthmark on his neck below his right ear. Both Hymes and Joe stood as Richardson entered, and Hymes made the introductions.

"Detective Erickson was wondering if someone remembered a couple of students...uh, sorry." He looked at Joe and asked, "What did you say their names were?"

"Amber Engstrom and Regina Fischer. They would have graduated eight years ago."

Richardson's face lit up. "Oh, yeah. I remember them."

"Good. Why don't you two go into my conference room so you can talk?" Hymes stepped to a door on the north wall of his office and opened it. Joe followed Richardson into the room, and Hymes shut the door. They sat down at the table.

"How is it you remember these two students?" asked Joe. "It's been eight years. A lot of students have passed through in that time."

Richardson removed his glasses and began wiping the lenses with a handkerchief as he spoke. "You tend to remember certain people who make an unfavorable impression on you."

Joe was surprised by Richardson's remark. "Unfavorable? In what way?"

"There was a clique made up of five white girls. Each one was very attractive, but they seemed to get their jollies out of bullying others, especially other white girls. They didn't pick on Latinos or African American kids. Probably afraid to. Anyway, they could be mean and nasty.

After writing this down, Joe asked, "Can you give me an example of what they did? If you can remember, that is."

"Oh, I can remember, all right. If anybody challenged them or somebody lipped off to one of them, they would gang up on the person and make their life miserable. Sometimes, they seemed to harass others just for the fun of it."

"How so?"

"Well, once, during a party while her parents were gone, it was rumored one of them slipped a girl a roofie. Reprisal for something she said or did. After she passed out, she was taken to a bedroom and stripped of her clothes. Pictures were taken of her posed naked on a bed, and they were posted on the internet. When she woke up early the next morning, she realized she'd been raped."

"What became of it?"

"She came to see me since I'm a counselor, and she told me about what happened. I encouraged her to tell her parents and go to the police, but she didn't know who was responsible. And it was too late for DNA evidence to be taken. After the photos were posted, she felt humiliated and received sneers and jeers from other students. She couldn't bear the shame and the embarrassment, and she ended up taking her own life. It was all very sad."

"That kind of criminal behavior should have been reported and investigated."

"I know. It should have, but it wasn't."

"Do you remember the name of the student who committed suicide?

"It was Shari McCarthy."

As Joe wrote down the name, Richardson continued.

"Another time, one of the clique supposedly took a photo of a girl as she got out of the shower after physical education class. She was buck naked, and that photo was also posted on the internet for all to see."

"That's not only cruel but criminal. Did anything come of it?" asked Joe.

"Nobody could prove who took the photo or who posted it. That was the problem. But the victim said she had confronted one of the girls about something, and when an argument ensued, she was told she'd regret it. Some kind of payback, evidently. Of course, the girl was mortified and extremely upset about the photo."

"That's vicious. And the school couldn't do anything?"

"You can't act on rumors and assumptions. Students were afraid of crossing any of those girls for fear they could be their next victim. The kids began referring to the clique as 'the...'"

"The Bitch Squad?" asked Joe, giving Richardson a skeptical look.

"You know how kids are. But yeah, that was the name they hung on them. I think students and teachers alike were relieved to see them graduate."

This information gave Joe a whole new avenue to pursue. Anyone who crossed the Bitch Squad, or became a victim of their wrath, could have a motive for killing Engstrom and Fischer.

"Were Amber Engstrom and Regina Fischer members of this Bitch Squad?" asked Joe.

"They were."

"You said there were five. Do you recall the names of the other three?"

"I do. There was, let's see...Stephanie Daniels, Madison Powell, and Tracey McNamara."

Joe finished writing the names down and said, "You have a good memory."

"Like I said, you tend to remember the troublemakers."

"And they all graduated the same year?"

"They did."

Joe looked at Richardson and said, "Anything else you can tell me?"

Richardson thought for a minute and said, "Well...ironically, they were all good students. Smart. Other than that..."

"You don't know what happened to them after graduation, do you?"

"I'm afraid not."

"Would you know anyone who would?"

"Not that I know of."

"Well...This has been helpful."

Joe was satisfied with Richardson's answers and closed his notebook. "I think I have what I need. What's a good way to contact you if I have a few more questions?"

"You can call me on my cell phone. 312-555-7272."

Joe wrote the number in his notebook. Rising from his chair, he said, "I appreciate your time, Mr. Richardson."

"No problem. You think these two girls were killed by somebody they knew from high school?"

"Right now, we're exploring several leads, but nothing substantial yet." He reached out and shook Richardson's hand. "Thanks again."

"Take care."

Joe left the conference room, followed by Richardson. Hymes was no longer at his desk. He stopped in front of Donovan's desk and said, "Please tell Dr. Hymes I appreciate his assistance."

"Certainly," replied Donovan. "Have a good day."

With this new information, Joe drove back to Area 3 and informed Sam about what he learned from Gary Richardson.

"The Bitch Squad? Wow, what an appropriate name," said Sam.

"Yeah. Did you get a call from Fischer's friend?"

"Uh-huh. But I didn't learn anything we didn't already know."

"We need to do some digging tomorrow and find these girls. If you want to locate Shari McCarthy's parents, I'll start searching for the remaining members of the clique."

"Sounds good."

Chapter Twenty-Three

When Joe got home, Autumn started barking as soon as Joe pulled his car under the carport. When he entered the kitchen, Autumn was doing her welcome-home dance. After locking up his Glock, he kneeled and petted her.

Destiny came out of the office and said, "I think you like her more than me."

"Not true," replied Joe, standing. "If you danced and wagged your tail when I got home, I'd pet you first."

"Fat chance of that," she said and gave him a peck on the cheek. "Thirsty?"

He sat on a stool at the island and said, "I am."

Destiny stepped to the counter and opened a bottle of Pinot Noir. As she was pouring out two glasses, she asked, "Good day today?"

"It was. We have a new lead to follow up on."

"Great. I hope it takes you somewhere."

"You and me, both."

She set the glass of wine in front of Joe while she sat on another stool and tasted the wine. Watching Joe take a drink, she asked, "What do you think?"

"It's good. Hints of fruit."

"It's from a vineyard downstate. The guy at the wine shop recommended it to me."

"Really. It's very good. We'll have to shop for this label again."

Joe tipped up his glass for another drink, and as he was putting it down, Destiny asked, "So, can you share your lead with me?"

"I shouldn't be sharing confidential police business," he kidded. She gave him a look that made him smile. "Okay. I'll spill my guts."

Joe told her about the Bitch Squad and where he was going with his search tomorrow. Destiny took it all in, nodding as if she was familiar with such cliques.

When Joe finished, she said, "We had cliques like that in high school, but they were never that cruel. I think every school has a clique of girls who would look down their noses at others. A "We're Special and You're Not Club," you know? There was one like that in my high school."

"You weren't in it, were you?" Joe asked, knowing that she would not have been.

"God, no. They were all airheads."

Joe laughed. "I think it's possible someone may be seeking revenge on members of the Squad. There were five members, and two of them are dead."

"It's possible. But since it's only two, it could be a coincidence, and the offender has a different motive."

"I know. But until I rule it out, I'm following my gut."

Destiny put down her glass and said, "Not to change the subject or anything, but you like the Beatles, don't you?"

"Yeah. But you know I prefer metal."

"I know. You still lamenting the breakup of Black Fast?"

"Yeah, but I've been able to move on."

"I'm asking because a group impersonating the Beatles is performing here, and there are still tickets available for tomorrow night. George Harrison's wife even endorsed them. I think it would be fun. So, my question is: Would you go with me?"

Joe knew Destiny liked the Beatles and could tell how much she really wanted to go. "Okay. I'm up for it." He had been spending a lot of time at home, and getting out of the house for an evening would be refreshing.

"Good, because I reserved two tickets."

"Will you go with me if I get tickets to see Warbringer? They're touring with Goatwhore and Havok."

"Goatwhore? There's a group called 'Goatwhore?'"

"Yeah. Blackened death metal."

"You're serious."

"Yeah."

"Oh, boy." She thought for a few seconds. "Okay. If you think they're good, I'll give it a try."

After Joe finished his wine, he took Autumn for a walk around the block. When they returned, Destiny was busy in the kitchen making dinner.

"What's on the menu?"

"Salmon with bearnaise sauce, asparagus spears, and a green salad. You want to whip up your Italian dressing?"

While Destiny was preparing the bearnaise sauce, Joe made his dressing from olive oil, balsamic vinegar, brown mustard, roasted garlic powder, onion powder, sugar, and Italian spices. It was his own special concoction, and Destiny, as well as her mother, were both fond of it.

Following dinner, Joe and Destiny adjourned to the living room, where they took their places on the couch. But before Joe could switch on the TV, Destiny spoke.

"From what you've told me, and given this is no coincidence, I'd be looking for someone who was harmed by these girls when they were in high school. It could be a family member of someone who was injured or harmed as a result. A parent, brother, sister, boyfriend, or someone close to that person."

"I appreciate your take on this. I was thinking the same thing. We know of two people they harassed. One suicide, and another who was humiliated by them."

Destiny continued. "If someone is selecting these women for payback, they need to be contacted and told they could be in danger."

"I'm going to be working on that first thing tomorrow," said Joe. "I'm going on the assumption this has more to do with their past behavior rather than their modeling careers."

"I've done a lot of profiles, but nothing quite like this. I think you're on the right track. Without digging deeper, I can't give you anything more specific."

"Thanks. Glad to know we're on the same page."

"It's only logical your offender has an axe to grind. Now…what would you like to do?"

"Forget about work, for starters."

Chapter Twenty-Four

The first thing Joe did when he got to his desk the next day was to begin researching the three remaining members of the Squad. He began with Tracey McNamara. He checked with the Illinois Driver's License database and found several records for a person with that name. After viewing them all, he settled on one record. Tracey Ann McNamara was 25, the right age, but her license was expired.

Joe assumed that since her license had not been renewed, she either stopped driving, moved to another state, or was no longer living. He checked the Social Security Death Index and found a record for Tracey A. McNamara. Her birth date matched what was listed on her driver's license, and her date of death made her 25. Her social security number was issued in Illinois, making it a good chance she was the person he was looking for.

After an online search, he found an obituary posting on a funeral home website. He read that McNamara was born in Chicago and graduated from Clinton Preparatory High School and the University of Indiana. She had been working for an insurance agency in Indianapolis before her death. The cause of death was not mentioned, but she died in Indianapolis. *At age 25?* wondered Joe.

Joe printed the obituary and searched the internet for additional hits. He found a newspaper article from the Indianapolis Star, which reported that Tracey A. McNamara, 25, was found dead in her apartment. Joe read the article, which stated police were treating it as a homicide. He printed the article and placed it in a file folder along with the obituary.

Curious, he searched for another Squad member in the driver's license database. Once again, several women named Stephanie Daniels pulled up. But only three were living in Chicago, and two were over the age of forty. The remaining license was for Stephanie Ellen Daniels, an attractive brunette, living at a River North address. The license information revealed she was 26 years old, but the license had not been renewed.

Again, Joe searched the Social Security Death Index but found no entry for a Stephanie Daniels with the corresponding age. *Hopefully, she's still alive*, Joe thought.

Not satisfied, Joe searched the internet for any information on a Stephanie Ellen Daniels. Lo and behold, he saw an entry for the Milwaukee Journal Sentinel. The headline read, "Woman Found Murdered."

Omigod thought Joe. The article was six months old and stated Stephanie Daniels, 26, was found by a friend who checked on her when she missed work for two days. It said she had been strangled and sexually assaulted.

Another hit in his search brought up her obituary. It stated she graduated from Clinton Preparatory School and the University of Wisconsin at Milwaukee. Survived by her parents and two brothers, she was employed by a major brewery at the time of her death. Joe printed the newspaper article and her obituary, placing them in the file with Tracey McNamara's information.

Joe took a drink from his coffee. It was clear someone was killing members of the Squad. Joe began a search for the fifth member, Madison Powell. The driver's license database showed a Madison Marie Powell, 26, and listed an address in Wicker Park.

Joe found no hits in the Social Security Death Index, and no deaths or obituaries were listed for her. One entry listed a Madison Powell as a faculty member at Traynor College, a community college on West Wilson Avenue. Further digging on the Traynor College website revealed she taught English courses. Could this Madison Powell be the only remaining member of the Squad?

After writing down Powell's contact information, Joe called the Indianapolis police department. He identified himself and asked to speak with a homicide detective. He was transferred, and the call was answered.

"Homicide, Detective Palermo," said a male voice.

Joe identified himself and asked if he had information on the death of Tracey McNamara.

"Why do you ask?" said Palermo.

"We believe her death could be related to one of our ongoing investigations," said Joe.

"That's still an open case."

"I'd like to speak with the primary."

"That would be me," replied Palermo.

"Ah. Well, let me ask this," said Joe. "Was she found strangled, and was there a box with dead roses found near the body?"

"Uh…there was a box with one dried-out rose."

"One?"

"Yeah. It seemed strange that a single dried flower would be in that large box."

"And was there a card that read 'sic semper scortilla?'"

Silence. "Yeah," he said, stretching out the word. "How did you know that? That information wasn't released."

He just confirmed what Joe suspected. The same offender killed three members of the Squad. "Because we have two identical homicides here in Chicago."

"No shit?"

"Yeah. Were you able to collect any evidence? Something that could link McNamara's murder to the two we have here in Chicago?"

"Our forensic people found microscopic red fibers in the chafed area on her neck. She'd been sexually assaulted, but the killer didn't leave any DNA. We think it's possible she could have been penetrated with an object since no hairs or skin cells were recovered."

"Same here," added Joe. "Just one more question. Was the victim tased?"

"Uh…yeah. Were your two women tased, too?"

"They were. I think that goes to prove we're looking for the same offender."

"Do you have a link between these women?" asked Palermo.

Joe explained about the five members of the so-called "Bitch Squad" and told him he found an obituary for another member in Milwaukee. He suggested Palermo's lieutenant contact his lieutenant about coordinating their investigations.

Palermo asked to be apprised of any progress Joe made in their investigation, and Joe asked Palermo for the same. Following his conversation with Palermo, Joe called the Milwaukee Police Department. He identified himself and asked to speak with a detective in their homicide division. A man with a gruff voice answered.

"Homicide, Sergeant Lisowski."

Joe identified himself and asked to speak with someone about the Stephanie Daniels homicide. Lisowski put him on hold while he checked. Then he came back on the line and said, "Detective Townsend's the primary on that one. Let me transfer you."

Moments later, a female voice answered, "Detective Townsend."

Joe introduced himself and said, "Your sergeant told me you're the primary on the Stephanie Daniels case. Is that correct?"

"It is."

"Is it still an open case?"

"It is."

Their conversation mirrored the one he had with Detective Palermo. Townsend was offended by the description of the clique as the "Bitch Squad," so Joe decided not to use it again during their conversation.

"Are you telling me there are three other murders with the same M.O.?" asked Townsend.

"Looks like it. All three victims were tased, raped, and strangled with a red ligature. Was there a box containing dead long-stem roses left at the scene?

"There were two withered roses found in the box."

"Two?"

"Yes. Two."

"And a card that read 'sic semper scortilla?" asked Joe.

"Yeah...are you telling me we've got a serial killer on our hands?"

"Maybe, maybe not," replied Joe. "We think the offender is someone with a revenge motive, someone who is seeking retribution by killing each member of the clique."

Townsend was silent for a few seconds and then asked, "Do you know how many girls made up this clique?"

"I was told by a school official there were five. Four are dead."

"So that leaves one still alive."

"As far as I know. I haven't tried contacting her yet. That's next on my list of things to do."

"I hope you'll keep me in the loop on this," requested Townsend.

Joe agreed. They talked for a while longer about the case. When the call ended, he walked to Sam's desk and told him what he found out.

"Two more?" said Sam, nearly choking on his coffee. "You telling me there's only one girl from the Squad who's still alive?"

"Yeah. And get this. The offender's been adding one more rose to the box with each murder. He seems to be indicating how many are dead. One rose with his first kill, two with his second, three with Engstrom, and four with Fischer."

"Strange way to send a message."

"I think we'd better talk with Madison Powell before she gets a flower delivery," replied Joe. "Let me try to contact her at the college and see if we can meet."

Chapter Twenty-Five

Joe called Traynor College's general number and was transferred to the secretary in the Department of English, Communications, and Journalism. After identifying himself, he asked to speak with Professor Powell.

"She's not in today," the woman stated. "She doesn't teach on Tuesdays and Thursdays."

"I see."

"Can I take a message for her?"

Joe declined but asked, "I know you can't give out her address, but can you confirm if she still lives on West Lawrence Avenue?"

"Since you're the police, I guess I can do that. Let me check." After punching her keyboard a few times, she said, "She does."

Joe thanked her and ended the call. Writing down her address from the driver's license record, he determined it was essential to reach her at home as soon as possible. Joe and Sam drove to Powell's West Lawrence Avenue address in the Uptown neighborhood. They stepped inside the triangular-shaped tan building and located the intercom. Joe pushed the button for Apartment 715. Eventually, a female voice responded.

"Yes?"

"Chicago PD," said Joe. "We'd need to speak with Madison Powell."

"That's me. What's this about?"

"We'd prefer to discuss that with you face to face."

"All right." The buzzer sounded, and the door unlocked. Joe and Sam took the elevator to the seventh floor and knocked on Unit 715. It opened as far as the chain would allow.

"Madison Powell?" asked Joe.

"Yes."

"Chicago PD."

"Can I see your badges?" she asked.

Joe and Sam held up their IDs for her to see, and a moment later, they heard the chain slide. The door opened to reveal Madison Powell standing in the doorway, but she did not invite them in.

"We need to speak with you," said Joe. "Can we come in?"

Without responding, Powell opened the door wide, inviting them to enter. As Joe entered her apartment, he was greeted by a place that was neat and expertly furnished in Scandinavian style decor, which is marked by a minimalist, uncluttered design emphasizing functionality.

After closing the door, Powell asked, "What is it you want?"

"Can we sit down?" asked Sam. "This could take some time."

"If this is about my brother, I haven't seen him in two years." She walked into a tastefully decorated living room, and they sat down, Joe and Sam on the couch and Powell on a matching chair. The coffee table was scattered with typed papers, some marked with red ink, and Joe assumed she had been correcting her students' assignments.

"This isn't about your brother."

"Oh?"

"You belonged to a clique with four other girls when you were in high school, is that right?" asked Joe.

"A clique? I wouldn't call it a clique. We were just a group of friends."

"Did you know four of them are dead?"

"What?" she gasped.

"All of them murdered."

"For god's sake," she exclaimed. "How...how can that be?"

"You hadn't heard anything about your friends' deaths?"

"I haven't kept up with them since high school. I read a story in the Sun-Times about Amber. But I didn't know about the others."

Joe noticed Powell's hands shaking as she picked up a bottle of water from the side table.

"I can't believe this," she said before taking a drink.

"We're investigating the deaths of Amber Engstrom and Regina Fischer. We discovered Tracey McNamara and Stephanie Daniels were killed while living out of state. We believe someone is getting revenge on your group of friends."

"And now, you're the sole surviving member of your group," added Sam.

Powell didn't respond. She seemed frozen, staring at the floor, seemingly processing the news. A few moments later, she looked up, saying, "So…are you saying I could be in danger?"

"We're concerned the offender could be targeting all of you based on something you may have done back in high school," said Joe. "We interviewed a teacher from your school who told us all about the so-called "Bitch Squad."

Powell's eyes flared with anger.

"So, you've heard that name before, huh?"

"We didn't deserve that."

"I don't know, given the hateful things the Squad did to other students."

"Like what?" replied Powell, clearly irked by Joe's implication.

"I'll tell you what. Like drugging a girl and photographing her naked in a bed. And taking a photo of another girl getting out of the shower and posting these photos on the internet for all to see. That's just the tip of this vicious iceberg, Ms. Powell. You see, we know all about you and your friends," said Joe.

"I wasn't responsible for those things. That was Amber and Tracey," protested Powell. "They wanted to teach those girls a lesson."

"And what did you do, stand there and giggle?"

Powell teared up. "I'm…I'm sorry. I…" she said as tears rolled down her cheek.

"Save the tears," said Sam. "A girl died because of you and your friends. And now, someone appears to be paying all of you back."

Powell began crying. Joe looked at Sam, who let out a sigh. He reached into his jacket pocket and handed her a handkerchief.

After wiping her eyes, she said, "I wasn't in on that, I swear. What they did went way beyond a prank."

"It certainly did."

"Look, it was Amber and Tracey. Tracey had the drug, and Amber took the pictures and posted them online."

"It's easy to blame somebody else when they're not around to defend themselves," said Sam.

"I'm telling you the truth!" she said, wiping her eyes and blowing her nose. "I might have said some things I regret now, but not that."

"You know who raped that girl after you stripped her naked and took that photo?" asked Joe.

"No idea. But I suppose anybody could have gone into the bedroom after we left."

"Someone is out to get all the members of your group. Do you have any idea who it might be?"

"No."

"Did your pranks cause anyone else to die?" asked Sam.

"No, not that I know of."

"What about the girl you snapped a picture of getting out of the shower?"

"I didn't take the picture!" There was a pause, and then Powell spoke. "She and Steph got into a fight during PE class. I don't remember what it was about. Steph was angry and took the picture to get even."

"You know what her name was?"

"I don't. Sorry. It's been eight years."

Joe and Sam explained about the killer's M.O.–the taser, flowers, rape, and strangulation. The expression on Powell's face grew more and more horrified as they went into detail.

"Do you live alone?" asked Joe.

"No. My boyfriend and I live together. He's usually here after five."

"I want to warn you. If someone rings and says he has a flower delivery for you, do not, under any circumstances, accept them and buzz him in," said Joe. "It could be the killer."

"I won't."

"And if someone does ring saying he has flowers for you, call me immediately. I'll send the police and have them arrest the guy while he's outside your building."

Joe gave her his card. "That's my cell phone, and I'll answer it day or night."

She looked at the card and said, "Thank you."

"You have any questions?" asked Sam.

"I...I don't think so. At least, not for now."

"Then, we'll be on our way," said Joe. "Call me if you remember something, like the name of the girl you can't recall. Any little detail could prove helpful."

"I will."

On their way back to the office, Sam asked, "You think she was telling the truth about not being part of the Squad's activities?"

"No. But I sensed she regretted what they did. Maybe after graduation, she grew up and developed a conscience."

"Probably why she chose not to keep in touch with the other members of the Squad."

"Yeah. If she's telling the truth."

Chapter Twenty-Six

Shortly after four o'clock, Joe received a frantic cell phone call from Desiree McMillan, one of the models from TGM Talent.

"I'm at home, and some guy just buzzed my apartment and said he had a flower delivery for me!" said a frightened McMillan. "What do I do?"

"Give me your address, and I'll call the police," said Joe. "Try to stall him until the police get there. And stay on the line with me. My partner and I will be there ASAP."

"Okay."

"And whatever you do, do not let him in."

Knowing her address fell within District #19, Joe called and sent police to her address.

"Sam!" yelled Joe, rising quickly from his desk. "We need to roll."

As they ran toward the exit, Sam asked, "What is it?"

Another one of the models called. There's a guy trying to deliver flowers to her."

"Jesus!"

"I called the police and told her to try and stall him."

Jumping into their squad car, Sam hit the lights and siren once they hit the street. McMillan's address was only five minutes away on Belmond Avenue.

When they were almost to the address, McMillan cried into the phone, "He's outside my door now! Help!"

"Don't open your door. Stall him. We are only a couple minutes away," said Joe.

When they pulled up to the address, uniformed officers were already on the scene and prepared to enter the building.

"We're here," he told McMillan." Buzz the door open."

Joe, Sam, and two uniformed officers ran up the steps to the second floor and saw a man standing outside McMillan's door, holding a bouquet of flowers. He was knocking on her door. When he saw them coming toward him with guns drawn, his eyes practically popped out of his head.

"FREEZE," yelled Joe, and the man stood there, not moving a muscle.

"Slowly put the flowers down and place your hands on your head." When he complied, Joe ordered one of the uniforms to cuff him.

He was patted down, but they failed to find a taser or any red material, and the flowers were a fresh bouquet, not dried roses in a box. This didn't look promising.

"What's your name?" asked Sam.

The delivery man, frightened and confused, stammered, "Aram Nazarian." Joe checked the man's wallet and confirmed that was his name.

"I not understand," said Nazarian with a thick foreign accent. "I do nothing wrong?"

Looking at one of the uniforms, Joe said, "Take him down and put him in your cruiser."

As they led him out, Joe spoke into his phone, "Ms. McMillan. You can open your door now. We're here."

He heard the chain release, and McMillan opened the door. Sam put on gloves and picked up the card attached to the bouquet.

"We've apprehended the man who was delivering the flowers," said Joe. "Were you expecting flowers from anyone today?"

"No," said McMillan.

"So, you wouldn't have received anything from a boyfriend or anyone congratulating you for something?"

"Oh. Wait a minute."

"Joe," said Sam. He had opened the envelope and was holding up a small card that read "Happy Birthday," followed by "Love, Mom" written on the inside. Joe closed his eyes and let out a breath. He was annoyed and relieved at the same time.

"What is it?" asked McMillan, a confused look on her face.

"Show her," said Joe.

Sam held up the card for her to read. "Make sense to you?" he asked.

McMillan looked at the card, and she closed her eyes and dipped her head down. She took an audible breath and looked up. "My mom…evidently, she sent them. It's my birthday tomorrow."

"Better a happy birthday bouquet than a box of dead roses," Joe said to Sam.

"This is embarrassing," said McMillan. "I'm so sorry."

"We're just glad that you're safe," said Sam. He picked up the bouquet from the floor and handed it to her. "Happy birthday."

Taking them, she blushed and said, "Thank you."

"We have some things to attend to," said Joe. "Enjoy your flowers."

On their way down in the elevator, Sam asked, "What about the delivery guy?"

"We've got some explaining to do."

As they exited the building, they walked over to the cruiser where Aram Nazarian was sitting. Joe opened the back door and said, "You can get out, Mr. Nazarian."

Nazarian got out of the cruiser and stood before Joe and Sam. He still looked frightened. While the two uniformed officers looked on, Joe apologized to Nazarian for what happened and explained why the woman got scared and called the police.

"How did you get inside the building? She didn't buzz you in," asked Sam.

"Somebody came out, I went in. I wait long time." Looking at Joe, he asked, "Can I go now? I got more stops."

"Yeah, you're free to go," replied Joe.

Nazarian hurriedly walked down the street while Joe stepped to the uniformed officers and said, "He was mistaken for an offender we're looking for. Sorry for the call."

"No problem," said one of the officers. "You need us for anything else?"

"No, we're done here. You can go."

As Joe and Sam watched them drive away, Sam said, "I guess we're done here, too."

"Yeah. Is it Miller time yet?" asked Joe.

"Way past," said Sam. "Way past."

As Sam drove them back to their office, Joe rang Destiny and told her he had been delayed and would explain when he got home.

"You remember I've got tickets for the Beatles show tonight, right?" reminded Destiny.

"I know. I'll get home in time."

"Problem?" asked Sam.

"We have tickets for a show tonight, that's all. "

"Ah."

"How are you and Carolyn getting on?"

"We're good," said Sam. "She's been talking about us moving in together, but I don't know if I'm quite ready for that yet."

"Why not? You've been seeing her for quite a while now."

"I kinda like things the way they are. But she can be pretty persuasive, so…"

"She know you're feeling hesitant about it?"

"She does. But she's not pushing it, so it'll happen when it happens, I guess. I like my privacy, and giving up some of that makes me feel uneasy, you know?"

"I know what you mean. I felt like that when Destiny and I made the decision to buy a house so we could live together. But I'm still able to have my privacy if I want it."

"Divorce ruins you. I guess that's why I'm uptight about it. I don't want our relationship to fall apart if we move in together."

"Is she worth taking a risk for?"

"Yeah."

"Then, take the risk. There's nothing like having a partner to share your life with."

As Joe drove home, he thought about the advice he gave to Sam and how lucky he was to have someone like Destiny in his life.

"You're one lucky SOB, Joe Erickson," he said out loud. A minute later, he turned onto their street. He would have just enough time to grab something to eat before heading out to see the Fab Four performance.

It turned out to be an enjoyable night in the theatre. Destiny loved it, and the actor/singers portraying the Beatles were impressive, not only in portraying their characters but also singing and playing their instruments. It was like witnessing the original Beatles performing.

Afterward, as they were leaving the theatre, Destiny said, "Thank you for going with me tonight."

"I enjoyed it," replied Joe. "I needed some fun after the hectic day I had at work."

Chapter Twenty-Seven

Two days later, Joe began searching the internet, hoping to find the name of the girl whose photo was taken as she was getting out of the shower. When numerous searches failed to turn up anything, he searched for the actual photo, thinking anything posted on the net never really goes away. He wasn't having any luck finding it and felt a little sleazy looking at nude and partially clad photos of teenage girls.

One of his fellow detectives, a young guy who worked property crimes, noticed the photos he had pulled up on his computer screen and piped up, "What the fuck are you looking at?"

"I'm looking for a photo taken eight years ago of a high school girl getting out of the shower at her school. One of her fellow students snapped the photo and posted it on the web to embarrass her. It's evidence in one of our cases."

"I wish I had a case like that," he said facetiously.

"No, you don't," replied Joe, who didn't find his comments amusing.

Joe went back to his search and spent another hour trying to find a candid photo of the shower girl. Finally, he'd had enough. Throwing up his hands in frustration, Joe walked out into the parking lot to blow off steam. This wasn't the only crime he had on his caseload. Others required his attention, too. So, he decided to refocus his attention on them.

Around two o'clock, Sam walked over and said, "You have any luck locating the name of the shower girl?"

"No. And I was unable to find her picture."

"Well, I found the mother of the girl who committed suicide."

Joe was pleasantly surprised. "Really. How did you do that?"

"It wasn't easy because she got divorced and remarried. Her name is now 'Marx.' Claudia Marx. She's living in Bisbee, Arizona, a small town southeast of Tucson."

"Way to go, Sam. You get her contact information?"

"Yeah. I tracked down a phone number, and I'm going to call her in a few minutes."

"See if she'll agree to a Zoom meeting so we can speak with her face to face."

Sam agreed and walked back to his desk.

Finding Marx lifted Joe's spirits, and he hoped she could provide a lead for them to pursue. But his sense of satisfaction didn't last long.

A short time later, Joe received a call from the Office of the Medical Examiner. It was Kendra Solitsky.

"I've got good news and not-so-good news."

"Okay," said Joe. "Let me have it."

"We got DNA results back from the hair found on Amber Engstrom's body. All I can tell you is it didn't belong to her. It came from a male."

"So, did it match any known offenders?" asked Joe.

"It was mitochondrial DNA because there was no root attached to the hair sample. CODIS won't allow mitochondrial DNA to be entered into their system since it can match multiple people. The only exception is in missing person cases."

"Great."

"But if you make an arrest, it could be matched to your suspect. Speaking of suspects, you have one yet?"

"No. No suspects at the moment," replied Joe. "But we're working on it."

"Well, good luck. Talk to you later."

That was disappointing. Nuclear DNA would have created a unique profile and could have been used to match an offender in CODIS, the FBI's Combined DNA Index System. But it was better than nothing. It was up to them to find the right suspect.

Sam made the call and confirmed Claudia Marx was the mother of Shari

McCarthy. She worked from home and was familiar with Zoom meetings. She agreed to meet virtually at four o'clock, and Sam told Joe he would set it up.

An hour later, Lieutenant Bellamy called Joe and Sam into his office. Joe thought he may be looking for an update on their double-homicide case.

They settled into the chairs in front of Bell's desk. He didn't waste any time letting them know why they were there.

"I got a call from our Commander a few minutes ago. What happened with the guy delivering flowers the other day?"

Oh, great! thought Joe.

Sam gave Joe a look which he interpreted as "go ahead."

"We received a panic call from one of the models we interviewed, saying a man was attempting to deliver flowers to her," said Joe. "That was the M.O. of the offender who killed two models working for TGM Talent. We warned the other models not to accept a flower delivery from anyone, and if a delivery came, not to open the door but to call one of us immediately. She called, and I stayed on the line with her and used my office phone to have District 19 officers respond. We got to her apartment building shortly after uniforms arrived. The woman was nearly hysterical when she called after the deliveryman knocked on her door. We found out he gained entrance to the apartment building when another person came out the door. We apprehended him and told one of the officers to place him in his cruiser so we could sort things out."

"I see. Did you arrest him?" asked Bell.

"No, we didn't. After we determined he was delivering flowers sent by her mother, for her birthday the next day, we knew he wasn't our offender. We went down to the cruiser, removed his cuffs, and apologized for the mistake. Then, we let him go."

Bell nodded as though he understood. "I can see why you responded the way you did. I probably would have done the same."

"What's the Commander have to do with this?" asked Sam.

"He informed me the delivery man has obtained an attorney and is threatening to sue the department for wrongful arrest."

"For cryin' out loud!" blurted out Joe.

"We never placed him under arrest, Lieutenant," said Sam. "The uniformed officers can attest to that. They witnessed everything."

"Good to know. Make sure you put everything in your report, including the names of the officers, if you remember."

"Engler and Goldman from the nineteenth," said Sam.

"Okay. Send me the report, and I'll follow up with the Commander. I don't think this guy has a leg to stand on. He's just angry about what happened."

"I guess an apology and an explanation doesn't cut it anymore," said Joe.

"It would be different if he was roughed up or something, but he wasn't," added Sam. "We didn't treat him badly."

"We can get sued for looking cross-eyed at somebody these days," replied Bell. "Don't worry, I'll handle this. You making any progress on these two homicides?"

"Four," corrected Joe.

"Four?"

"Yeah. We found that two other girls from this high school clique were murdered–one in Indianapolis and one in Milwaukee. Same M.O., same evidence found at the scenes."

Bell sighed as if this was one more thing that would complicate his life.

"Of the five girls in this clique, only one remains alive," said Sam.

"And these murders were confined to members of this clique?" asked Bell.

"Yeah."

"Any suspects?"

"The two we investigated provided alibis. They couldn't have done it," said Sam."

"We're working on it, Lieutenant," assured Joe. "We're interviewing people hoping to find a lead. By the way, you may be getting a call from the lead detective's lieutenant in Indianapolis. Sounds like they want to coordinate investigations."

"Okay. Keep at it," said Bell as he rose from his chair. That was his cue the session was over.

"We will."

"And have the report on my desk tomorrow morning."

"Yes, sir."

As they walked back to their desks, Sam said he was going to set up the Zoom meeting, and they could access it from their desk computers. Joe had plenty of experience with Zoom meetings and said he would be ready whenever Sam told him to go online.

Sam sent Joe the link for the meeting, and five minutes before four o'clock, he told Joe to log in to the Zoom link. Sam's face appeared on the screen, and Joe checked that his audio and video were working. At four o'clock, a woman's face appeared on the screen. Sam introduced Claudia Marx to Joe and thanked her for agreeing to their meeting. After a few pleasantries, they began.

"When your daughter, Shari, was in high school, were you aware of a clique of girls who bullied your daughter?" asked Sam.

"I was. She confided in me that they were being mean and bullying her. You see, Shari was an excellent student—straight As. But she lacked self-esteem because she had a problem with acne. She was being treated by a dermatologist, and her complexion was getting better."

"Did they tease her about it?"

"Eventually. What brought her into their sights was when one of the girls asked Shari for the answers on a test. She refused, and when pressured, she purposely gave her the wrong answers. Of course, the girl failed the test."

"I can see why that would anger the girl," said Joe. "What happened after that?"

"The entire group began bullying her. Once they beat her up in the restroom. They slid obnoxious stuff into her locker, knocked books out of her hand as they passed by, cornered her by her locker to intimidate her, and they began referring to her as 'Zitface' and 'Pizzaface.' Mean-spirited stuff like that."

"She must have hated going to school every day," said Sam.

"She did. She reported the bullying to her guidance counselor, and the girls were called on the carpet for it. That just made matters worse. After that, they not only picked on her but began picking on my son, too."

"He was in high school at the same time?" asked Joe.

"He was a year younger than Shari. He stuttered from the time he was a child, and with speech therapy, he'd made progress dealing with it, but the girls zeroed in on his disability. Like the vultures they were. They began bullying him, too. Calling him 'D-D-D-Daniel' to his face. And saying things like, 'You have a nice voice, Daniel—when it works.' But they didn't see him as often as Shari."

"How long did this go on?" asked Sam.

"For over a year. It carried into the next year in school. Her junior year. But then it started to taper off. I thought maybe they got tired of bullying Shari and moved on to others."

"Could you tell us what happened at the party Shari attended?" asked Joe. "We heard she was drugged."

"It's still not easy for me to talk about this," said Marx.

"Take your time."

"Well, Shari made the mistake of going to a party at a girl's house when her parents were away. Alcohol and drugs were available. Shari wasn't a wild kid, but she liked to socialize once in a while. The girls—Shari told me other kids called them the 'Bitch Squad'—they came in later. Shari said she tried to avoid them, but one of the girls cozied up to her. She knew Shari didn't drink, so she handed her a can of Coke. She didn't remember much else after that."

"You suspect her drink was spiked?" said Joe.

"Yeah. She woke up around two in the morning. She was on a bed with no clothes on, and she realized she'd been raped."

"When did she discover her picture on the internet?" asked Sam.

"About three days later. Kids were giving her funny looks at school, and one of her friends gave her the link. She was horrified, of course. When she showed it to me, I contacted the police. But they told me they couldn't find who took the photo or who posted it. They were eventually able to have the website delete the photo, since she was a minor. But the humiliation couldn't be undone."

"Is that what led to her taking her life?" asked Sam.

"She missed her period and began to feel sick. Finally, I took her to the doctor, and we found out she was pregnant. At that point, she told me what had happened to her at the party. She was inconsolable."

"That must have made this bad experience worse," said Joe.

Joe could see the emotion on Marx's face, and she sniffed back tears before saying, "It did. She couldn't handle the humiliation and the stigma of being pregnant. I told her I would approve her ending the pregnancy if she wanted. But before we could go through with it, she…she swallowed a bottle of Vicodin that was prescribed for my ex-husband's back injury. I found her… the next morning. By then…it was…too late. She was gone."

Joe and Sam passed along their condolences. She nodded her head. They gave her time, allowing her to speak when she was ready.

"It's been eight years, but it doesn't get any easier," said Marx. "I still get emotional." She dried her eyes with a tissue as Joe and Sam looked on.

When he felt she was ready to answer another question, Joe asked, "If I could ask you another question…How did your son handle his sister's death?"

"He took it really hard. They were pretty close. Because of the bullying and what happened to his sister, we had him transferred to another school. He spent his final two years in high school there."

"How's he doing now?"

"Daniel's fine. He graduated from college and works as an assistant to a well-known fashion photographer. He's traveled with him to Europe, Japan, New York."

A light bulb flashed in Joe's mind. Bose's assistant was named Daniel. "That wouldn't be Damian Bose, would it?"

A surprised look registered on Marx's face. "How did you know?"

"We encountered him when we visited Bose's studio some time back."

"Really. What a coincidence."

"Yeah, it is. Small world."

"Detectives," Marx began. "I may have despised the girls who bullied my kids. But I would never have wished them harm. I just hope they grew up and realized their actions had consequences. And they regretted what they did."

"We do, too," said Sam.

They thanked Marx for her time and wished her well before logging out of the Zoom meeting. Joe walked to Sam's desk.

"What do you think about Daniel McCarthy?" asked Joe.

"I think we may have a new suspect," replied Sam.

Chapter Twenty-Eight

Joe's research revealed Daniel McCarthy was born in Chicago twenty-five years ago, making him a year younger than his sister, Shari. He graduated with honors two years ago from Columbia College with a BFA degree in photography. The Illinois Vehicle Registration database indicated a black four-year-old Nissan Sentra registered in his name, and that it stated he lived at an address on North Ashland Avenue in the Wicker Park neighborhood, a trendy, bustling place for young adults. His residence is less than fifteen minutes from the Greektown neighborhood where Bose's studio is located.

Further searches showed he had no criminal record and no traffic violations. He did not possess a FOID card from the Illinois Firearm Owners Identification system, so it appeared he did not own a registered firearm and could not legally purchase ammunition. All in all, he appeared to be an upstanding citizen. But facts can often be deceiving. Joe remembered seeing McCarthy at Darian Bose's studio and decided to check the Illinois Driver's License database. McCarthy's height and weight were consistent with the description Jim Wells provided of the person he saw delivering flowers to Regina Fischer. The address on his license was the same one listed on his Vehicle Registration.

Finally, Joe sought out McCarthy on social media, beginning with Damian Bose's website and Facebook page. But there was nothing about McCarthy on either one. Next, he looked up McCarthy's Facebook page and found a lot of photos he had posted. There were several of McCarthy himself, and Joe printed the best one. His information did not indicate any questionable posts, and there was nothing about his sister or anyone named Shari. His posts mainly consisted of photos he had taken, many of them quite impressive, in Joe's opinion.

After completing his research, he called Damian Bose's studio, but his call went to voicemail. No surprise there. Not wanting to leave a message, he hung up. No phone number was listed for McCarthy's residence, so he figured he had no landline. As he thought about what to do, he glanced up and saw Sam walking back to his desk with his coffee cup in hand. Standing, he stepped toward him.

"Hey."

"What's up?" said Sam.

"Daniel McCarthy is physically similar to the description provided by Jim Wells. I think we need to bring him in for questioning."

"When?"

"I tried calling Bose's studio, but my call went to voicemail. I'm thinking we should leave in a few minutes. See if he's at work."

Sam agreed, and Joe checked out a squad car for the trip. Fifteen minutes later, Sam had polished off his coffee and was ready to go. They drove to Bose's studio in Greektown, arriving at 10:15 a.m. Joe figured if they were like most businesses, they would open at ten o'clock.

The door was locked, but they could see a light on through it. Joe rang the bell, and a short time later, Daniel McCarthy appeared.

Opening the door, McCarthy said, "If you're looking for Mr. Bose, he's in Law…Los Angeles today and tomorrow." Apparently, his stuttering had not gone away completely.

"We aren't interested in speaking with Mr. Bose," replied Joe. "We want to speak with you."

"I don't know what you want…with me."

"Could we come in?" asked Sam. "We can do this here or at our office."

McCarthy opened the door for them, and they entered. He led them down a hall to a small office and indicated two chairs for them to sit. The walls were decorated with framed pages from magazine ads and covers.

After sitting, McCarthy asked, "What is it you want from me?"

"Are you familiar with a clique of girls in your high school known to students as "the Bitch Squad?" asked Joe.

A surprised look came across McCarthy's face. After a few seconds, he nodded and said, "They made our lives miserable."

"We know about the tragedy of your sister, Shari. We spoke with your mother about what happened to her."

"They killed her, you know. The B-Bitch Squad. What they did to her was...horrible."

"We agree," said Sam. "Did you know someone has been killing them?"

Again, a look of surprise. "Really."

"Really. Amber Engstrom, Regina Fischer, Tracey McNamara, and Stephanie Daniels were all murdered."

"There's only one remaining member of the Squad still alive," said Joe.

McCarthy was silent.

"What did they do to you, Daniel?" asked Sam.

"Your mother told us they bullied you, too," said Joe. "What did they do to you?"

After a moment, McCarthy said, "They made fun of my speech impairment. Called me Da-Da-Da-Daniel. And they'd giggle if I stuttered, and they called me names like 'retard' and 'fungus.' You...You know what it's like to hear that almost every day? 'Daniel Retardo.' They made my life hell. I'm not sorry they're...dead."

"I can see you're still angry," said Sam.

McCarthy didn't say anything.

"Are you angry about their bullying of you or what happened to your sister?"

"Both!" exclaimed McCarthy, barely containing his rage. "They should have gone to p-prison for what they did to Shari."

"So, have you been getting even with them?" asked Joe. "Tracking them down and acting as an executioner."

"I wish I had," replied McCarthy, seething with anger. "As far as I'm concerned, they d-deserved what they got."

"Did you kill Amber Engstrom?" pressed Joe.

"What? No! I never killed anybody."

"Where were you on June 4th and June 26th?"

"Wha…W-What do you want to know for?" asked McCarthy, suddenly becoming belligerent.

"Because…those are the dates when Amber Engstrom and Regina Fischer were killed, Mr. McCarthy," said Sam.

"Fuck you guys!" yelled McCarthy.

That was the last straw. Joe and Sam simultaneously stood, and Sam began walking around the desk with cuffs out, saying, "Stand and put your hands behind your back."

McCarthy was shocked by their actions.

"Wa-Wa-Wait. Wait," he said.

Sam stopped at the side of the desk and said, "Wait for what?"

"I can…find those dates on my computer."

As Joe and Sam looked on, McCarthy used his keyboard to call up information on his computer. After a few moments, he looked from Sam to Joe.

"On June 4th, I was on a plane to New York with Mr. Bose. I have the ticket receipts if you want to see them." He punched a couple of keys on his keyboard, and the printer pushed out a sheet of paper. McCarthy handed it across the desk to Joe, who looked it over.

"What about the 26th?" asked Joe.

McCarthy punched a few more keys, and after seeing what appeared on his screen, he sighed. "It appears I was home on that day."

"Can anyone verify that?"

"No. My calendar says I was home that evening."

"What are your normal working hours?" asked Joe.

"It varies. I come in by ten to take care of business, make phone calls. Mr. Bose comes in when he pleases. Sometimes I'm done at five. Other days we may work into the night on a shoot."

"Can you take time off if you want?"

"I have to plan around Mr. Bose's schedule. But if I have a…dentist appointment or something, I can if I plan ahead."

"I see your plane left O'Hare at 6:30 in the evening," said Joe, looking up from the printout."

"So?"

"Amber Engstrom was killed around four o'clock. That would still give you time to kill her and make your plane."

"I'm sure Mr. Bose can confirm I was here at the studio."

"Do you know what time Mr. Bose will be back?" asked Sam.

"Sometime day after tomorrow. He usually doesn't come in on the day he travels."

Joe rose from his seat. "We'll be speaking with you again, Mr. McCarthy."

"Fine. I'm sure you can find your way out," replied an indignant McCarthy.

Joe and Sam left, and once they were outside, Sam asked, "What do you think?"

"He's angry enough, and he has plenty of motive. I'd like to know if he traveled out of state on the dates when McNamara and Daniels were killed."

"I don't think Bose would be a good alibi. He strikes me as somebody who would lie to protect his assistant or just to spite us."

"Agreed. Let's go deeper on McCarthy. I printed out a photo from his Facebook page. I'll get you one. See if anyone from the florist shops we checked recognizes him. Maybe they can call us if he comes in to buy more flowers."

We can canvass the same shops we did previously. Still have your list?"

"Yeah. Good old-fashioned shoe leather."

"You got it. I'll make copies of McCarthy's photo so we can hand them out to florists. If we leave our cards with the photo, maybe someone will call us if he comes in to make another purchase. Sound good to you?"

"Well, it's a start."

Joe could tell Sam was not too keen on approaching florists again. But the link between the offender and roses should not be overlooked.

Chapter Twenty-Nine

That afternoon, Joe and Sam set out to visit the florists they had previously contacted. Joe plotted out his shops on a map so he would not waste time crisscrossing the city.

By late afternoon, he had visited four different shops. None of them recognized McCarthy from the photo or had his name in their customer databases. If McCarthy was the offender, he would probably purchase roses with cash rather than a credit card—assuming he was smart, that is.

The fifth shop on Joe's list took him to Bucktown Custom Floral, located at West Fulton Street. Upon entering the red brick building, a bell above the door tinkled. As he walked toward the counter, a woman entered through swinging doors next to a cooler full of flower bouquets. Her heavy eye makeup detracted from her otherwise good looks. Joe pegged her age around forty-five. She was not the same person he spoke with the last time he visited this establishment.

"Good afternoon," she said cheerfully.

Joe noticed the name Casey embroidered on her apron and said, "Should I assume you're Casey?"

"You can assume that. What can I do for you?"

Joe produced his ID and said, "I'm Detective Joe Erickson with Chicago PD."

Casey raised her eyebrows and said, "Oh. I didn't know detectives came in such attractive packages."

Joe chuckled and noticed there was no wedding ring on her finger. "Well, I'm homely compared to some of our detectives."

"Oh, I doubt that."

Returning his ID to his pocket, he pulled the photo of Daniel McCarthy. "We're working a case involving a person who left long-stem red roses at a crime scene. Do you recognize this person?"

After he handed her the photo, she put on the glasses that were hanging from a chain around her neck. As she looked the photo over, she nodded. "He's been in here. I remember because he bought two dozen long-stem red roses. We don't normally get many purchases like that. Besides, he was kind of cute."

"Did he say anything while he was standing here?"

"I remember I asked him if it was for his wife, and he said, 'Something like that.' Kind of strange. So, I assumed he may have been trying to impress a girlfriend."

"Do you have any records of the purchase?"

She started to hand back the photograph while removing her glasses. "Keep the photo," said Joe.

"Okay. To answer your question, we would normally have a record of the purchase if he paid with a card, but I remember he plunked down cash, so his information wouldn't be on file."

"Do you recall when he was here?"

"Oh, boy…it was a while back. I can't give you an exact date. Uh… Sometime in May, I think."

"You have a good memory."

"I do," she said, giving him another smile.

"You've been very helpful. Thank you, Casey." Handing her his card, he said, "If this person comes in to buy long-stem roses, I need you to call me right away. This guy is a person of interest in a homicide, and it's important we know about it."

"Oo. Really?"

"Really."

After reading the card, she looked up, seemingly concerned, and said, "Is this guy dangerous?"

"Probably not to you."

"That's good to know."

"And please let your employees know about this, too."

Casey placed his card and McCarthy's photo in her apron pocket. "You sure I can't interest you in some flowers for your 'significant other?' We have long-stem roses in the back. I can give you a 'special deal.'"

"Not today. Maybe another time."

As he turned to go, she said in a sultry voice, "Come back again, hon."

"I might just do that," said Joe, smiling to himself as he turned and walked out the door. *Well, she's a trip,* he thought.

Out on the street, Joe called Sam to let him know he found that Daniel McCarthy bought two dozen long-stem roses from Bucktown Custom Floral a few months ago.

"That's great," said Sam. "Because I struck out in the four places I checked. Out of curiosity, did you happen to buy more potpourri?" he teased.

"Not this time. My squad car must have been deodorized recently. It smells like a pine forest."

"I'm going to keep checking my list to see if he bought any roses more recently," said Sam. "I can make one more stop before quitting time."

Joe checked with one more store on his list as well. No one there recognized Daniel McCarthy's photo or had his name in their records. He had six more shops to check tomorrow, and if McCarthy was planning on attacking Madison Powell, he might still be using roses he purchased in the past.

The next day, Joe and Sam continued canvassing florist shops. By mid-afternoon, Joe had finished questioning the last florist on his list. Nothing. He called Sam, who said he had no luck either but had one more establishment to check out before he completed his list.

Joe returned to his desk and began planning a strategy to further explore Daniel McCarthy as a suspect. At some point, McCarthy would make a move to kill Madison Powell, the last remaining member of the Squad. He would have to find out where she lived and observe her coming and going so he could plan his attack. Since Madison Powell lived with her boyfriend, Joe felt more confident about her safety. The rest of the Squad lived alone, making them vulnerable to the offender's attacks. And Powell had been made aware of the offender's M.O. and knew not to accept any flower deliveries. Joe wondered if the offender knew about her living arrangements and if he did, what it might take to lure her boyfriend away from the apartment.

When Sam returned to the office, he told Joe that the last florist shop could not identify Daniel McCarthy from the photograph. He was frustrated that his dozen shops were of no help.

"The important thing is we confirmed McCarthy bought two dozen roses, which he could have dried out to leave at the scenes of the crimes," said Joe.

"But he may need more if he plans to eliminate the last member of the Squad," replied Sam.

"Not necessarily. If he continues with his M.O., he will be leaving five roses in a box for Madison Powell. Five for the fifth member. If he bought two dozen roses, he will have needed fifteen of them for all five women."

"We left our cards and McCarthy's photo with each florist, asking them to call if he comes in to buy roses. That's twenty-four shops that have his information."

"Hopefully, they'll call if he shows up," said Joe. "But he may not need to buy from another shop if he has enough."

"I know," replied Sam. "That's what I'm afraid of."

Joe arrived at home and found Destiny working at her computer. Autumn came running from the room they used as their office, happy to see him.

"I'm home," he announced.

"I'll be another minute," called Destiny.

Joe walked to the kitchen counter and saw an open bottle of Pinot Noir. It was tempting, but he decided to skip it so he could have a glass with dinner. Opening the refrigerator, he poured himself a glass of cold water instead.

Sitting at the island, he picked up Autumn, who was pawing at his leg, demanding his attention.

"And how are you, Miss Dog?" he asked as he petted her head. She gave him a couple of quick licks on the cheek before he pulled his face away. "That's enough, Autumn." He continued petting her for a minute or two. Then he put her down and picked up his glass to take a drink as Destiny walked into the room.

"I see which girl you like best," she joked, leaning over and giving him a kiss.

"One has to have priorities."

Destiny smiled and kissed him again. "You know I like you best," said Joe.

Autumn, who was sitting near his stool, looked up at him and woofed.

"You shouldn't say that in front of her. You'll hurt her feelings," said Destiny. Then she squatted down to pet Autumn. "It's all right. How about a treat?"

Autumn barked a response and began turning in circles. Destiny gave her a treat and came around the island to sit next to Joe.

"You have a good day today?"

"I think we made some progress today with our person of interest. He's the brother of a girl the Squad bullied. She's the one who later committed suicide."

"I remember. You told me about that."

"Well, we found out he bought two dozen long-stem red roses, possibly in May, which would have given him time to dry them out and use them at both crime scenes. An over-sexed florist identified him as a person who bought them."

"Over-sexed florist?" was Destiny's incredulous response.

"You had to be there," said Joe, chuckling.

"Male or female?"

Joe scoffed, "Female. But you don't have anything to worry about."

"I'm not worried," she said.

"I know what side my bread is buttered on."

"And what side is that?" asked Destiny, trying to put him on the spot.

"Your side, of course."

Chapter Thirty

During his morning jog, Joe thought about Daniel McCarthy as a person of interest in their case. The elimination of four members of the Squad took a pretty sophisticated plan, and carrying out each murder would have taken nerves of steel. He didn't get that impression from McCarthy when they interviewed him. Yes, he was angry about the bullying and what happened to his sister. But would this twenty-five-year-old photographer have the nerve to execute four women he clearly despised and leave no evidence at the scene?

Since all of the murders took place sometime in the afternoon, Joe and Sam decided to surveil McCarthy and see if he would try to gain entry to Madison Powell's apartment building. Since she taught courses at the community college, he would need to know her class schedule and office hours. To be sure, he would probably need to stalk her, following her from the college to her home. And he would also need to monitor what time her boyfriend was at work, so he would know when Powell was alone.

Joe and Sam took turns surveilling McCarthy, following him from his apartment to Bose's studio. After a week, nothing out of the ordinary happened. McCarthy drove to the studio, arriving shortly before ten o'clock, left for lunch at noon, and ate at the same bistro each day. Occasionally, he would leave the bistro with a woman about his age, and after a kiss, he would return to the studio and remain there until six o'clock. One day, when Joe was surveilling him, he remained at the studio until after nine o'clock in the evening. Observing several women enter Bose's studio that day, Joe assumed there must have been a photo shoot taking place.

Each day, they followed McCarthy back to his apartment in Wicker Park. Nothing stuck out as suspicious. Was McCarthy biding his time, letting the murders of Engstrom and Fischer settle, hoping Powell would become complacent? They couldn't surveil him forever. Other homicides on their caseload demanded their attention, too. If he tried to gain entrance to Madison Powell's apartment under the guise of delivering flowers, she would alert them immediately so he could be arrested. At this point, it was the best they could hope for.

* * *

A month went by, and it was now the first week in September. Progress on the Squad murders amounted to zero, but Joe and Sam successfully closed one case and investigated one new homicide, the stabbing death of a woman found in an alley behind a bar. Since there were no surveillance cameras in the area and they had no suspects, they awaited forensic information that could possibly provide them with a lead. Homicides were rife in Chi-town.

On a Thursday afternoon, Joe received a call from an officer investigating an assault at Traynor College. Alarm bells went off since that was where Madison Powell was employed.

"The victim asked me to call you since you're investigating a related case," said the officer.

"Who's the victim?" asked Joe.

"A professor here by the name of Madison Powell."

"I'm on my way."

Joe walked quickly to Sam's desk and said, "Let's go. Madison Powell's been attacked at the college."

Joe drove their squad car with lights flashing, attempting to get to Traynor College as quickly as possible. Arriving at the building where she maintained an office, they saw two police cruisers and an ambulance parked nearby.

As they exited their squad car, EMTs were wheeling a gurney out of the building. Powell was conscious but had her head bandaged. They learned she was being transported to Holy Cross Hospital for treatment. Joe followed the gurney as the EMTs pushed it toward the ambulance.

When Powell saw Joe, she said, "I was tased."

"We'll talk with you later. Right now, you need to get checked out," Joe reassured her.

When Powell was loaded into the ambulance, Joe and Sam badged their way inside the building and followed a college police officer to the hallway where Powell's office was located.

A uniformed officer from District 19 was interviewing a man outside Powell's office. A second officer was standing by, taking notes. Yellow crime scene tape had already been placed across the door.

The officers were concluding their interview with a middle-aged man with a gray beard. As they approached, the man walked away with one of the officers. Joe and Sam produced their IDs.

"Joe Erickson, Area 3 Homicide. This is my partner, Sam Renaldo. We're investigating a case that's connected to Madison Powell."

"John Nixon," replied the officer. My partner and I were called in by college security.

"What happened here?" asked Sam.

"Professor Powell was assaulted in her office. The offender tased her and began ripping off her clothes when one of her colleagues opened the door and interrupted the assault. The offender tased him, too, and then left the building. We're checking for any surveillance video that might show people entering or leaving the building before and after the assault."

Joe was aware of the variation in the M.O. The offender attacked all the other girls in their apartments using the ruse of delivering flowers. But Powell was the only one who lived with a boyfriend. Maybe the offender knew she lived with a guy, and he had to find another way to carry out his vendetta. He may also know that law enforcement would be looking for someone delivering flowers and chose not to use that ruse anymore.

"How badly was she injured?" asked Sam.

"She hit her head on the edge of the desk when she fell backward. She may have a concussion, and the cut on her head may need stitches."

"She was tased, you said?" asked Joe.

"Yeah. There was a burn mark visible on her abdomen," said Nixon. "Same with her colleague, Professor Garland. That's who we were speaking to when you walked up. He refused treatment."

"It's a good thing her colleague opened the door and interrupted things. It could have been murder rather than assault."

"Anyone get a look at the offender?" asked Sam.

"We're still checking with people in the building. Garland said he was tased before he got a good look at him. All he can remember is a blue baseball cap. We weren't able to interview Professor Powell."

"Was there a box of flowers left in her office, by any chance?" asked Joe.

"Box of flowers?"

"You know, the kind of box used for long-stem roses?"

"No, I didn't see anything like that. We're waiting on Evidence Techs. Maybe they can turn up some prints."

They spoke for a while longer before Joe and Sam left for the hospital. They were hoping Madison Powell was not seriously injured in the attack.

"I don't envy the Evidence Techs. Can you imagine the number of different prints in a professor's office?" commented Sam.

"Yeah, and I'd be willing to bet the offender was wearing gloves," replied Joe. "Probably a waste of time pulling prints."

After arriving at Holy Cross Hospital, Joe and Sam were directed to the Emergency Room. When they asked about Powell, the attending nurse told them she had already been moved to a private room. They knocked on Powell's door. A moment later, a nurse came to the door. Showing their IDs, Joe told her they needed to speak with Powell.

"Let me check with the patient," said the nurse.

The door closed, and a few moments later, the nurse opened it and said, "You can go in."

As they entered, they saw Powell lying in bed with a gauze bandage wrapped around her head. She tried to manage a smile when she made eye contact with them.

"How are you feeling?" asked Joe.

"I could be better," replied Powell. "Seven stitches to the back of my head and a slight concussion. My head hurts like crazy, but I'll live."

"The officer on the scene reported you'd been tased. Is that right?" asked Sam.

"I was."

"Do you remember what happened?"

Powell nodded. "I was in my office grading papers when there was a knock on the door. I assumed it was a student, so I said, "Come in." But it wasn't a student. It was a middle-aged guy. He told me he was with the maintenance department and needed to check my internet connection. So, I got up from my desk so he could check the line, and when he started to move around me, he tased me. It knocked me out, and I don't remember anything until I came to a few minutes later."

"What do you remember when you came to?" asked Joe.

"Well...my head hurt, and it was bleeding, and I saw that my blouse was ripped open, and my slacks and underwear had been pulled down. Some kind soul saw fit to throw a blanket over me so I wouldn't be exposed to the world."

Joe could understand the humiliation she must have felt being partially stripped and lying injured on the floor of her office.

"Who was there when you came to?"

"Professor Garland was kneeling over me, telling me not to move. That I was going to be all right. He said EMTs were on the way."

"What do you recall about the offender? Can you give us a description?"

"Middle-aged guy. He was wearing one of those black medical masks. He apologized for the mask, saying he had a bad cold."

"Anything else you can remember? Height, weight, clothing?"

Powell paused and closed her eyes. Joe assumed she was trying to picture him in her mind. After a few moments, she said, "He wore a blue baseball cap, a gray work shirt, gray pants, and a lightweight jacket. Blue, I think."

"That's good, thank you. Tall? Short?"

"Average height. A little tubby if you know what I mean. And he had short, dark hair and glasses. Plastic rims."

"Any identifying marks like tattoos, scars..."

"He had one of those little red birthmarks below his ear—right ear, I think—but I can't be sure."

"Can you describe it? The size or shape?" asked Sam.

"No, not really. It was small, but I only saw it for a split second."

Joe's mind immediately flashed back to Gary Richardson, the guidance counselor they interviewed at Clinton Prep. He had a small port-wine stain birthmark on his neck below his right ear. He was also middle-aged, medium height, dark hair, and had a paunchy belly. Richardson was the one who alerted them to the students who made up the Squad. Why would he do that if he was the offender?

Joe's reaction caught Powell's attention, and she asked, "Do you know someone like that?"

Joe glanced at Sam, who also picked up on Joe's reaction to her description. "Possibly," Joe replied, not wanting to reveal Richardson as a suspect. "But it could be a coincidence. I mean, port-wine stain birthmarks are fairly common."

"We'll check it out," said Sam. "Your description's very helpful. Up until now, we haven't been able to get a decent description."

Placing his notebook back into his pocket, Joe said, "Do you know how long you'll be in the hospital?"

"They're holding me for observation. Because of the concussion. The doctor said if there aren't any complications, I can go home tomorrow."

The door to the room opened, and a handsome young man started to enter. He stopped when he saw Joe and Sam.

"Oh, sorry," he said. "I can come back later."

"No, it's all right," said Powell. "You can come in." Looking at Sam and Joe, she continued, "This is my boyfriend, Sean Kellen. Sean, these are Detectives Erickson and Renaldo. They're investigating what happened."

"I left work as soon as I heard," said Kellen, in a slight Irish accent. "What happened?"

Rather than stay for a rehash of the incident, Joe and Sam wished her well and promised to be in touch before driving back to their office.

During the drive, Sam asked, "You remembered something in there, didn't you? Your eyes lit up like a lightbulb went off in your head."

"You recall when we interviewed Gary Richardson, the guidance counselor who told us about the Bitch Squad?" asked Joe.

"Yeah."

"You remember what he looked like?"

As Sam considered it, he nodded. "Yeah, the description fits. And he had a red birthmark on his neck."

"I lied back there. Those birthmarks are not that common. I didn't want Powell to think that I recognized a specific person with those characteristics."

"This is weird. A high school teacher killing former students? That's extreme."

"I know. What would make him do that?"

"It can't be because he doesn't like a particular group of students," said Sam. "There has to be more to it than that."

"And why would he tell us all about the Squad if he was the one killing them?" asked Joe.

"Yeah, that doesn't make sense."

"Yet."

Chapter Thirty-One

Back at his desk, Joe began looking into Gary Richardson. He found he graduated from Northern Illinois University with a bachelor's degree in education and a master's degree in counseling. He has been employed as a guidance counselor with Clinton College Prep High School for the past eighteen years. His address showed he lived in Rogers Park.

According to records, Joe found Richardson and his wife, Brenda, had three children: Joel, Anthony, and Carrie. Joel and Anthony both graduated from Clinton Prep, but there was no record that Carrie did. In fact, there were no records of her graduating from any high school. Strange.

Joe wondered if Carrie could be a person with special needs who was unable to complete a high school degree. Or worse. Maybe she was deceased. He searched the internet for the name Carrie Richardson and found an obituary from a year ago. The article stated she had attended Clinton College Preparatory High School and listed her parents, Gary and Brenda Richardson, along with two brothers, and two grandparents as survivors. However, it did not state a cause of death.

He needed to contact a family friend or relative to find out about her. After a considerable amount of digging, Joe found a sister of Richardson's wife Brenda. Rebecca Tunney was employed as a teacher at another school. She and her husband, Ashton Tunney, also lived at an address in Rogers Park. Since there were no entries under their names in the phone directory, Joe would need to knock on their door.

Following the end of his shift, Joe drove to the Tunney's West Sherwyn

Avenue address. It was a well-maintained two-story white stucco house, a style built in the early 1900s. Joe walked up the sidewalk and climbed the steps onto the porch, where he pushed an antique button next to the door. He hoped the doorbell was in working condition.

A few moments later, a woman opened the door.

"Are you Rebecca Tunney?" Joe asked.

"That's right," she replied with a skeptical look.

Joe produced his ID and introduced himself.

She remained behind the screen door and asked, "Did something happen?"

"No," explained Joe. "We have an ongoing investigation, and a name came up while we were working on the case. I need to speak with you since you're a relative."

There was a look of concern on her face, and Joe sensed she did not trust him.

"We can talk inside or out here on the porch. Your choice."

Tunney thought about it for a few moments and then released an eyehook on the screen door and stepped out onto the porch. She appeared to be in her mid-forties and was dressed casually in jeans and a T-shirt.

"I don't understand what you might need from me," she said.

"Information to help clarify some things," assured Joe. "I won't take up too much of your time."

"Okay."

"Gary Richardson...he's your brother-in-law, is that right?"

"Yes. My sister's husband."

"We found the Richardsons are the parents of three children. A question arose regarding their daughter, Carrie. We could not confirm the circumstances of her death. Was there a health issue or accident of some kind?"

Tunney nodded and took a deep breath. "Why don't you come in?"

She led Joe to the living room, where they sat facing each other on matching couches separated by a large coffee table.

"My niece was in a nursing home for several years before she passed," said Tunney.

"Really. She was only twenty-five years old. Could you elaborate?"

"It's a rather sad story. Carrie was very creative and a wonderful artist. But she was quite sensitive. She didn't have a lot of confidence, and I don't think she had a strong self-concept. Things would bother her, and she'd take them to heart and fret about them. During her junior year, a group of girls began bullying her. She was a little overweight, and they began picking on her because of her size. She wasn't obese or anything. Just needed to lose a few pounds, you know. These girls made fun of her, called her names…And after some time, she evidently couldn't take the bullying any longer. One day, she swallowed an entire bottle of her mother's Xanax pills in an attempt to kill herself."

"I'm sorry to hear that," said Joe.

"Her mother found her unconscious and called an ambulance. They got her to a hospital and pumped her stomach, but not before it caused serious brain damage. She was in a coma and on a ventilator, fed through a feeding tube. She was alive…but only because her heart was still beating. She was never going to wake up." Tunney began to tear up. "But Gary never gave up hope."

"I assume she died after several years?" asked Joe.

"She was in a coma for about eight years before Gary and Brenda made the decision to let her go. She was in a vegetative state. Her brothers came home so they could say their goodbyes, and then they had her ventilator turned off. She passed peacefully a few minutes later. Very sad."

"I can't imagine how hard that must have been."

"It'll be a year next week."

"How did her parents find out about the bullying?"

"She left a note. I never read it, but Gary and Brenda said they were surprised about what was going on at school. They were quite distraught about it. Brenda went to the school and filed a complaint. But it was a sticky situation since Gary worked there."

"And they had no idea she was being harassed?"

"No. Carrie was the kind of kid who kept a lot of things to herself. She didn't talk a lot about school, but she kept a diary, and it was quite explicit about what was happening to her."

"What about her father? How did he take it?"

"Gary clammed up. Seemed to keep it bottled up inside. He refused to talk about it to anybody. Including me or my husband. As a counselor, he should have known that wasn't healthy."

Joe felt he needed to speak with Destiny about this and get her take on Richardson's behavior. She would know if he might fit the profile. Then Joe's cynical side surfaced, and he thought this could turn into another wild goose chase. But the birthmark—it was strong evidence that could identify Richardson as Powell's attacker.

"What kind of guy is Gary?"

"Up until what happened with Carrie, he was an affable guy. He and Ash—that's my husband—they used to go to Cubs and Bears games together. All that stopped. His personality changed, and he became remote and seemed to isolate himself from family. I hardly see him anymore, and they live just a short distance away from us."

"It sounds like the counselor needed counseling."

"I know. Brenda tells me he's become a different person. I thought maybe grieving for Carrie would serve as a way for him to get back to normal. But from what Brenda told me, it hasn't."

"Do you think Gary could become violent? Seek revenge on those who bullied her? "

"Violent? I don't think so. At least, I'd like to think not. He never struck me as a violent person."

"But you said he'd changed," said Joe, trying to dig deeper into Richardson's behavioral issues.

"True, but I don't believe he would do something crazy."

Joe knew that individuals acting out revenge are first motivated by anger, but later get an emotional release and a sense of satisfaction out of their actions. Whoever was responsible for the murders of these women may have found satisfaction in raping and strangling his victims.

"Do you think your sister would be open to my interviewing her?"

"Is Gary suspected of a crime?" she asked, growing suspicious of Joe's questions.

"At this point, we don't know. We're widening our investigation, and we're looking for anything that could lead us to a suspect."

"Well...She may be willing to speak with you. She and Gary have a strained relationship, and I think they're only staying together for the sake of their kids. We were brought up Catholic, and divorce isn't something she would want to go through."

"I understand. She's a teacher, right?"

"Junior high math and science."

"So, she and Gary don't work at the same school?"

"No. She teaches at Pierce Middle School."

"I'll need her phone number. I assume you have it?"

Tunney complied and gave Joe Brenda Richardson's cell phone number.

"Well...I want to thank you for your time, Mrs. Tunney, and for being so candid."

He began to leave when Tunney added one more comment.

"Gary was devastated by what happened to Carrie. He was a wonderful father, and what happened to her affected him deeply."

Joe acknowledged her and continued on his way. What he learned from Tunney was definitely helpful, and he wondered if Tunney would be making a call to her sister to alert her about his interest in Gary. Even if she did, he still planned to question Brenda Richardson, one way or another.

That evening after dinner, Joe needed to pick Destiny's brain about his suspicion that Gary Richardson could be the person responsible for killing members of the Squad. After adjourning to the living room, Joe explained what had gone on with Carrie Richardson—the bullying, suicide attempt, coma, and eventual death. Destiny found the story upsetting, calling it a tragedy.

"Madison Powell described her attacker as having a small port-wine stain birthmark on his neck. And Gary Richardson has such a birthmark on his neck below his right ear. I'm thinking that his daughter's death may have provided a catalyst for him to take revenge on the Squad members."

"Revengeful thoughts coupled with his actions could be providing a distraction, albeit temporary, from the suffering he's experiencing about his daughter's death," replied Destiny.

"So, do you think it's more than a distraction, that he's finding enjoyment in taking revenge?"

"Very possible."

"This is different than the motivation behind a serial killer, isn't it?"

"It is. Most serial killers have underlying issues. This reminds me of the revenge murders we encountered in Storm Lake several years ago. A grieving family member desiring retribution may evolve into a cycle of revengeful acts. In other words, acting out once may lead him to acting out again and again."

"Getting even with all those he views responsible for bullying his daughter."

"Precisely. The first successful kill bolstered his confidence, enabling him to continue. He may have missed the first time with Madison Powell, but that probably won't stop him. He may be shaken by that unexpected intervention, but it wouldn't surprise me if he tries to kill her again."

"Obsessed with completing his crusade?"

"I'd say more than likely."

"One thing I've found puzzling. Why would Richardson tell us all about the Squad if he was the one killing them?"

Destiny thought for a few seconds and said, "Maybe he wanted to disparage them, to reveal to you how evil their actions were. It could have been a way for him to justify what he was doing to them."

Joe thought about what she had said. His silence intrigued Destiny.

"What are you thinking?" she asked.

Snapping back into the moment, he said, "Hoping this doesn't lead us to another dead end."

Chapter Thirty-Two

As Joe was jogging the next morning, he was thinking about what he and Destiny had discussed the night before. The port-wine stain birthmark alone was not enough to implicate Gary Richardson in the attack on Madison Powell. And they had no evidence to tie him to the Squad murders. Did he have motive? Yes. Means? Probably. Opportunity? Possibly. He and Sam would need to prove Richardson had means and opportunity before they could think about making an arrest. Proving his attack on Powell may be easier than proving he killed the Squad members. Unless…DNA swabs collected from Engstrom's and Fischer's bodies produced results. He needed to call Kendra to see if she received any DNA results back.

Joe waited until after ten o'clock to call Kendra at the Office of the Medical Examiner. She picked up right away.

"Good morning, Joe. What can I do for you?"

"I'm hoping this will be a good morning. I have a question about the Amber Engstrom autopsy."

"Okay. Let me pull up her file."

After a few keystrokes, she replied, "Got it. What's your question?"

"During the examination, you swabbed her skin for DNA. Has the DNA analysis come back on any of the swabs you took?"

"I think so. Let me see." There was a pause as she searched the file. "It did. Swabs from her thigh area showed DNA that was not a match to the victim."

"That's interesting. Was it nuclear DNA by chance?"

"It was. We ran each through various databases attempting to find a match, but we were unsuccessful. It belonged to an unknown offender."

"Okay. I think we may have a viable suspect. We'll see."

"Good luck. I've got to go—I have an autopsy scheduled in a few minutes."

Joe felt positive about the DNA, but if Amber Engstrom had intercourse with someone earlier that day, the DNA may not necessarily be a match to Gary Richardson. He hoped that wasn't the case.

He picked up the phone and called Madison Powell's cell number. She picked up after a couple of rings.

"Ms. Powell, this is Detective Joe Erickson calling."

"Oh. Do you have a break in the case?" she asked.

"Not yet, but I have a question for you."

"All right..."

"When you were in high school, do you remember a girl named Carrie Richardson?"

"Oh, yeah. I remember her. She was the girl who tried to kill herself. We got into a lot of trouble over that."

"And rightly so. Did you know she died last year?"

"No. Does my attack have something to do with her?"

"We don't know. But we're investigating something possibly related to her."

"Okay."

"Since you are the only remaining member of your group, we believe the offender is obsessive about eliminating every one of you. I'm convinced he will make another attempt on your life, so be very careful."

"I will."

He let Sam know about the DNA evidence from Amber Engstrom, and they decided to question Richardson's wife before going any further. It was summer, and since she would probably not be in the classroom, they decided to drive to her address in Rogers Park to see if she was home. Because Gary Richardson worked the year around in his position as a guidance counselor, he probably would not be at home. But they needed to make sure before knocking on their door.

Five minutes before reaching their address, Joe called Brenda Richardson's cell phone, hoping she would not ignore it since it was an unknown number. His call rolled over to voicemail. *Damn!* Joe decided to call Clinton Prep to find out if Gary Richardson was in his office. He let out a sigh of relief when he was informed Richardson was in today.

They arrived at Richardson's North Boswell Avenue address, which was only a few minutes from the Tunney home. The three-story brick house was like many others on the block that were built in the early years of the twentieth century. It was expertly maintained and landscaped.

The front steps were narrow and led to a small platform facing the front door. There wasn't room for both men, so Joe took the lead and rang the doorbell while Sam remained on the steps. He waited and then rang the bell again. This time, a woman opened the door a crack and said, "Yes?"

Joe held up his ID for her to see and said, "Detective Joe Erickson, Chicago PD. My partner and I need to speak with you."

"What about?"

"Your late daughter."

Brenda Richardson considered it for a moment and asked, "Why?"

"We would prefer to discuss this with you inside."

She sighed and opened the door for them, saying, "All right. Come in."

They followed her to the living room, which was located in the hexagonal area that jutted out on the front of the house. A large brick fireplace was flanked by double bookcases filled with books on each side. Indicating the couch for them to sit on, she sat on the adjacent matching chair.

"You said you wanted to talk about Carrie?" she asked.

"Yes. I'm sorry for your loss," said Sam.

"Thank you."

"We're investigating a case involving a person who bullied your daughter at school," said Joe. "Were either you or your husband aware Carrie was being bullied?"

"No. It came as a complete shock. She was quiet, an introvert, and she didn't discuss it with us. We didn't find out until we saw the note she left and read her diary entries where she named names and documented what they did. They fat-shamed her. Called her names like 'Blimpie' and 'Fatso.'

She wasn't fat, just a little pudgy."

"I see."

"She was in a coma for some time, is that right?" asked Sam.

"Seven years."

"That must have been hard. How did you and your husband deal with that?"

"We were hoping against odds that she would wake up. We knew she'd suffered brain damage, but no one knew to what extent. I visited her as often as I could. Gary would go there almost every day and read to her, hoping she could hear him and respond in some way."

"Did she?"

"No, but it didn't deter him. After a while, his visits tapered off to three times a week or so. But he never gave up, bless his heart."

"For seven years he read to her?" asked Joe.

"He did. He hoped hearing him read would eventually stimulate her to the point she'd begin to respond."

"I'm sorry I have to ask you this, but what motivated you to remove her life support, given your husband was still hoping she'd come out of her coma?"

"Well, that was a very difficult decision. We discovered her kidneys were failing, and she would only have about a month or so before she went into total kidney failure. We didn't want her to suffer through that...and we thought it would be more humane...to let her go before that happened."

Brenda was fighting back tears at this point and reached in her pocket for a handkerchief. "Sorry," she said before blowing her nose.

"How did your husband respond to her passing, given he'd spent so much time with her?" asked Sam.

"He took her accident—we call it an accident rather than a suicide attempt—it's easier than saying what it really was. Anyway, he took her accident pretty hard, and he changed. He never seemed to have fun anymore. You know, I don't think I ever heard him laugh after that. I got worried about him."

"How so?" probed Joe.

"He pretty much stopped talking to me. I don't mean he was silent, but he didn't seem able to initiate a conversation anymore. He would keep to himself and work out in the garden shed, potting flowers and taking care of the yard."

"Did he ever travel out of town? Maybe to distance himself from his memories?"

"Not very often, but he did a few times."

"Where did he go?"

"I don't know. He told me he just needed to get out of the city for a few days. I was concerned he wouldn't come back, but he did. And he was in a better mood afterwards. At least for a while."

Joe didn't want her to think they were only interested in Gary, even though they were. So, he felt he should change the focus to her. Maybe she was complicit in the Squad murders.

"How did you deal with Carrie's passing?"

"This is going to sound strange, but I felt relieved. Seven years of watching your child simply exist in a vegetative state. You have no idea how was hard that is. Letting her go…I grieved for her…but it released a burden I'd been carrying for a long time."

"You said Carrie documented the bullying in her diary. That she named the persons harassing her. Did you confront the school?"

"I photocopied the passages and filed a complaint that included those pages."

"Did you get any satisfaction from school officials?"

"They said they would discipline the girls involved, but according to Gary, they received a slap on the wrist. I wanted to sue the school, but since Gary worked there, it would have created problems for him."

"So, you let it go?"

"If I was going to heal emotionally, I had to."

"Did you ever think about getting even with the girls who bullied Carrie?" asked Sam.

"No. I was angry with them for what they did. But doing something to them? What good would that do? They were just immature kids being mean to others."

"Did you know that someone has been systematically killing each of the girls in the clique who harassed your daughter?" asked Joe.

Brenda's jaw dropped, and she seemed stunned, saying nothing for a few seconds. Finally, she whispered, "Oh my god…"

Joe and Sam observed her and waited for her to speak. Then it appeared to dawn on Brenda that they viewed her and her husband as suspects.

"You don't think we had anything to do with this, do you?"

"Did you?" asked Sam.

"No! Absolutely not," she exclaimed.

"Have you or your husband purchased any long-stem roses?" asked Joe.

"No. What's that got to do with—"

"Do either of you own a taser?"

"No. Why are you asking?"

"Because four of the five members of the clique that bullied your daughter were tased, raped, and strangled within the last year." Then he added a piece of disinformation. "But we have no idea how the offender may have gained entry into their apartments."

Sam gave Joe a look and then a nod, realizing Joe was planting some erroneous information for her husband.

"The last remaining woman is so paranoid and upset that her boyfriend moved out. Evidently, he couldn't take living with her behavioral issues anymore. Not a nice guy, in my opinion."

Silence. After a few seconds, Brenda began slowly shaking her head. By the look on her face, she appeared genuinely surprised by the details Joe provided. He didn't get the impression she was faking it for their benefit.

"So, you can understand why we're investigating anyone who had a motive to eliminate each one of these girls. Someone wanted to make them pay the price for something they did."

"I'm sorry, but this has nothing to do with us," said Brenda. "We aren't criminals."

"Perhaps not. But it would be irresponsible of us as investigators not to look at every possibility."

After a moment, Brenda nodded.

Joe felt it was time to leave. They had gleaned the information they wanted about Gary Richardson. It confirmed what Rebecca Tunney had told them.

Rising from the couch, Joe said, "Thank you for your time, Mrs. Richardson. And again, I'm sorry for your loss."

Brenda stood without replying and led them to the door, where she saw them out. While walking to their car, Sam asked, "When did you come up with the idea to set up Madison Powell?"

"The plan flashed in my mind as we were speaking with her."

"You think Richardson will tell her husband about Powell's paranoia and her boyfriend moving out?"

"I'm counting on it."

Chapter Thirty-Three

On the ride back to their office on Belmond, Joe explained his plan to Sam in detail. He wanted to capture Richardson making an attempt on Madison Powell's life.

"Sounds like it'll work," acknowledged Sam. "It all depends on Powell going along with it."

"I'll talk her into it. She knows what's at stake."

"He'll never try for her again at the college. Especially given what happened the last time."

"If he thinks her boyfriend has moved out and she's living alone, and if he thinks we have no idea how he gained entry into their apartments, I think he may use the flower delivery ruse one last time. That fact has never been released to the media. If he's obsessive about killing every one of them, he won't stop until he completes his objective."

"You'd think he'd be wary about using the same flower delivery business since he's used it twice already. Think he could use another tactic, like he did at the college?"

"I know that could be a possibility," replied Joe. "He's smart, but I think his need to kill Powell will blind him to that consideration, and he'll fall back on what worked."

"I hope you're right. You know what I'd like to see? His garden shed. Ten to one, there are dead flowers and a box for them in there."

"Yeah. I was thinking the same thing, but we don't have enough evidence for a search warrant. And we don't dare try to see what's in there without one."

"I'll bet his wife never goes inside that shed. She probably has no idea."

"Could be. I just hope she passes along the disinformation I gave her about Powell."

"Yeah. Fingers crossed on that."

"And I'd like to know when he took his vacations or had a few days off," said Joe. "See if they match up with the dates those women in Indianapolis and Milwaukee were killed."

"Another search warrant?" asked Sam.

"Let's wait on that."

Back at Area 3, Joe called Madison Powell again.

"Detective Erickson," she said. "Two calls in one day. What's going on?"

"I need to meet with you and your boyfriend today."

"What's this about?"

"I'll explain when I see you. It's not something I can discuss on the phone. When will you both be at home?"

"After five o'clock."

"Okay, I'll meet you at your apartment at a quarter after five. See you then."

Joe texted Destiny, saying he would be late getting home. Then he drove his Camaro to Madison Powell's address. After finding a parking place a block away, he walked to her building and rang her apartment. He identified himself, and she buzzed him in.

Powell introduced Joe once again to her boyfriend, Sean Kellen, a well-built man in his twenties with a movie star face. They had met briefly in Powell's hospital room.

"Nice to see you again," said Joe.

"The pleasure is mine," Kellen replied with his subtle Irish accent.

"What do you need to discuss with us?" asked Powell.

"We have a suspect. Given what we know, we think he will make another attempt on your life, Madison. I have a plan to not only keep you safe but also catch him in the act. It will mean you'll need to move out of this apartment for a time."

"But where will we live?"

"I'm thinking you could live where we do. We could exchange residences for a short period of time. We live in a house in the Lincoln Square neighborhood. My significant other and I would stay here and wait for the offender to attempt to gain entrance into your apartment. We'll be waiting for him, and when he makes his move, we'll apprehend him."

Powell looked at Kellen and said, "What do you think?"

"It is up to you of course, but if they can apprehend this yob, I say do it," he replied.

She thought for a moment and said, "All right. I'll go along with it."

"Thanks," said Joe. I'll get back to you tomorrow. In the meantime, be careful."

As he was walking down the street toward his car, Joe had only one concern: convincing Destiny to go along with it.

When he arrived home, Autumn greeted him. Destiny was eating dinner seated at the island.

"I was hungry and didn't know when you'd get home," she said. "The rigatoni aglio olio is in the oven. I've been keeping it warm for you."

After giving Autumn some attention, Joe dished up his pasta. He sat at the island next to Destiny. Her rigatoni aglio olio was always very good, and this was no exception.

After a few bites, Joe said, "I have an idea to catch the offender who killed members of the Squad."

"Oh? Tell me about it."

"When we were speaking with the wife of our suspect today, I lied and told her we had no idea how the offender gained entrance to the victims' apartments. I'm hoping she'll tell him what I said so he'll use his flower delivery ruse one more time with Madison Powell. To complete his mission to eliminate all the members of the Squad. I also told her a story that her boyfriend had moved out because he couldn't deal with her paranoia and behavioral issues any longer."

"So, you're inviting him to attack Madison Powell?" she asked.

"I am, but instead of Powell and her boyfriend, it will be you and me in her apartment, prepared to take him down."

Destiny thought about it for a few seconds and then said, "So, how do we know when to be in her apartment?"

"I can't predict that, but I was thinking that Powell and her boyfriend could move in here while we move into her apartment. Just for a short period of time."

"You want us to turn our house over to complete strangers?"

Not surprised by her reluctance, he said, "I know what you're thinking, but we'll be living in their place, too."

"What if they're slobs? And what about Autumn?"

"I've seen their apartment, and it was neat and clean. There are no signs of them being slobs. As for Autumn, she can go with us. She's housebroken and well-behaved. It's not like she would chew up their furniture."

"Oh, man. I'm going to have to think about this."

"And you can work from anywhere."

"I know."

"Give it some thought. But keep in mind, we'll be apprehending a killer."

"How long do you plan for us to live there? A week? A month?"

"There's no way to know when he'll make a move. But it will be sooner rather than later."

"I don't like it."

"Okay. Can you come up with a plan to prevent this guy from killing Madison Powell? If you can, I'm all ears."

"I'll think about it."

"The only other option I can think of is for her boyfriend to move out and for me to move in with her."

"Live with her?" Destiny gave him a disapproving look. "I suppose she's pretty."

"Not as pretty as you."

"Very politic, Joe."

Joe kissed her and said, "You don't have anything to worry about. You know that."

"I'm not worried about you. But I don't want you moving in with someone who, for all we know, could be a nymphomaniac."

"I'll have myself injected with saltpeter."

"Oh, very funny."

Joe laughed. "I'll tell you what. I'll let you come up with an alternative plan. How's that?"

"Deal."

Chapter Thirty-Four

As Joe approached the house from jogging, he saw Destiny and Autumn returning from their walk around the block. They arrived at the front steps at the same time. Destiny had her key out and unlocked the front door for them.

"I need to get rid of this," said Destiny, referring to the plastic bag she used to clean up after Autumn. She handed Autumn's leash to Joe, who removed it and let her run into the house. Then, he walked to the bedroom and got ready to jump in the shower.

After he got dressed, he entered the kitchen to prepare a breakfast of two slices of whole wheat toast spread with roasted red pepper hummus. Destiny was already sitting at the island drinking a cup of coffee.

"I just poured you a cup," she said.

"Thanks," said Joe, sitting next to her.

"I did some thinking while you were jogging, and I think I may agree to your plan if I can meet Madison Powell first. I want to know what she's like before I agree to let her live here."

"Good idea," replied Joe. "Before I leave, I'll give you her phone number so you can set up a meeting."

"Great."

When Joe was sitting at his desk at work, he accessed Gary Richardson's Facebook page. The thing about Facebook is that you cannot necessarily see a person's posts without being a "friend." However, you can look through their photos. That's what Joe did. He looked for a photo of Richardson he could use to show people. There wasn't one. He was not very active and had posted very few photos since he'd been on Facebook. But that was not true of his wife, Brenda. Her Facebook page contained many images over time, and as he looked through them, he found a recent formal photo taken of her and Gary.

Joe copied the photo onto his computer. Then he cropped out Brenda, so he had a photo showing only Gary. Fortunately, the photo was created in a large format, so the picture did not look blurry or pixelated. After printing two copies on white card stock, he handed one to Sam.

"What's this?" asked Sam before looking at it.

"Take a look. It's a photo of Gary Richardson we can show around."

"Show around…Who'd you have in mind?"

"Now we have a suspect, I think we should re-canvass the florist shops and show them his picture. See if anyone remembers seeing him."

"Okay."

"You still have my list?"

"Yeah. What did Destiny think of your plan?"

"She's skeptical. But she hasn't ruled it out. She wants to meet with Madison Powell first."

"Can't blame her for that. I wouldn't want a complete stranger living in my place."

"Yeah. Let's hope they hit it off."

Joe and Sam began canvassing the florist shops they had previously visited. On his second stop, he showed the photo to a young woman at the counter.

"Oh, yeah," she said. "He looks familiar."

"So, he's been in here buying flowers?" asked Joe.

"Let me get Phoebe. Maybe she remembers him better than I do," she said, and walked through swinging doors into the back part of the shop. After a few moments, an older woman with pure white hair entered along with the young woman Joe was talking to.

Joe had spoken with her the first time he came in. "Remember me?" he asked.

She smiled and said, "Of course I do, Detective…Erickson, right?"

"That's correct." He handed her the photograph and asked if she recognized the man pictured. Phoebe slipped on her reading glasses and examined the photo.

After a minute, she removed her glasses, looked at Joe, and said, "Uh-huh. I remember him. He bought a dozen long-stem roses. Paid in cash."

"You remember him after all the customers you've seen since?" asked Joe, amazed by her attention to detail.

"I have what's called a photographic memory." Handing Joe the photo, she smiled and said, "I remember everybody."

"Thank you," replied Joe. "Is this something you could testify to in court if it became necessary?"

"If I needed to, I suppose I could."

Joe asked for her full name and found it was Phoebe Coleman. "I don't suppose you remember when he bought them?"

"I can't be specific about the date. Sorry. But it was recent."

"How recent?"

"Oh…I'd say sometime in the last couple of months."

"Thank you, Ms. Coleman. You've been a big help."

Before leaving, Joe acquired Coleman's contact information. Even though he now had a witness attesting to Richardson buying long-stem roses, Joe continued to canvass the remaining florists on his list, hoping someone else would recognize Richardson. He had to have purchased roses earlier in the year. Tracey McNamara and Stephanie Daniels were killed eight and nine months ago. But no such luck. By the end of the day, Joe had obtained only Phoebe Coleman's recollection of Richardson's purchase. But she was a strong witness whose precise recollection of Richardson and what he purchased provided important evidence.

When he finished checking the last shop on his list, Joe called Sam as he was walking to his car. "You have any luck?"

"I had one person who thought she remembered him," said Sam, "but that's it. She couldn't be specific about when and what he bought. How about you?"

"I struck gold," said Joe.

"Yeah?"

"I found a witness who not only remembered him as a customer but also recalled he bought long-stem roses. Sometime in the last two months."

"Wow," replied Sam. "That's some memory she has."

"Yeah. Are you done?"

"One to go."

"Okay, I'm done. So, I'll meet you back at the office."

When Sam returned, it was almost quitting time. No one at his final stop recognized Richardson's photo, so Joe shared Phoebe Coleman's contact information with him before clocking out for the day.

As Joe was returning home, he saw an unfamiliar car parked in front of his house. When he entered, he heard women's voices. Stepping into the kitchen, he looked into the living room and saw Destiny and Madison Powell engaged in an animated conversation punctuated occasionally by laughter. After locking up his Glock, he made his way to the edge of the living room.

"Sounds like you two are enjoying yourselves," he said.

"We are," said Destiny.

"That's great."

After glancing at her watch, Powell rose and said, "Gosh, I didn't realize it was this late. I should probably be heading home."

"Don't run away on my account," said Joe.

"I need to get back to my apartment. I didn't leave a note, and I don't want Sean to start worrying about me."

Destiny rose and said, "I'll see you tomorrow." She followed Powell out onto the front porch and said goodbye. Entering the house, she returned to the kitchen, where Joe was now sitting at the island with his laptop open.

"So, you're seeing her tomorrow?" asked Joe, looking up from the screen.

"I am. She invited me to their apartment."

"So, what do you think?"

"Well, so far it's looking positive. I'll let you know tomorrow."

Chapter Thirty-Five

When Joe returned home from work the next day, he found Destiny in the kitchen cooking brown rice while something simmered in the wok.

"Smells wonderful," said Joe.

"Thai Chicken with Basil. I've substituted seitan for the chicken. Hope you don't mind."

"Not at all," replied Joe. He had grown used to eating seitan, a wheat meat substitute, since it had the texture of actual meat and was packed with protein. When he was the chef for the evening, he would cook portions with meat separately so Destiny could eat a meatless version or, in the case of seafood, ask ahead of time to see if she was agreeable to eating fish. Destiny would often ask Joe if he was agreeable to eating her vegetarian choices.

Once they sat down to eat, Joe asked, "Did you meet with Madison Powell like you planned?"

"I did."

"What do you think?"

"I like her. She's highly intelligent and well-spoken. And that Irish boyfriend of hers...what a hunk!"

"He isn't ugly, I'll say that," replied Joe.

"Their apartment is quite attractive, too. Neat and tastefully decorated, although I'm not crazy about Scandinavian decor. But to each his own."

"So, what's the verdict?" asked Joe.

"I think we can go ahead with your plan—for a couple of weeks, anyway. Any more than that will prove problematic, don't you think?"

"Yeah. I guess we'll have to hope for the best. If something doesn't happen with Gary Richardson in that amount of time, I'll need to rethink how to apprehend him."

"Surveil him during the day?"

"Him or Powell's apartment building when she's at home," replied Joe. "At least we know he uses his flower delivery ruse during the day and not at night. I think we can work something out with our lieutenant regarding time for surveillance."

"The problem you'll have is that he can't be observed every hour of the day."

"I know."

"He works, so he would need to take time away from school to observe her or to execute his plan. I suppose he could use a few of his vacation days to do that. But since it's summer and school's not in session, that shouldn't be a problem for him. He can leave early any afternoon she isn't teaching."

"Given the first attack, he already knows she only teaches on Monday, Wednesday, and Friday this summer," said Joe.

"But he would need to determine when she's at home on Tuesdays and Thursdays," said Destiny. "That could be difficult. When he makes his move, he'd need to verify she's at home. He could do that if he had her landline phone number. He could make a call and hang up if she answers. Then he would know."

"If she has a landline. And he would have to assume she would answer an unrecognizable number. If she has caller ID. If she only has a cell phone, he wouldn't know if she was at home or not if she didn't answer."

"You could follow his car to the vicinity of her apartment, so you know when he's observing her and when he decides to deliver flowers."

"Chances are, he's done with observing her already," said Joe. "He's had plenty of time."

"After she finishes work, she can't drive directly to our place. If he is following her, he'll know something's up. She'll have to go to her apartment like she always does. What time does her last class end?"

"Two o'clock. She should be able to leave for our place after six o'clock.

He won't try to deliver flowers after six."

"So, his window of opportunity is from about 2:30 to let's say 5:30. Three hours."

"And I doubt he'll follow her when she leaves," replied Joe. "She could be going anywhere. He's not going to deviate from his plan. It's been successful too many times."

"Agreed."

"I think he's been biding his time and will make his move sooner rather than later. But either Sam or I will have to monitor where he is any time he's not at school. That's going to be tricky."

"Maybe you could track him using his cell phone," suggested Destiny. "There's technology available for that. As long as he has it turned on. It could save you a lot of surveillance time. I'll ask about the best app for my laptop from one of my contacts at the FBI. I can help you by tracking the location of his cell phone."

"But it won't give us his exact location, only the approximate area he's in based on his cell phone bouncing off towers."

"That's true, but it would tell us if he had entered an area near Powell's address."

"Good idea," said Joe. "But it's illegal to track his cell phone like that."

"You'll need to obtain a warrant."

"Figures."

"You have sufficient cause."

"We do."

"You know, what might work even better than the cell phone trace would be a tracking device attached to his vehicle. It would be precise and wouldn't go dead if he turned off his cell phone or removed the location services on his phone. It wouldn't hurt to track him both ways."

"I'll talk to Sam about it tomorrow. If we send the warrant application downtown first thing, and if Sam rushes it, we could have it the same day."

"Is Judge Warner back in his office now?"

"I don't know. I hope so because he's always been quick about issuing a warrant, especially if we need it right away."

"Perfect," said Destiny. "Because if you think his attempt could be imminent, we need to move into their apartment as soon as possible."

Destiny called Powell to set up a meeting tomorrow when she returned from work. The following day would be a Thursday, and they could exchange residences when Powell had the day off.

"I'll contact my FBI friend tomorrow about the best software to use," said Destiny. "And let me know right away when the search warrant's been approved so I can load the software onto my laptop."

"I hope to hell this works," said Joe.

Destiny replied, "Fingers crossed."

Chapter Thirty-Six

The next morning, Joe and Sam put their heads together and discussed what they needed. Afterward, Sam began writing the request for a warrant. When he finished, he ran it downtown to Judge Warner's office. Warner, who had been on medical leave following bypass surgery, had recently returned to work. Sam explained their critical situation to Warner's administrative assistant, who asked Sam to wait while he took the warrant request to the judge. After several minutes, Sam was escorted into Warner's office. He had never appeared before the judge regarding a search warrant application. He had always handed off the paperwork to his assistant and received it back once it was signed.

As he entered, Sam saw Warner reading the search warrant application and frowning. The look on Warner's face shook his confidence.

As he stood in front of Warner's desk, Sam thought that the sixty-plus-year-old man looked good for someone who had undergone major surgery just two weeks ago. The judge looked up from his reading and asked for clarification. "I've read over your application, Detective. My assistant told me you need this as soon as possible. Can you explain the circumstances regarding the immediacy of this warrant?"

Sam detailed Joe's belief that the offender's attack could happen at any time. They needed to track him to know when an attack could be imminent. Knowing the offender's location was crucial in protecting Madison Powell and apprehending the attacker.

"So, what are you saying?" asked Warner, "That this possible attack could happen as soon as today?"

"It could, your honor," replied Sam.

Warner nodded, and a moment later, he picked up a pen and signed the application. Sam breathed a sigh of relief. He thanked the judge and was ushered out of the office by his assistant.

As soon as Sam was outside the building, he called Joe to let him know that Warner had authorized the search warrant. In turn, Joe called Destiny, informing her of the warrant's approval.

When Sam returned to the office, he and Joe went to speak with Lieutenant Bellamy about obtaining a tracker for Richardson's car. Bellamy looked over the search warrant.

"How soon do you need it?" asked Bellamy.

"Yesterday," replied Joe. "We believe the suspected offender could act as soon as today."

Bellamy looked a little displeased by this last-minute request. After a few seconds, he replied, "All right. I'll have to call in a favor, but I think I can have the equipment to you by this afternoon."

"Thank you," said Sam.

"Who's going to be doing the monitoring?"

Joe responded, "I will." He wouldn't be, but he didn't want Bellamy to know that Destiny would be doing it. That would not go over well, even if she was a former FBI agent.

"Very well," said Bellamy, standing and walking them to his door. "Good luck with this."

Early that afternoon, Joe received a package. In it, he found a small device to be attached to Richardson's car, along with the device's corresponding software, and additional software to monitor Richardson's cell phone's location. Joe checked his notebook and found the cell phone number Richardson gave him during their first meeting. Hopefully, he would not be using a different phone.

Joe looked up Gary Richardson in the Illinois Vehicle Registration database and found two cars registered to Gary and Brenda Richardson: an eight-year-old blue Taurus and a two-year-old white Camry. He wrote down their license plate numbers. The question remained, who drove what vehicle?

Joe drove to Clinton Prep High School and looked for one of the two Richardson cars. He found the eight-year-old blue Taurus with a matching plate in the parking lot. He needed to affix the electronic tracker to the car, a place where there was metal, so the magnet could attach. So many parts on new cars are made of plastics and composites, making it hard to find a place to attach a magnetic tracking device. Joe decided that inside the trunk would be the best place for it. Using a Slim Jim tool, he unlocked the driver's door and checked the back seat. No flower box. That was good news.

Looking around to make sure no one was watching, Joe pushed the button that popped open the trunk. The tracker, which he placed on the metal framework, would not only adhere well but also remain out of sight. He pushed the trunk lid closed and locked the doors.

Just as he finished, he looked up and saw Gary Richardson walking out of the building toward the parking lot. *Shit!* Ducking down and assuming a hunched-over position, Joe quickly moved between vehicles and made it back to his squad car. He watched Richardson unlock his car with his key fob and get in. Joe opened his driver's door and slid into the seat, observing Richardson as he pulled out of the parking lot.

Joe pulled his squad car out onto the street and began following Richardson's Taurus. Maintaining a safe distance, he tailed Richardson to within two blocks of his home. At that point, Joe turned left onto a side street and headed back to Area 3. Given the time, he was reasonably certain Richardson would not be going after Madison Powell today.

Back at his office, Joe called Destiny and told her he had successfully planted the tracking device and would be heading home soon with the software for her to download onto her computer.

"We're going to be busy," said Destiny. "We have to pack if we're moving into her apartment tomorrow."

"It's a good thing I start my two days off tomorrow," replied Joe. "It'll give me time to pack my stuff."

Joe found Destiny waiting for him at the kitchen island, her laptop open and ready to download the software.

"Looks like you're ready to work," he said.

"I am."

After giving her a quick kiss, he handed her a flash drive. "The software is all on this."

"Oh. Okay, let me get my cable adapter."

Destiny stood and walked into their office. As Joe locked his Glock away, Autumn jumped up, putting her paws on his leg. Joe kneeled down, stroking Autumn's head. "You going to be a good girl when we move to Madison's apartment?" She looked at him and then pawed his knee one time. "Oh, so you want more attention, huh? Have you had a 'treat?'" Hearing the word, she perked up and wagged her tail.

Destiny returned with her cable adapter and said, "No, she hasn't."

"Okay. Let me get one for you." Joe stood up and got a treat from the bag on the counter.

Holding up the treat, he said, "Speak!" Autumn gave a short bark, and he rewarded her with the treat.

Destiny plugged in the flash drive and began downloading the software file onto her desktop. She looked at Joe and said, "It's a big file. It'll take quite a while for it to download."

"Like watching paint dry, huh?"

"More or less. I'm going to start the laundry. I don't want dirty laundry sitting in the hamper when Madison is here."

Destiny went into the bedroom and began sorting laundry. Joe went into the garage and brought in his large duffel bag from storage.

When the file had finished downloading, Destiny placed the application on her hard drive. At that point, she opened the app. It brought up a map of Chicago streets with a red dot indicating where the tracker was located. The dot was not moving.

"It's working," she said. "Look."

Joe looked at the screen. "This is amazing."

"It's located on North Boswell Avenue. You know where that is?"

"Yeah," said Joe. "That's where his home is."

"We can now tell exactly where his car is located at any given time."

"Does the app do anything like beep to let you know the car has started moving?" asked Joe.

"It does. I read up on the system's features this afternoon. These GPS trackers are pretty sophisticated."

"Hopefully, when he decides to make his move, he'll be driving his Taurus rather than the car his wife drives."

"You think he's that smart? To switch cars?"

"He hasn't been caught yet. So, yeah. He could be that smart."

"Well, we have this other software that will track his cell phone. I'll download that, and we'll have another way to track his location."

When the file had been downloaded, she placed it on her hard drive. Once there, she opened the app, and Joe gave her Richardson's cell phone number. The software responded, giving her an area where his phone was located. Richardson's home address was within the parameters disclosed. It was not as specific as the car's tracker, but it would tell them if he was near Powell's apartment building.

Chapter Thirty-Seven

After completing his jog, Joe hit the shower and got ready for moving day. By the time he entered the kitchen, Destiny was already up, had finished folding their clean laundry, and had walked Autumn. "Coffee?" she asked.

"Please."

He petted Autumn and then sat down on a stool at the island as Destiny poured him a cup from their drip coffee maker and sat down beside him. He thanked her, and after he had taken a sip, he asked, "How much are you packing?"

"More than you need to," she said. "You don't have makeup, hair products, lotions, and all the things we girls need every day."

"That's true. I figured a toothbrush, razor, and a change of underwear should do it."

"For a week?"

"I'm kidding," laughed Joe. "I think I can get most of what I need into my large duffel bag."

He took another sip of his coffee. Then he got up to make his usual slices of whole wheat toast spread with roasted red pepper hummus.

"Once we get settled in, we'll need to get groceries," said Destiny. "We can't eat her food."

"Chances are, she doesn't eat what we do, anyway. I guess we should take any of our stuff that won't keep."

"Right."

After breakfast, they began packing. Clothes for one week and personal items filled Joe's large duffel bag so full, he had trouble zipping it shut. He was fighting with it when Destiny came into the bedroom.

"One change of underwear, huh?" she smiled.

Looking up at her, Joe said, "After some thought—"

"I know. I was able to squeeze everything I needed into my largest suitcase. Except for my computer. I'll have to carry that separately."

"I'll have to do the same. And we can't forget Autumn's stuff."

They looked to the corner where Autumn's carrier, bed, box of toys, bowls, and food were packed.

"Geez, she has more stuff than we do," remarked Joe.

"Right. Looks like we'd better take both cars."

After their suitcases were ready to go, they moved to the kitchen and checked the refrigerator. Some things were placed in the freezer, but others could not be frozen and would spoil if left for a couple of weeks. Joe got a cooler from the garage, and they began filling it with items to take with them.

"What about wine?" asked Joe.

"We could do without for a week, I suppose. It won't kill us."

"I don't know about that," quipped Joe.

"Or if we would like some, I can go to the Wine Sellers and pick up a couple of bottles."

"Sounds good."

It was now 10:15, and Destiny called Madison Powell to review logistics. They decided Joe and Destiny would move into Powell's apartment first, and then they could assist her move into their house since her boyfriend was not available to help. They agreed to meet at her apartment and begin moving in around one o'clock.

After running the dishwasher and putting away the clean dishes, they decided to eat a quick lunch at a bistro not far from their house. That saved them from re-cleaning the kitchen and washing more dishes.

Shortly before one o'clock, Joe and Destiny arrived at Madison Powell's address. Following instructions, they parked in the visitors' spots in the apartment's parking garage. Destiny had called Powell as they were pulling up to her apartment building. Once they parked, Powell met them, and they began the task of moving their stuff into her seventh-floor apartment. *Thank God for elevators*, thought Joe. He carted Autumn in her carrier first. With Powell's help, they had everything moved in after several trips.

Powell looked into Autumn's carrier and said, "Cute dog. What breed is she?"

"Lhasa Apso," replied Destiny.

"Really? I've heard good things about them and always wanted to see one."

Joe reached down and opened the door to Autumn's carrier. Picking her up, he said, "Our little prima donna."

"Aww," responded Powell. She reached over and let Autumn sniff her hand. "Can I pet her?"

"Sure," said Joe. Powell petted Autumn, saying, "What a pretty girl you are."

After Joe returned Autumn to her carrier, Powell showed them around her apartment and explained where things could be found and how things worked. The kitchen was small, but it had everything they would need to prepare meals.

"I'm no Julia Child," said Powell. "But I think you'll find I have the basics." She opened the cupboard doors and showed Joe and Destiny where she kept various items. When she opened the refrigerator, they saw it was almost empty. Only a few condiments and fruit juice remained, and just a handful of food items were in the freezer. There was plenty of room for the food they had brought.

After they got squared away, Joe and Destiny helped Powell load her suitcases into her car. They drove to Joe and Destiny's residence, brought Powell's things into the house, and gave her a quick tour. When they had finished showing her around, Powell said she would feel more comfortable sleeping in their guest bedroom rather than on Joe and Destiny's bed. They were fine with that and told her she could park her car in the garage if she liked. Joe handed her the remote to open and close the garage door, and they exchanged keys.

"I'll be coming to my apartment after work on Monday, Wednesday, and

Friday, right?" asked Powell.

"That's right," said Joe. "In case you're being followed, you need to return to your apartment. After six o'clock, you should be able to drive back here. If the offender will be using his ruse about delivering flowers, he won't try to make a delivery after six."

"Do you think he'll try to attack me? In my apartment and not somewhere else?"

"My gut's telling me he won't stop. He's obsessed with eliminating all five girls who were part of the clique. Each one was attacked and killed in her apartment."

"And we'll be there to apprehend him when he does," assured Destiny.

Joe and Destiny drove back to Powell's apartment, and Destiny began unpacking. Joe took Autumn for a walk around the block, allowing her to investigate new smells. When he returned, he spent some time helping her get acquainted with the new environment by showing her where her bed, food dish, and water bottle were located. After giving her a treat, he went into the bedroom and began unpacking. Luckily, Powell lived in a two-bedroom apartment, but there was only one queen-size bed. The second bedroom had been transformed into an office. But it did have enough space for Joe to stack his clothes on a card table he had found and set up.

Once they finished settling in, Destiny called Powell and asked if she had any questions. They chatted for about twenty minutes. Meanwhile, Joe pulled out the bottle of Pinot Noir he smuggled in with his clothes. He went through Powell's cupboard and found wine glasses. Using the corkscrew he brought from home, he opened the bottle and poured a glass.

When Destiny ended her phone call, she asked, "Are you drinking her wine?"

"Of course not! I brought one bottle from home."

"You had me worried for a minute. Can you pour me a glass, too?"

Joe got up and filled a glass. He handed it to her, clinked her glass, and said, "Here's to catching this guy."

"To catching this guy," Destiny repeated. "May it be sooner rather than later."

Chapter Thirty-Eight

T hat evening, Destiny called in an order to their favorite Chinese restaurant and had it delivered to their new address. It was relaxing not having to cook after all the hustle-bustle associated with moving.

The only problem with moving into Powell's apartment involved their cars. Powell had only one parking place reserved, and Joe and Destiny had two cars. The next morning, Joe spoke to the apartment manager, showed him his ID, and explained there was a police stakeout going on, so they temporarily needed another parking place. Fortunately, the manager was willing to help the police with their situation. He told them one of the apartment's residents was in Europe for a month, and they could use her spot since her car was at the airport.

Late in the afternoon, Joe walked Autumn around the block, stopping occasionally while she sniffed the sidewalk, streetlamps, car tires, and the walls of buildings, curious about her new surroundings. Inside the apartment, she continued checking out their accommodations. Finally, she calmed down, lying between Joe and Destiny as they watched television.

Around nine o'clock, Joe was starting to nod off now and then.

"Why don't you go to bed?" suggested Destiny.

"Maybe I will," he said, rising slowly from the couch. He walked into the bedroom, undressed, and pulled back the covers on the bed. When he slid in, he was greeted by one of those memory foam mattresses that supports the contours of the body. Joe found it comfortable, but he missed his own pillow. *Should have brought it. Just have to tough it out.*

Joe woke up to his wristwatch's alarm. Destiny was sleeping much closer to him since their own bed was a California King. Slowly getting up so as not to wake her, he walked into the office where he had placed his clothes and slipped into his jogging outfit. As he rode the elevator down to the main floor, it stopped on the fourth floor, and a woman in her thirties wearing jogging togs got on. Her blonde hair was pulled back in a ponytail.

"You jogging this morning?" Joe asked.

"Nearly every morning," she replied. "You, too?"

"Nearly every morning," Joe replied with a smile.

"I haven't seen you here before. Are you new?"

"So to speak," replied Joe. "We're apartment-sitting for a friend."

"We," she asked.

"My partner and I. We're taking care of a friend's apartment for a week or two while she's away."

Sensing she was the curious type, Joe changed the subject. "We can jog together if you like."

"That sounds nice. How far do you usually go?"

"Three miles."

"Oh. That's a bit too far for me. I only go about a mile and a half."

"That's fine. I'll just continue after you're done," said Joe.

The elevator reached the ground floor, and they exited the building and began jogging up the street. It had been years since Joe had a jogging partner. The last time was when he was in Iowa to settle his father's estate, and a precocious teenager named Melissa began running with him each morning. He wound up saving her from a psychopath who kidnapped and sexually assaulted her. Joe had not thought about Melissa for a while and wondered how she was doing. *Maybe I should give her father a call and see what she's up to.*

"What's your name?" the woman asked as they jogged along together.

Jolted out of his thoughts, Joe said, "What? Oh, it's Joe. What's yours?"

"Zoe."

"Nice to meet you, Zoe."

"Likewise."

They didn't speak for the next half a mile. Joe liked to use his jogging time to think about his cases, and that's what he was doing when Zoe spoke up.

"You don't talk much, do you?"

"I usually use this time to think. I'm not used to having someone to jog with."

"Your partner doesn't run?"

"No. But she works out a lot. She has two black belts, one in Jiu-Jitsu and another in Muay Thai."

"Wow. I guess I'd better treat you right," she chuckled. "If you don't mind me asking, what's Muay Thai? I've never heard of it."

"It's a form of hand-to-hand combat from Thailand."

"And she has a black belt?"

"Just recently. She's been studying with a master teacher for a long time."

"Sounds wicked."

"It can be. She's never been in a situation where she's had to use it, thankfully."

After they jogged farther, Zoe asked, "What about you? What do you do?"

Joe knew it would come up sooner or later, so he decided to be honest with her. "I'm a police detective. I work homicide."

"Really."

"Really," said Joe, amused by her reaction.

"I guess I should feel safe jogging with you early in the morning, huh?"

"Have you ever felt unsafe?"

"Not so far."

"That's good. Do you carry pepper spray with you?"

Zoe patted the right pocket of her pants. "Yup. I come prepared, just in case."

Joe followed Zoe's lead on where to turn and run down another block. After jogging for about fifteen minutes, they ended up in front of their building. Zoe stopped, and Joe followed suit.

"I'm done," she said. "It's been fun jogging with you, Joe. Tomorrow? Same time?"

"Why not?" replied Joe. "See you then." They parted company, and he began the second half of his jog.

After he showered, shaved, and dressed for the day, Joe walked into the kitchen. They had brought coffee, bread, and hummus with them, so he was able to fix his breakfast. Destiny had made a pot of coffee, and after pouring himself a cup, he sat on the couch. Destiny joined him.

"How was your first jog in this neighborhood?" she asked.

"I met a fellow jogger on my way down in the elevator, and we jogged together for fifteen minutes. She only runs about half as far as I do. Zoe's her name."

"That must have made things interesting."

"She asks a lot of questions."

"What did you tell her? About our presence here."

"We're apartment sitting for a friend."

"Ah. I'll use that if someone asks."

Joe and Destiny discussed their strategy regarding Gary Richardson. Destiny would keep track of him on her laptop, and if he seemed to be driving near the apartment building, she would alert Joe. Since Joe would not go back to work until tomorrow, he would be around all day.

"I'll go with you to the grocery store," said Joe. "We'll probably have a lot to carry in."

"We should wait to go until we know Richardson's car is at the school," replied Destiny.

At nine o'clock, Destiny tracked Richardson's car to Clinton Prep. Shortly after, her cell phone rang. Madison Powell was calling.

"Hello, Madison."

Powell asked how things were going at her apartment. Destiny told her everything was fine and asked how she was getting along in their house.

"I love your kitchen. I wish I had a kitchen like this one."

"Did you find everything you needed?"

"I did. Did you sleep well?"

"We did. We like your mattress."

"Comfy, isn't it?"

They chatted a while longer and agreed to check in once a day. Since today was a Friday, Madison would be returning to her apartment following her last class. They would talk more then.

An hour later, Destiny and Joe drove to the supermarket and bought groceries. They tried to keep it simple, with no lavish meals, but they ended up with a lot of bags to carry onto the elevator. Once they had everything safely in the apartment, Destiny checked her laptop. Richardson's car was still at the school, and his cell phone pinged off three towers, indicating the school's approximate location.

They put away the groceries, and Joe volunteered to make lunch. He made the green salad that Destiny requested and made a BLT sandwich for himself. Following lunch, Joe selected a mystery novel by Robert Parker from Powell's bookcase and began reading it. Destiny had interested him in reading novels as opposed to watching television, and he found he enjoyed mysteries and thrillers the most.

Around two o'clock, Destiny alerted Joe to Richardson's car moving away from the school. She tracked him to an office that sent out parcels via FedEx and UPS. After that, he parked his car near a neighborhood pub. His car was stationary for about an hour. Then it was on the move again, until he arrived home.

Madison called forty minutes later and said she was about to take the elevator up to the apartment. A short time later, Destiny heard the doorbell. Taking no chances, she opened the door as far as the chain allowed and saw it was Madison.

Destiny grinned and opened the door. "Welcome to your apartment."

Joe was on his feet and greeted Madison as she came in. "Hi. Can I get you anything?" he asked.

"No, thanks. I'm fine," she replied. "I guess I'll have to get used to parking on the street. I had a two-block walk."

"Let me talk with your super," said Joe. "There may be other spaces open."

Given the size of the apartment, Joe couldn't avoid listening to Destiny and Madison talking about various things that didn't interest him. They seemed to hit it off, after just knowing one another for a short period of time, and after this meeting, Joe got the impression they might remain friends.

Madison left shortly after six to drive to Joe and Destiny's house. Joe walked her to her car, parked two blocks away, and said he would contact her after speaking with the super about access to another parking space.

That night, it was more of the same: dinner, television, reading, bed. The only difference was that Destiny went to bed at the same time Joe did. Sleep came easily an hour later.

Chapter Thirty-Nine

For a week, nothing changed. Their schedule was the same day after day, and Joe was concerned they would be lulled into a kind of complacency. Madison continued returning to the apartment after she finished her teaching duties and left for Joe and Destiny's residence after six o'clock each Monday, Wednesday, and Friday.

As they began their second week, Joe was getting discouraged about his plan succeeding. He knew that Richardson was most likely biding his time and would make an attempt on Madison's life sooner or later. But how soon? They could not continue these awkward living arrangements forever. Destiny suggested two weeks, which was reasonable. He didn't want to extend the time since she had been supportive of his plan. And Madison probably wished she could be back living in her own place.

If there was an upside to this difficult arrangement, Destiny and Madison were becoming closer. A year ago, Destiny's best friend, Liz, was killed when a small plane piloted by her husband crashed while they were returning from North Carolina. Liz and Destiny were like sisters when they were growing up, and they maintained their friendship through college and beyond. Although Liz could never be replaced, Joe sensed that maybe Madison could be the person to fill that void in Destiny's life. Could an English professor and a criminal profiler have enough in common to cement a friendship? And has Madison purged the undesirable qualities she had during her high school days as a member of the Squad? He hoped so.

When Joe was at work, Destiny kept him updated on any changes to the location of Gary Richardson's car and cell phone. On Wednesday,

Richardson's car left Clinton Prep and returned to his home shortly before two o'clock. But half an hour later, his cell phone location was changing, despite his car remaining at home.

Destiny alerted Joe, who informed Sam.

"You think he may be making a move using his wife's car?" asked Sam.

"It's possible. I think we'd better get in place in case he is."

Joe called Destiny back and told her he and Sam were on their way. He put a portable emergency light on top of his squad car and quickly drove to Madison's apartment building. They arrived much sooner than Richardson could have, and Joe parked in his temporary spot. While he went up to the apartment, Sam took up a position across the street where he could monitor the building's entrance.

Joe called Destiny to let her know he was in the building. He rang the apartment's bell, and Destiny peered out. Seeing it was Joe, she removed the chain and let him in. As soon as he entered, he saw Madison standing near the window.

"Madison returned from the college not long before you arrived," said Destiny. "I made her aware of the situation, but let her know this could also be a false alarm."

Joe looked at Madison, who appeared apprehensive. And who could blame her? It could be a confrontation with the man who wanted her dead.

"How are you doing?" he asked.

"I'm glad you're here," she replied.

"My partner is in place across the street, and he'll let us know if anyone enters the building carrying a box of flowers. We'll buzz him in and take him down when he tries to deliver them. You won't be in any danger."

"Thank you."

Waiting was nerve-wracking for everyone. Joe began questioning whether Richardson was going to make an attempt after all. He began second-guessing. Maybe they were overreacting. Maybe Richardson was taking his wife's car in for an oil change. Or to a car wash. Or maybe he was taking his wife to a doctor's appointment. There could be a myriad of reasons why he was not driving his own vehicle.

Destiny was watching her computer screen and tracking the position of his cell phone. Then, his cell phone suddenly stopped pinging off towers. "Crap!" she said.

"What is it?" asked Joe.

"His cell phone's no longer visible. It's like it disappeared."

"You think he could be in an area where there's no service? Or in some underground facility?"

"Do you think he turned it off?" asked Madison.

Destiny gave her a look and said, "I don't know. Maybe."

"He'd be smart if he did," replied Joe. "That way, the police couldn't trace his phone and place him here. How far away was he when you lost his signal?"

Scrutinizing her screen, Destiny said, "About twenty blocks."

Joe called Sam and informed him of the loss of signal when Richardson was twenty blocks from their location."

"I'll be watching for that white Camry. See if it goes by," said Sam.

Everyone was on pins and needles. For the next half an hour, there was nothing.

Then Sam called Joe. "Uh, there's a UPS delivery guy approaching your building with a package."

"UPS?" asked Joe.

"Yeah. Brown uniform and cap."

The package could be for anyone who lived in the building. Joe looked at Madison and asked, "Are you expecting a delivery from UPS?"

"Maybe. I ordered something from Amazon a few days ago."

"Okay," replied Joe. "We'll have to sit tight and see if we get a message."

A moment later, the buzzer for the intercom sounded, and Destiny answered it, saying, "Yes?"

A male voice stated, "I have a UPS delivery for a Madison Powell."

"That's me. Can you leave it downstairs?"

"I'm sorry, but it requires a signature."

Madison looked concerned. Looking at Destiny, Joe said, "Go ahead and buzz him in. It may be legit."

CHAPTER THIRTY-NINE

"What should I do?" Madison asked, trembling.

"Destiny will answer the door. You stay back by me just in case."

"He knows what Madison looks like," said Destiny. "And my hair is nothing like hers."

Joe looked at Madison and ordered, "Quick! Get a large towel from the bathroom."

A moment later, she returned. Joe handed Destiny the towel and said, "Wrap your hair up like you've just washed it. Maybe he won't remember Madison's face."

As Destiny was finishing wrapping her dark brown hair under the towel, the doorbell rang. She looked at Joe, who had drawn his Glock, and then opened the door as far as the chain would allow. She saw a middle-aged man wearing a brown cap and uniform with a medical mask over his nose and mouth.

"UPS, ma'am," said the male voice. "I have a package for you."

"Oh, good," she replied as she removed the chain. She opened the door, and as the man handed her the package, Destiny suddenly batted it away, revealing a taser in the man's hand.

Her move surprised the man for a split second, but it didn't deter him. As he made a quick jab to get the taser close to Destiny's midsection, Joe moved in. But before he got there, Destiny had grabbed his wrist, pushed it into the air with one hand, and in a lightning move, slammed the heel of her other hand into his elbow as she yelled. Her powerful blow dislocated the joint. The taser fell from his hand onto the floor as he screamed in pain.

Autumn started barking incessantly from inside her carrier, alarmed by the ruckus.

Kicking the taser away, Joe grabbed the man and threw him face down onto the floor. He pulled off the medical mask and cap, revealing the face of Gary Richardson.

"Gotcha, asshole!" growled Joe as he pulled Richardson's arms behind his back to cuff him. Richardson screamed again, uttering some obscenities through the pain. Joe placed him under arrest and read him his rights. Richardson was barely able to acknowledge it as he was in extreme pain from his dislocated elbow.

Searching through his pockets, Joe found a red silk scarf about twenty inches long. Pulling an evidence bag from his pocket, he handed it to Destiny and said, "Here, bag this scarf. We'll need to have it checked for DNA." Destiny complied.

Joe looked over at Autumn, who was still barking. "No bark!" he said sternly, and then repeated it. Then in a soothing voice, he said, "It's all right, Autumn. It's all right." She quit barking and only uttered an occasional "woof" after that.

Looking up at Destiny, Joe said, "That was a nice move."

"Glad to be of service to the Chicago PD," said Destiny with a smile. Glancing over at Madison, Destiny saw she was crying, so she moved to comfort her.

With his knee firmly on Richardson's back, Joe called Sam. "Come on up, Sam. We got him."

"Seventh floor, right?"

"Seven fifteen."

Looking over at Destiny, he saw she was hugging Madison. Joe waited a few seconds. He hated to interrupt them, but he had no choice. "Sam's on his way. One of you needs to buzz him in. I'm a little preoccupied here."

Once Sam entered the apartment, he looked down at Richardson's brown work shirt and matching pants, which he had used to emulate a UPS driver's uniform. Seeing the cap Richardson was wearing, he picked it up and looked it over, saying, "I've called it in. Uniforms should be here shortly."

"You'd better call for EMTs, too. Destiny dislocated his elbow."

Looking her way, he said, "You did?"

"You know she has dual black belts in martial arts, right? She put that training to good use."

Tossing the cap next to Richardson's head, Sam said, "She ever use it on you?"

"Not yet," called Destiny from the next room.

"Open the box, Sam. Let's see what's in it."

Sam gloved up and opened the box with a small knife he carried. Inside were dead roses, which Sam counted.

"Five for the fifth victim," said Sam. "And here's a card."

"What's it say?" asked Joe.

"Surprise, surprise. It says 'sic semper scortilla.'"

Sam made the call, and EMTs were there ten minutes after uniformed officers from the 20th District arrived. After Richardson's elbow was immobilized, he was placed on a gurney. The cuffs had been removed from his injured arm during treatment, and his other hand was cuffed to the gurney's sidebar. He was transported under armed guard to a nearby hospital, where they determined if his elbow would eventually require surgery.

A search of Richardson's pockets also revealed handcuffs and a condom, probably in anticipation of the rape he was going to commit.

Before they answered questions posed by the uniformed officers on the scene, Joe called Lieutenant Bellamy and told him about the arrest of Gary Richardson for the attempted murder of Madison Powell.

"You think you can link him to the other two murders?" asked Bellamy.

"The ME found a loose hair on one victim, and DNA on the other. I think it will be a match to our offender. We also found dead roses and a card with a Latin message inside the box he was carrying. Just like we found at the other scenes. We've nailed him, sir."

"Good work, you guys. We'll talk tomorrow."

Several hours later, after the police officers had gone, Joe and Destiny began packing for the return to their home. Joe packed up the food they purchased and transferred it from the refrigerator to the cooler. The day before, Destiny had washed their clothes, so they were already folded and ready to pack. While Joe was packing his clothes, she washed the bedding, so Madison would have clean sheets and pillowcases.

Joe walked Autumn around the block so she was prepped for the ride back home. Once everything was loaded into their cars, they exchanged keys with Madison.

Madison looked at Joe and Destiny and said, "I have a request, and I hope you don't mind." She hesitated before continuing.

"What is it?" asked Joe.

"Well, I'd rather not be alone tonight. And I was wondering if it would be all right with you if I slept in your guest bedroom one more time?"

"Of course," replied Destiny. "You don't mind, do you, Joe?"

"Not at all. You can sleep over tonight and pack your things tomorrow."

"Thank you," replied Madison.

Chapter Forty

Madison followed Joe, Destiny, and Autumn to their home on North Leavitt Street. Joe placed Autumn's carrier back where it usually sat and put away her food, treats, and toys. While Joe was unloading his duffel bag, Destiny unpacked her suitcase. Madison began packing a few things she kept in the guest bedroom.

With his unpacking finished, Joe looked over the house. The kitchen was immaculate, and the rest of the house appeared as if it had just been cleaned. He was happy to see that Madison had been quite particular about taking care of their home.

Once everyone finished their tasks, they met in the kitchen. Madison and Destiny sat on the stools at the island while Joe opened the cabinet that held several bottles of wine. He looked at Madison and asked, "Would you care for a glass of wine?"

"That would be nice, thanks."

"Red or white?"

"Red, please."

Joe removed a bottle of Cabernet Sauvignon and set out three glasses. Once he had poured a generous amount in each one, he set glasses down in front of Destiny and Madison.

When Madison picked up her glass, she held it high. "I want to propose a toast." Looking at Destiny, she said, "To both you and Joe, Destiny. I owe each of you my life, and for that, I'll be forever grateful."

They clinked their glasses and sipped the rich Cabernet.

"What I don't understand is why this man would want to kill all of my former friends."

"Gary Richardson was one of your high school's guidance counselors. Do you remember ever being in his office while you were a student?" asked Joe.

"No, I don't think so. The guidance counselor I talked with about college was a woman. Mrs. Carnahan, I think."

"Do you remember a girl in your school named Carrie Richardson?"

"No. Why?"

"What about a girl your friends fat-shamed, and called 'Blimpy' and 'Fatso?'" Joe's tone was more accusatory than he intended.

The shock of recognition showed in her face, and she hung her head. "Now, I do. Yeah."

"Did you know she attempted suicide because of the bullying she received?"

"No," Madison whispered as she studied the wine in her glass. "I'm so sorry."

"Long story short, her suicide attempt failed, but it left her in a coma for seven years. She died last year, and it appears her death affected her father immensely. As a result, he blamed the girls who bullied her, and he began taking revenge on members of the so-called 'Bitch Squad.' He managed to kill every one of them but you."

"Omigod," said Madison. "We...We were so immature back then. Pretty little...bitches. All of us. I have to tell you, I'm ashamed of my behavior during that time. I should have parted company with those other girls when they started doing really mean stuff, like posting the nude photos. But if I had, I was afraid they would turn on me and make me a target. So, I laughed with them and played along, but I kind of stayed in the background and wasn't an active participant in some of the despicable things they were doing." She took a drink of wine and then said, "You may not believe me, but it's the truth. After high school, I made sure I never saw them again."

"I'm not blaming you," said Joe. "We all have regrets growing up. And it seems as though you turned your life around after high school and put your past behind you."

"I tried. I never saw any of the other girls once I went off to college. I didn't want anything to do with them."

"That shows maturity," said Destiny.

"But it didn't undo what I'd done."

"Nothing can do that. The things we experience, both good and bad, help to mold who we are. How we handle adversity is what builds character. Don't let Gary Richardson's crimes negatively affect your life."

"People who have character are more prone to doing the right thing," said Joe. "What you and your friends did led to harmful consequences. I can tell you are a better person now. I'm sure you'll find some way to atone."

"Thanks for the pep talk," replied Madison, her eyes still on the wine glass.

"And remember, if you need anything, you can always call on me," said Destiny.

"I'll keep that in mind. Thanks for being my friend during this time."

"It doesn't have to end here, you know," replied Destiny.

Madison looked at Destiny and held her gaze for a moment. "Thanks. I appreciate that."

Joe was hungry and decided to bring up the question of dinner. "I don't know about you, but I'm hungry."

"I am, too," said Destiny. "Should we cook or have something delivered?"

Joe looked at the refrigerator's contents. Looking at Madison, he said, "How about vegetarian lasagna?"

"Sounds lovely."

"He's a good cook," added Destiny. "Let's go into the living room and let him get to work."

Destiny grabbed the bottle of wine, and she and Madison picked up their glasses and moved to the living room.

Joe's lasagna came out of the oven an hour later, and it was a big hit with Madison. Destiny had eaten this many times in the past, but even she agreed Joe had outdone himself.

After dinner, they talked for over an hour. They had eaten a lot, and combined with a second glass of wine, Joe was becoming drowsy.

"I'm all in," said Joe. "If you'll excuse me, I think I'm going to hit the hay." He stood.

"Sleep well," said Destiny. "It's been quite a day."

"Good night, Joe," added Madison.

"Good night, Destiny. Madison."

"My friends call me Maddie."

Joe couldn't help but smile. "Okay. Good night, 'Maddie.'"

* * *

The next morning, Joe realized he missed having Zoe jog with him. She was a pleasant distraction, and their conversations made the first mile and a half fly by. But as enjoyable as that was, he still preferred running alone so he could think about a case he was working on. And today, he was thinking about interviewing Gary Richardson.

It was Saturday, and Joe expected Maddie to be at the house when he returned, but her car was no longer parked out front.

"Where's Maddie?" he asked Destiny.

"She said she didn't want to impose on us any longer," explained Destiny. "She was eager to get back to her own place."

"Can't blame her for that, I suppose."

"She told me to tell you thanks...for everything."

"You two seemed to get along really well," said Joe. "You think you'll continue to see one another?"

"We've already set a date to have lunch next week, so...yeah. I'm hoping we can become friends."

* * *

Gary Richardson had been released from the hospital and was being held in a jail cell at the 20th District. Joe and Sam drove over to interview him. Richardson was led into the interrogation room, his right arm in a sling. His good hand was cuffed to the table.

Joe looked at him for a few seconds before asking, "What motivated you to attack Madison Powell?"

"I want to speak with a lawyer," said Richardson.

When he lawyered up right away, Joe could not hide his annoyance. "Fine," he said. "How's your elbow feeling?"

Richardson just glared at him.

"You're now under arrest for attempted murder. But I know you killed Amber Engstrom and Regina Fischer. And I'm going to do my best to prove you killed Tracey McNamara and Stephanie Daniels, too. I will make you my personal crusade."

Richardson looked him in the eyes and said, "Lawyer."

"You're one sick son-of-a-bitch," said Sam.

Richardson repeated, "Law-yer."

Joe looked at Sam, and they simultaneously got up and left the room.

"We're not going to get anything out of him," said Sam. "Even with his lawyer present."

"He knows he's toast," replied Joe. "Let's get out of here."

The following Monday, Gary Richardson was arraigned on a charge of attempted murder. He pleaded not guilty, and his bail was set at five hundred thousand dollars. He wasn't going anywhere.

Shortly afterward, a court order was issued to obtain a sample of Richardson's DNA so it could be compared to the loose hair found on Amber Engstrom's body and the DNA found on Regina Fischer.

Later in the week, while he was sitting at his desk, Joe received an unexpected call from Art Casey, the evidence technician they had worked with many times.

"We found something you might be interested in," said Art.

"Oh?" replied Joe. "I hope it's good news."

"We were able to get a partial print from inside the box. We got an eight-point match to your suspect. Thought you'd like to know."

"Thank you, Art! That makes my day!"

When Joe told Sam, he said, "Wow! That's an additional link we need to connect him to the other murders. I'd be willing to bet the DNA will be a match, too."

"We've got him," replied Joe. "We've got him."

When the prosecuting attorney heard about all the evidence found, two counts of first-degree murder were filed against Gary Richardson. Sixty days later, Richardson's DNA profile came back, and testing determined his DNA was a match to the hair found on Amber Engstrom's body and the DNA swabbed from Regina Fischer.

When news of Richardson's arrest was publicized, Clinton College Prep High School terminated his employment. In a statement expressing how horrified they were that he was implicated in such crimes, they also went on to offer thoughts and prayers to the families of his victims.

Those who had been friends with Richardson mourned for his family and the tragic circumstances that led to his daughter's death, but nothing could excuse what he did.

When DNA results came back on the red silk scarf Joe pulled from Richardson's pocket, forensics revealed DNA had been matched to Richardson and four women: Amber Engstrom, Regina Fischer, Tracey McNamara, and Stephanie Daniels. All of the deceased Squad members had been strangled with the same red silk scarf.

After being presented with the evidence against him, Richardson took a plea deal offered by the prosecuting attorney. He pled guilty to two counts of second-degree murder as well as one count of attempted murder. Given the circumstances and a lack of remorse shown by Richardson, the judge sentenced him to the maximum penalty under Illinois law: twenty years on each murder count and another twenty years for attempted murder. Because of the heinous nature of the crimes, the judge also ordered the sentences to be served consecutively. A total of sixty years in prison. Richardson would spend the rest of his life incarcerated since he had no chance of parole.

Since the same notes were found at the murder scenes of Tracey McNamara and Stephanie Daniels, and their DNA was found on the scarf ligature, the state's attorneys in Indiana and Wisconsin filed first-degree murder charges against Richardson.

Brenda Richardson filed for divorce and requested her name be changed back to "Mueller," her maiden name. She sold their home and moved away from the city in an attempt to put the past behind her and start a new life.

In one of his poems, Carl Sandburg called Chicago, "the City of Big

Shoulders." As a homicide cop, Joe knew how powerful those shoulders could be. They could endure the tough, cruel, corrupt, and evil acts perpetrated in their midst. With Gary Richardson off the street, Joe felt those big shoulders relax a little. Justice had been served.

Acknowledgments

Joyce Johanson; Detective Timothy O'Brien, Chicago PD; Shawn Reilly Simmons; Verena Rose; Deb Well; and the staff at Level Best Books.

About the Author

Lynn-Steven Johanson is an award-winning playwright and novelist whose plays have been produced on four continents. Born and raised in northwest Iowa, Lynn holds a Master of Fine Arts degree from the University of Nebraska-Lincoln. His five previous Joe Erickson mysteries, *Rose's Thorn*, *Havana Brown*, *Corrupted Souls*, *One of Ours*, and *Sins Revealed*, are published by Level Best Books. He lives in Illinois with his wife, and they have three adult children.

SOCIAL MEDIA HANDLES:
  Facebook: https://www.facebook.com/streetsofmarathon
  Twitter: https://twitter.com/JohansonLS
  Instagram: https://www.instagram.com/lsjohansonIK ju
  LinkedIn: https://www.linkedin.com/in/lynn-steven-johanson-0542841
4/

AUTHOR WEBSITE:
  https://LSJohanson.com

Also by Lynn-Steven Johanson

Rose's Thorn

Havana Brown

Corrupted Souls

One of Ours

Sins Revealed